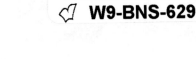

LOVE ON LOCATION

CASSIDY CARTER

Love on Location
Copyright © Cassidy Carter

print: 978-1-947892-42-2
eBook: 978-1-947892-30-9

Hallmark
PUBLISHING

www.hallmarkpublishing.com

CHAPTER 1

Beams of morning sunlight flashed through the tall pine trees surrounding the empty parking lot. Sipping the last of her coffee, Delaney Phillips stared at the front door of the main office of the rustic Cabins in the Pines. She sat in her modest, seen-better-days hatchback, steeling herself for what was ahead. She was quite early for work, not that she needed to be. Judging from the vacant spaces around her on this summery Friday morning, she didn't have high hopes that there would be a great influx of patrons.

"Come to the Cabins in the Pines—beautiful vistas, relaxing, remote location—and hardly any campers!" She sighed. Maybe having the place so deserted today was better. Only the staff would be around when she made her confession to her boss.

I have to do it. No more putting it off. I really have *to tell Wyatt.* Delaney wondered how he'd react to what she'd done, and her heart dropped again—as it had every time she'd thought about the envelope that had come in the mail yesterday.

At least she was making it into the office before he

did. His text had come bright and early, waking her before her alarm.

I've got to run an errand this morning. Can you handle opening?

She'd barely been coherent, but she'd shot back a quick text.

I can handle it. After all these years, I could probably handle it in my sleep—and get a few extra hours of shut-eye.

His reply had come quickly. It had brought a sleepy smile to her lips.

Point taken. Thanks, Friday. I owe you.

You do know there were movies made after 1940, right, Wyatt?

I don't believe you. But I appreciate you. Thanks again.

Her breath had caught, and she'd stared at the text, reading and rereading it. Ah, yes, there was also *that* complication to their working relationship. They'd always been friends, but since returning to the Pines after her divorce, she'd started to feel something new for Wyatt.

Wyatt had always been obsessed with old movies— as long as Delaney had known him—and though she used to be mystified at his use of *His Girl Friday* to nickname her, she'd come to see that it was an endearment, one that meant he equated her with something he loved.

It was only the first in a string of dozens of things she'd begun to notice about their friendship, things that seemed significant to her—and made her feel that there could be more between them.

And now things might change again.

Delaney glanced over at her passenger seat. There,

lying on top of a pair of soccer cleats and the sparkly pink duffel bag that held her daughter's dance things, was the evidence of Delaney's recent sneakiness. Oh, sure, the manila envelope looked harmless, but the three words stamped across the front in bold letters could be either just what the Cabins in the Pines needed—or a case of Delaney seriously overstepping her bounds.

Only one way to find out, she thought. She took a deep breath, dropped the envelope into her purse, and grabbed her coffee cup. She couldn't delay any longer. What few patrons they did have would be wanting to check out soon.

She climbed out of her hatchback, straightened her short-sleeved, button-up camp shirt, and crossed the parking lot, taking in the scents of the forest and the sounds of the birds chirping happily in the fresh green trees. She climbed the steps of the rustic log building that served as the office for the Cabins in the Pines and unlocked the front door.

"Good morning!" she called out as her entry set off the cheery bell attached to the doorframe. There was no response to her greeting. She hadn't seen Ursula's car in the parking lot, but the receptionist sometimes parked out by their camp restaurant to grab a bite before she walked over to the office, so Delaney had hoped to find her already at work and busy. No such luck.

Delaney dropped her purse under the front desk and powered up the antiquated computer. As it whined and sputtered to life, Delaney nearly whined along with it. The ancient machine barely ran the scheduling software that the resort relied on for reservation tracking, but it couldn't even do that efficiently. If it wasn't started up early enough, she'd have a line of two, maybe even three whole people waiting to vacate the property.

"Ursula?" she tried again, hoping the longtime receptionist was just in the back making coffee. Delaney's cup was empty, and she'd need a heavy dose of caffeine to keep her courage up to talk to Wyatt. But she didn't smell any coffee in the air, and again, she was met with no reply.

Delaney made short work of checking the phone messages, vacuuming, straightening the lobby, and finally starting a pot of coffee in the break room. Thirty minutes later, when the first guests came through the door and set off the bell again, Ursula still hadn't shown up—but neither had Wyatt. His office door was still closed tight, and the interior was still dark. Delaney was thankful for the small sliver of extra time before she'd have to face him.

"Good morning! Checking out?" she asked the elderly couple who'd come in. She remembered checking them in just yesterday when they'd gotten lost on their cross-country RV trip and happened upon the campground by luck.

The husband sniffed the office air. "I smell coffee!" he replied grouchily, hoisting up the waistband of his blue golf pants. "You got any coffee?"

Delaney smiled at him. "I do. Would you like some?"

His wife, the tip-top of her rhinestone baseball cap only coming up to her husband's chin, gave him a soft swat on the arm. "Oh, Harry, stop it. This poor woman is not your waitress. Can't you see she's tryin' to run a business?"

"There's no one here, Audrey. Look around," Harry groused back.

Delaney winced. Harry wasn't wrong.

Where is Ursula?

"Let's get you all checked out, and then I'll be happy to get you both a cup of coffee for the road. Better yet, I'll call over to the Bean Pot and tell Maisie to fix you both breakfast before you take that RV back out on the road—on the house. How does that sound to you?"

Harry's demeanor changed instantly. His face lit up with a wide smile. "That's mighty nice of you, young lady. What's the Bean Pot?"

"The Bean Pot is our camp's on-site restaurant." Delaney pointed to the map on the wall behind the check-in desk. "Just on the trail bend where the RV parking spots end and the cabins start. Red tin roof. You can't miss it. We have lots of amenities you folks probably haven't had a chance to take advantage of."

"Oh, that's why I thought I smelled biscuits and bacon this morning," Harry said, nodding. He gave his wife a see-I-told-you-so look. "Well, we were just going to go on up the road to try and search up some grub. I suppose we can stay a bit longer."

Delaney knew their camp chef was always ready to surprise unsuspecting guests with her wicked culinary skills. And Delaney knew that unlike Ursula, who was sometimes in her own world and on her own schedule, Maisie would've been in the kitchen since sunrise.

Working as quickly as the computer would let her, Delaney marked the now-vacant RV site as available—though it was only one of three that had even been taken—and printed off a receipt for the couple's stay.

"Here you are," she said cheerfully as she passed

the receipt over the counter to Harry. "I'll call right over to Maisie and let her know to expect you at the Bean Pot. You can just leave your rig parked in your campsite for now."

No one else is going to need it.

She shook off the negative thought. She still had her secret, and she hoped Wyatt would agree that what she had in mind was a good way out of their current slump.

As the couple left, Audrey reached over the desk and took Delaney's hand. "Thank you, dear. You just changed his whole mood. We've got that fancy, high-tech, expensive RV he's always grumbling about, and you made his day with a plate of biscuits and bacon." The woman squeezed Delaney's hand. Delaney found herself smiling back and forgetting about the stress of her morning.

"You're welcome. Please come back and see us. And tell your friends."

Audrey drew her hand back, patted the top of Delaney's, and breezed out of the office after Harry, who, Delaney thought, must have been halfway to the camp kitchen already. Delaney looked down to find a twenty-dollar bill in her hand.

Laughing at Audrey's attempt at slyness, Delaney stuffed the bill into the donation jar for the local Lion's Club that sat on the edge of the reception desk. Then she picked up the phone and called Maisie to warn her about Harry.

"Hey, sugar, you hungry?" Maisie almost always answered the phone this way when she saw the line ring over from the office; sometimes it was Delaney, sometimes Ursula, sometimes Wyatt, but Maisie didn't worry about who was on the other end when she asked. She just asked in that slow Southern accent of hers.

"No, Maisie, thanks. I'm sending some guests your way. Can you set them up with breakfast and comp it?"

"No problem, Del. Hey, you seen Wyatt yet?"

Delaney sputtered a bit. "No, why?" Maisie knew Delaney's secret—but not that Delaney was going to drop the bomb today. Maisie had been so excited when Delaney had told her the news: a reality show that saved failing businesses had chosen the Pines for an episode. Delaney had been sure that day that her friend's ecstatic whooping would tip Wyatt off. She was surprised and grateful that, despite all their elation, not one of the crew had revealed the secret yet.

"I thought he'd be in already, but I guess I should have known he wasn't. Haven't seen Duke anywhere. You know that furry little beggar's usually running around here, sniffing for food."

"Kind of like his daddy," Delaney interjected. "And Wyatt's running an errand. He'll be in a bit late."

"Yes, well, I'll try Wyatt on his cell, but if you see him, send him my way. One of the coolers is acting funny."

Delaney's stomach turned a little at the prospect of another repair needed at the restaurant. *Please let it be nothing*, she thought, just as her cell phone rang in her purse. She reached for it. "Will do. Got to go, Maisie."

"Bye, sugar."

"Bye." Delaney hung up, plopped her purse in her lap, and pulled her cell phone out. She swiped quickly to answer the incoming call when she saw the caller ID.

"Hey, sweetheart, everything okay?"

"Yeah, Mom. I'm fine."

"You get to school okay? Did you forget your lunch? What's wrong?"

"Mom, yeesh, nothing's wrong. Yes, I got here fine. I just want to know if I can spend the night at Bridget's house tonight. Her mom is letting her buy the whole third season of *Lovestruck High*, and we want to stay up really late and watch as much as we can."

Delaney chuckled at the eagerness in her daughter's voice. At eleven, Rachel was on the edge between being a little girl and tipping into tweenhood, and her tastes in entertainment were getting more and more cringeworthy. Delaney pictured her flaxen-haired, fair-skinned daughter, eagerly waiting on the other end of the line.

"I don't see why not."

"Thank you! Thank you! You're the best!"

Delaney could hear another squealing voice in the background. Bridget, Rachel's best friend, had obviously gotten the good news.

"Just have Bridget's mom call me so I can talk to her first. And homework before you start the marathon."

"Mom, there's no homework. This is literally the last day of school this year."

Delaney had almost forgotten. "Well, that's even better. But if you're going to binge on terrible reality TV, save me a spot in your schedule. We still have the latest season of *The ABC's of Business* at home."

"I will. Promise. Hey, Mom?"

Delaney heard the bell over the door chime again.

She looked up, her heart leaping into her throat. But it wasn't Wyatt, as she'd expected. Instead, Ursula sauntered in.

"Yes, Rach?" Delaney asked distractedly, glaring at the receptionist.

"Did you tell Wyatt about the show yet?" Rachel asked.

Delaney's eyes dropped from Ursula to the purse that sat open in her lap. She didn't want Ursula to see the block letters glaring at Delaney from inside. *Location Release Forms.*

"Not yet, honey. Listen, I've got to go. Have Bridget's mom call me."

"Ok. Love you."

"Love you, too. Have a good day. Eat those carrots I put in your lunch!" Delaney dropped her phone into her purse and shoved it quickly back under the desk before Ursula made it behind the reception area. She stood, smoothing her sweaty palms on the front of her khaki hiking shorts. The desk phone next to the computer rang, and Delaney answered.

"Cabins in the Pines. This is Delaney. How can I help you?"

Delaney tapped her watch, shooting a mock-evil glare at Ursula as the older woman put up her own bag and plopped into the rolling chair next to her. Delaney felt a little burst of excitement when the caller started talking.

"Three weeks? I'll be happy to check those dates for you. One moment, please." She turned to the computer and brought up the scheduling software. When the machine didn't respond and the silence stretched on the call, Delaney settled for pretending to type, clicking the keyboard loudly.

"Oh, yes," Delaney said cheerfully. "We do have availability, but our rooms are filling up fast."

Ursula made a face and whispered, "We *always* have availability."

Delaney stuck her tongue out. Ursula swiped Delaney's coffee mug and headed toward the break room with it. Delaney waited for the caller's response, grabbing a pen to take down the reservation details to add to the schedule later. The response had deflated her good mood.

"Yes, sir, I understand. There are other campgrounds closer to the highway, but I assure you, none are quite like us."

The caller's next question made her grimace. "No, we don't have a website. When you're ready, just give me a call. Mm-hmm. I see. Well, we'll look forward to hearing from you when you're ready to book."

Deflated, she hung up just as Ursula returned with two mugs—Delaney's travel mug and a flowery, oversized ceramic cup with the word *Namaste* emblazoned across the side in gold glitter. The phone rang again, and Ursula shooed Delaney away from it.

"Thank you for calling the Cabins in the Pines. This is Ursula. How can I help you?"

Delaney picked up her refilled coffee and sipped, humming gratefully. Leaning against the reception counter, she shuffled through a stack of yesterday's mail, her heart sinking further at the sight of bill after bill, many of them marked *Overdue, Second Notice,* and one that was even ominously labeled *Final Notice.*

She checked to make sure Ursula was still absorbed

in her phone call and caught her own reflection in one of the office windows. Her fair skin, something Rachel had inherited from her, was flushed from her morning chores, her dark hair was escaping her ponytail in several places, and the expression on her face reflected what she was feeling—worry.

She got up, walked to the window nearest her and opened it to let the fresh breeze through. The rustle of the branches calmed her. She listened, amused, as Ursula flirted a bit with the caller. When she hung up, Delaney turned to her.

"Who was it?" Delaney asked hopefully.

"Telemarketer. He sounded cute, though."

Delaney cracked a genuine smile, turning back to the picture window and taking in the lush green view just past the empty parking lot. She watched traffic on the small, two-lane road and counted cars for a few minutes. If she'd been using her fingers to count, she wouldn't have needed both hands.

"That darned bypass," she huffed. "Not much can get past progress, I suppose."

"We really need a website," Ursula opined.

"Yes," Delaney agreed. "And an online booking system. And WiFi for the campground." Not having WiFi also meant they relied on old-fashioned walkie-talkies for communication. "And cable run through the whole place. And a receptionist who comes to work on time."

Ursula tutted over the rim of her mug, grinning. Her wild red hair was fanned out around her head in a tumult of curls, and her bright purple glasses fogged over as she sipped. Ursula's hair color was not natural, but Delaney knew it suited her quirky, sixty-something-year-old friend.

"You know it takes longer to get here now since the bypass was finished. There's not even an exit that gets straight to us! Besides, I figured you and Wyatt always like an extra ten or fifteen minutes to have your morning chat. You know, alone time. That's got to be easier if I'm not around to distract you."

Delaney didn't miss Ursula's implication. And, despite Delaney's own growing awareness of Wyatt as more than just the boy she'd grown up with, she wouldn't dream of risking their friendship. And he was her boss. And he would probably freak out if she ever expressed an interest in him romantically.

She bristled slightly as she answered Ursula. "We've been talking a lot about camp improvements, but they're expensive. And if you can't tell by the parking lot, we're not exactly flush right now."

"Speaking of flush," a voice cut in.

Delaney turned toward the voice to see the camp's maintenance man-slash-groundskeeper standing at the mouth of the hallway that led to the break room. In his hand was a length of rusted pipe. With his tanned, boyish good looks, his brown hair brushing his collar, he looked more like a model in an outdoors catalog than a handyman.

Slater loved the cabins as much as the rest of them. When he wasn't fixing up something on the property, he could be found hiking, climbing, kayaking, or riding his extremely tricked-out mountain bike on the vast spread of land the cabins were built on. It was too bad love of the camp didn't pay the bills.

"Hey, Slater. What's that?" Ursula asked. Delaney fought the sense of dread creeping up on her.

"Cabin six's bathroom is out of commission," Slater

supplied. "I didn't see Wyatt's truck out front. I was hoping *you* could tell him." He made a pleading face at Delaney.

Delaney narrowed her eyes. "You want me to be the bad guy?"

Slater grinned sheepishly, shrugging. "I had to ask him for cash to fix three fifty-amp plugins that went bad at the RV park last week. Maybe if you take a look, you can think of a different way to fix things?"

Delaney knew what Slater really meant was *a different way to pay for things*. It was worth a shot. She'd gotten good at the last-minute campground Hail Mary. Delaney groaned.

"Well, it's not as though we'll need the cabin this weekend. How much do you think it's going to cost to fix?"

Slater squinted and scratched at the nape of his neck. "Don't know. Just takes time. It's more about the materials."

"Drat," Delaney said.

"Yep," Slater agreed. "Any ideas?"

"Yeah, I have some ideas," she assured him. "One for right now, at least. Do you have the number for Albert at the hardware store handy?"

Delaney thought of all the potential benefits of inviting the show to the Pines. She thought of what it could mean for the cabins and for all of them. Still, her breath caught when she thought of the possibility that Wyatt would be upset at how she'd gotten to this point in her plan without him. She sent up a little prayer that Wyatt would see the same thing Delaney had when she'd forged ahead at the opportunity—the chance for a miracle.

In her back pocket, Delaney's phone buzzed with a text. Wyatt's name flashed on the screen.

Hey, Friday, running late. Everything okay there?

Delaney's stomach dropped. She would have to talk to him, but not until she'd sorted all of this other mess out.

CHAPTER 2

Wyatt Andrews paced back and forth in an office at Fairwood Financial, staring at his phone. He ran a hand through his sandy hair—sprinkled with a few grays that had crept in over the last few years—and willed Delaney to text back, if only to distract him from his anxious wait. He'd been here for half an hour already. Realizing his rapid movement wasn't doing anything but making him even more anxious, he stopped pacing and sat back down for the fourth time.

His phone dinged with her reply. *Everything's good, boss.*

He relaxed slightly. The cabins were in good hands with Delaney, and the other crew members were all capable and had been with him for years—ever since he'd taken over the cabins from his father, who had taken them over from his grandfather. Wyatt was itching to find out what the branch manager had to say about his loan request. He was optimistic about his chances of securing the new loan. After all, not only had he been born and raised here in Fairwood, but his family had been here for generations. His family's legacy just needed a bit of an upgrade if he was going to make sure that people *kept* enjoying it for generations to come.

At least there was a window in the office with a picturesque view of the surprisingly busy main thoroughfare of Fairwood. Wyatt recognized nearly everyone who bustled past the window on their way to one of the many quaint shops flanking the courthouse at their center. The bank was only one of about a dozen local businesses that made up the town square, and Wyatt smiled as he recalled many a summer day just like today spent tagging along with his mom in this very town square, all the while wishing he could be back at the campground running wild. He pictured Delaney as a little girl, her dark braids flying out behind her as he chased her around the very statue that still stood in the green space between the bank and courthouse steps.

"Mr. Andrews, good morning! Sorry to have kept you waiting."

Wyatt stood to greet the man who entered. Bob Abernathy held out his hand for a shake, and Wyatt took it. The older man appeared much the same as when Wyatt had been a child, save the snow-white hair and deep laugh lines that fanned out around his wide grin. That famous smile was something he'd come to be known for around town over the years, and it was only the start of what made him such a welcoming part of the bank.

"Mr. Abernathy, you don't have to call me Mr. Andrews—you know that. Wyatt's fine."

"A professional courtesy, young man. Don't think I've forgotten that time you and the football team covered the bank windows in shoe polish." Bob put on a mock-stern expression that quickly broke back into his trademark smile.

"Hey," Wyatt protested, "they were the team colors. We'd made the playoffs. And I'll never forget the time it took all of us to *clean* that same shoe polish off all these windows—or how angry my parents were."

Bob's face clouded slightly. "They were good people, your folks. I was so sorry to hear about their accident."

Wyatt felt his chest tighten, and he took a deep, steadying breath before he replied.

"Thank you. That means a lot. It's been two years, and I still miss them every day. But that's why I want to improve the Pines. I think they would have wanted people to keep coming, keep enjoying what they helped build. Site improvements, a new website and booking system, advertising—we just need a little boost."

Bob took a seat behind his desk and motioned for Wyatt to sit. When Wyatt had resumed his place in the uncomfortable chair, Bob drew a folder out of his desk drawer and opened it on his desktop.

"I understand what you want to do, Wyatt. I really do. But, unfortunately, looking over the financials of the campground from the last year, I just can't give you a loan as substantial as you'll need without significant collateral."

Collateral? Wyatt didn't like the sound of that. He was a simple guy with simple belongings. His old truck probably wasn't worth anything to anyone but him, and his house was a modest cottage just a mile or so from the Pines.

"What did you have in mind?" Wyatt asked cautiously, not ready to give up hope.

"Let me show you this first," Bob suggested. He flipped the folder around and began running down numbers for Wyatt. After the first few minutes, the words ran together in an overwhelming jumble of *profit, depreciation, market valuation,* and endless others. Wyatt put up a hand to stop the onslaught.

"Mr. Abernathy, with all due respect, can we just get to the bottom line here?"

Bob paused, his pen hovering over a number labeled *Loss.* Wyatt knew that number all too well.

"Yes, well… Wyatt, uh, the bottom line is, the only way we can provide your requested loan amount is if you take the amount out against the Cabins in the Pines."

"And what does that mean for the business?"

"Shorthand, if you default—if you aren't able to make the payments on the loan—the bank owns the campground." Bob spread his hands out over the papers on his desk. "And what I'm getting at here is that, based on your numbers, you'd be on shaky ground regarding those payments if you continue losing money the way you have recently."

Wyatt nodded, his mind racing. Bob was right. He'd struggled to make payroll some months, forgoing his own paycheck several times instead of allowing his employees to go without. Ever since the big bypass had rerouted travelers around the Pines, there wasn't an easy exit that dropped customers off close to their entrance. With the exit gone, the big, kitschy billboard depicting three cheerful cartoon pine trees—which had proudly pointed campers in the right direction—went away, too. The loss of both had caused a dramatic drop in customers.

Wyatt was hoping that finally getting the place online would take up the slack. But that—plus the amenities modern campers seemed to demand—took money. Money he didn't have.

It was a circle that was making him dizzy. He needed the money to make more money, but in order to get the money, he had to risk the business. There were so many depending on him: Maisie, Ursula, Slater, Delaney. Especially Delaney.

When he thought about what she would do if she had to leave Fairwood for work, the stress it would put on her while she was trying to raise Rachel on her own, it squeezed his heart even harder. And then there was the way Wyatt's heartbeat practically stuttered when he thought about how little he would see Delaney if she weren't at the Pines. He couldn't fathom losing either of them as part of his everyday life.

A day without Del ribbing him, laughing with him? A day without her familiar, welcoming presence, her wide, bright smile? No way.

He couldn't put the Pines up as collateral if the risk was so high that he would lose it, that his staff and his best friend would lose their jobs. But if they didn't start making more money, the land would be just that—just land, and he wouldn't be able to employ anyone at that point, either. *It's a Wonderful Life*, he thought wryly. *But am I George Bailey at this point or Uncle Billy?*

"Wyatt?" Bob said gently, breaking in on Wyatt's train wreck of thoughts.

Wyatt pinched the bridge of his nose.

"Sorry, Bob. I need some time to think. Is that okay? Can I take the particulars with me and have a few days?"

"Of course," Bob said, seeming relieved that Wyatt

was going to consider his options. "Take your time. There's no hurry."

On your end, Wyatt thought. Wyatt stood and held his hand out first this time.

They shook hands, and Bob looked earnestly into Wyatt's eyes as he said, "Whatever you decide, you've done a great job with your folks' place. No one could have stopped that bypass."

Wyatt nodded, accepted the folder from Bob, and thanked him before leaving.

The bright sunshine blinded him a little as Wyatt stepped outside from the bank's artificially lit interior. As he walked to his truck, several people greeted him, and he returned their hellos in a bit of a daze. A face or two he recognized from last night's chamber of commerce meeting.

His mind swirled. He wished his dad were here to tell him what to do about the Pines: whether to keep fighting, or to just give up and admit defeat. His father had told him once that he'd know when things were worth fighting for and when it was okay to fail—and not be ashamed of the failure. Wyatt wished he had that wisdom now.

He pulled out his phone and checked his messages. Nothing new. He started to text Delaney to confide everything that had just happened, but everything he wanted to say would be easier to explain in person.

His heart lightened a little at the thought of talking with her. Maybe she would have a solution—she always did. She jokingly called it her "mom superpower." She had a knack for deconstructing a problem and finding a (sometimes unconventional) solution.

Delaney chalked her ability up to single-handedly

wrangling the ups, downs, comings, and goings of a rambunctious daughter, but in the past couple of years, the skill had really been put to the test working at the Pines, and it was just something that was inherently Delaney. She'd been his rock since childhood.

It was also where he'd come up with the nickname she professed to hate. His grandpa and his dad had been avid movie buffs, and he'd grown up fascinated with rousing depictions of stalwart heroes and feisty heroines. Delaney's quick wit, resourcefulness, and pluckiness were traits straight out of one of his favorite films.

She made fun of him for his old-fashioned taste in movies, but she always smiled when he used the endearment. He would talk to her when he got back to the Pines. Wyatt sent off a quick text.

Hey, Friday, I'm on my way. Can we talk when I get there?

She wrote back almost instantly. *Sure. Bring Duke. I think Maisie misses him.*

He slipped his phone back into his pocket. He had one more stop to make before he could book it to the Pines.

CHAPTER 3

"Thanks, Albert. I really appreciate it. And just let your daughter know she can come out anytime to see the lake and plan the reception."

Delaney hung up. One crisis averted. She walked back into the cabin, surveying the dated décor. Though it made her nostalgic, she knew it wasn't exactly a selling point of the facility. She ran a hand over the wall, dreaming of soft, neutral colors and big skylights. Slater was just finishing up clearing the drywall scraps from the bathroom. He stood from tying a large black trash bag as Delaney came in, his expression questioning.

"We got it," she said, not trying to hide the relief in her voice. "Think you can get everything for under six hundred at Albert's hardware?"

Slater surveyed the bathroom, nodding slowly. "Yeah. Actually, I think I can fix everything here and swap out the ceiling fan in the main room for that. It's been a little iffy."

"Great. Thanks. You staying here?" Delaney shook her thumb over her shoulder in the general direction of the office. "I've got to get back."

"Yeah. I'm going to rip out everything bad, go ahead and take down the old fan, and make a list for Albert."

Delaney nodded and headed for the door. Just as she reached the threshold, Slater called her back.

"Oh, Del?"

"Yeah?" She turned to look at Slater.

"If you see Wyatt, ask him to bring that big adjustable wrench out of his truck, will you?"

Delaney nodded. "I will. He's on his way in now. Said he had an errand. Maybe it's to do with that meeting with the chamber of commerce last night."

"Hmm...I hope that went well. Lots of folks in town hurting lately." Slater got a mischievous glint in his eye. "So, when are you going to tell Wyatt about the TV show?"

Delaney opened her mouth to speak, closed it, and then opened it again. "Well, you know, about that..."

"You've got to tell him, Del. What're you so afraid of? It could fix a lot of troubles around here."

Delaney frowned slightly, nervously playing with the end of her ponytail. She worried the dark brown wisps between her fingers, avoiding eye contact with Slater. "It'll have to be soon, obviously. Between you, Rachel, and Ursula, I can't even take my time."

Slater burst out laughing, throwing his hands up in surrender. "No pressure from me. Just wait until the production crew shows up. Then you won't even have to tell him."

Delaney bristled slightly. "I'll have you know that they won't just show up. Not until he signs the release forms for them to film here."

"He's not going to be mad, Del," Slater reassured her, lugging a heavy toolbox from the bathroom into the main sitting area of the cabin. Delaney watched as he unfolded a ladder, climbed up, and began efficiently taking apart the antiquated ceiling fan that Delaney was sure had been in cabin six since she'd come to Cabins in the Pines as a child.

"He *is* our boss, Slater. He might think it's none of my business. I don't know. He's quiet lately."

Slater's expression was incredulous. "You guys have been best friends since you were ten. Don't give me that 'boss' stuff. Look, we both know he's not the type to ask for help. Sometimes, he needs help dropped in his lap. Sort of like someone else I know." He now stared pointedly at her.

Delaney knew Slater was right about Wyatt—and her own stubbornness, though she chose for the moment to ignore that friendly barb. Just like Rachel had been right when she'd encouraged Delaney to submit the Cabins in the Pines to the infamous reality TV series, *The ABC's of Business*. The same way Ursula and Maisie had been right when they'd suggested that Delaney film the audition video not on a cold, sterile backdrop like the audition examples they'd researched online, but moving through the campground on one of the camp carts, showcasing the land and wildlife and ending at the wide, solid jetty that jutted out twenty yards into the center of sparkling Lake Fairwood.

"You're right, of course. I was planning on doing it today anyway," Delaney confessed.

"Wait until I leave for Albert's," Slater quipped.

"Thanks for the support," Delaney replied dryly. "First you're pressuring me to tell, and now you want to stand out of the potential blast zone."

Slater shrugged, grinning.

Delaney's phone buzzed again. There was a text from Ursula containing several emojis—all variations of "nervous" or "thumbs up."

Wyatt's here!

Delaney knew he was likely waiting at the office to have their morning meeting. She pushed off of the doorframe and gave Slater a little salute.

"Just ask for Al directly when you get there. And let me know when everything's good to go again. You don't have to tell Wyatt about this. I'll tell him about it when I drop the bomb about the things that have to do with *the thing*."

"Tell me what?"

Delaney turned fast, nearly falling down the front steps of the cabin. She caught herself on the railing and tried to rein in her knee-jerk panic. Wyatt stood in the well-worn dirt driveway of cabin six. Dressed in scruffy jeans and an old, faded camp shirt emblazoned with the Pines logo, his dark-blond hair a little mussed, he still kind of took her breath away.

They'd always been friends, but lately she'd started to feel something new. Why was that? *When* had that happened? She wasn't even sure herself.

It could've been when she'd contemplated dating after her divorce but couldn't imagine anyone else who would compare to her best friend. Or it could've been the afternoon a few months ago when a sudden, violent rainstorm had stranded them in one of the cabins furthest from the office.

Wyatt had built a fire, and the uninterrupted hours of conversation, the feeling of being completely cozy—completely *safe*—along with the thrill of being the focus of his undivided attention... Well, it had all certainly been potent.

Whatever had started the new awareness, she'd never let it endanger her friendship with Wyatt. He'd meant too much to her through the years. And still did.

How much did he hear?

"Hey, Wyatt. I was just coming back up to the office." Delaney hoped her voice didn't betray her anxiety.

A sharp, excited bark drew Delaney's attention. She glanced over Wyatt's shoulder to see his Red Heeler bouncing around the cab of his ancient pickup.

"Duke!" Delaney used the dog as a distraction. She jogged down the remaining two steps, rushing to the truck to bury her hands in Duke's soft fur. She'd always loved the marbled red and cream of his coat. The dog licked her face, ecstatic as she scratched his face and behind his pointy ears.

Wyatt came to lean against the truck beside Delaney. She tried to act normally, ignoring the possibility that he'd caught her talking to Slater about the show. She could feel Wyatt's eyes on her.

"Good thing you asked me to bring him. He was seriously moping when I ran by the house."

Delaney rubbed behind Duke's ears and was rewarded with another series of doggie kisses. "He loves having the run of the campground. You should take him to the vet and have him chipped in case he ever really does get lost out here, though," she suggested.

"Listen, kid," Wyatt quipped, "I don't keep up with all your newfangled technology. I'm a simple man. Old trucks, old movies, and dogs that don't have robot parts. That's good enough for me."

Delaney felt another spike of panic. *What about reality TV shows? Cameras? Having your name and face broadcast around the world and across social media?*

"Del? You okay?"

She focused. "Uh…yes. I…uh, have some stuff to… uh…go over with you."

Slater picked that exact moment to appear in the doorway of cabin six, lugging his tools. He waved at Delaney and Wyatt but quickly scurried toward his own SUV, which was parked nearby. *So much for needing that wrench*, she thought dryly as Slater loaded up and started his vehicle.

Wyatt's face clouded slightly. "Do I want to know what's wrong with cabin six?"

Delaney moved a hand from petting Duke to resting on Wyatt's arm. She gave his forearm a quick squeeze. There was another difference—contact she never would've even noticed before now made her breath catch. "That's all taken care of. I'll explain on the way back to the office. Mind if I hitch a ride?"

"Shotgun's always your spot, you know that. But first, I need to swing by the Bean Pot. Maisie called me on the drive over. Do *you* mind?"

"Not at all. She told me something was up in the kitchen."

They got into the truck, and Delaney found herself relaxing as she buckled her seat belt. Wyatt didn't seem as tense as he had recently, which made Delaney feel a little better. But something was off about him still. Where had he been for the last couple of hours? Then there'd been his text—*Can we talk when I get there?*

"You know," she teased, "you could always let me

drive every once in a while. Then I wouldn't always be in shotgun."

Wyatt fired up the old Ford and made a mock-disapproving face at her. "Blasphemy. This baby's a classic!"

"And you don't trust me to drive her?"

"Uh, I didn't say that."

The expression on his face told her that he was scrambling for an excuse. She laughed, letting him off the hook. "It's okay. I like this side of the truck." And she did. It felt natural, *right*, being by his side. She avoided looking at him, worried he'd be able to read the emotion in her eyes. "Got any details about the problem at the Bean Pot?"

"There's something wrong with one of the fridges. I tried getting Slater on his walkie-talkie when I pulled up, but now I see you had him occupied already. Thought I'd go out and take a peek at the fridge myself."

They started down the winding dirt road to the Bean Pot. Between the age of Wyatt's truck and the slightly uneven grade of the path, the ride was a bit of a rough one. The old vehicle creaked and rocked as they bounced ahead. Delaney laid her head back against the bench seat and watched the sunlight as it dappled through the canopy above. Duke wiggled into her lap, and she welcomed his warm weight, scratching him behind the ears as they bumped along. There was nowhere else on earth like this place. There was nowhere else that took her back the way this place did.

The closer they got to the Bean Pot, the stronger the smell of Maisie's cooking got. Biscuits, sugar-cured bacon, and that hash brown casserole. Truth be told, Maisie's cooking and the local crowd that frequented the Bean Pot were major factors in keeping their heads above water nowadays. Delaney's stomach growled. Her coffee, which was probably cold as ice back at the office, was all she'd had during her rushed morning.

"You said you had some stuff to tell me?" Wyatt said.

Delaney decided to just lay the light news on him for now. "Yeah, about cabin six. We had a pretty major leak in the bathroom. Slater's having to rip out a bunch of drywall." Wyatt's posture changed; his hands tightened on the steering wheel.

"I talked to Albert down at the hardware store, and he gave us plenty of store credit to get the supplies to fix it. In exchange, I told him his daughter could use the lakeside decks and the jetty for her wedding reception next month."

Wyatt seemed impressed. "Really? Wow. How did you know he'd go for it?"

"I didn't know for sure, but he coaches Rachel's soccer team, and I remembered him complaining last week about how his daughter wouldn't let him contribute any money to the wedding at all. But her soon-to-be husband is being deployed a couple of weeks after the ceremony, so they're bound to want to save some money on the wedding. I just offered him a way to help her without paying."

"That's my Friday," Wyatt said. "Always getting us out of trouble before trouble knows what hit it."

She felt her cheeks grow warm at the affectionate nickname—or, rather, the significance she now assigned to it.

"Your love of old movies would be annoying if it weren't so endearing," Delaney teased.

They arrived at the Bean Pot, a rustic lodge-style building that had been modeled to match the cabins. They climbed out, and Wyatt let Duke loose from the truck with a stern warning to stay away from possums. Duke leapt down as though he'd sprouted wings and tore off ecstatically around the back of the building, where Maisie always left a bowl of water and some leftover breakfast for him.

Maisie came out onto the screened-in dining area at the front of the restaurant, waving to them. "Hey, y'all! I see you brought the troublemaker."

"Yes, ma'am," Wyatt called back, "and I brought Duke, too."

Delaney rolled her eyes at the corny joke. "Look, Andrews, that wasn't funny in middle school, and it's not funny now."

The loose gravel and dirt crunched under their boots as they hiked up the slight incline to the restaurant. Wyatt held the door for Delaney and Maisie as they all moved from the porch into the main dining room. "I have a wonderful sense of humor. People like it."

"What people?" Maisie asked as they walked, her green eyes full of disbelief as she glanced back over her shoulder. Delaney waved to a few patrons, a little relieved to see that Harry and Audrey weren't still there.

"People," Wyatt supplied weakly. Both women laughed, and Maisie shook her head.

Back at the first of two walk-in coolers, Maisie gestured to a temperature gauge mounted to the thick steel door. "Here's the patient. Haven't been able to get it to drop to proper temp all morning. I moved everything to the other fridge, so we didn't lose any food, but if you managed any big party bookings from that chamber of commerce meeting, I'm going to need this space back and working."

Wyatt rubbed the back of his neck. He seemed to be thinking.

"Got any commercial refrigerator repairmen on your list who want to go camping, Del?"

Delaney shook her head. "Not today."

The flicker of stress that crossed Wyatt's features made Delaney's heart squeeze in her chest. It also shored up her resolve to convince him, even if he protested, to take a chance on *The ABC's of Business*. There would be time for pride and a go-it-alone attitude later; right now, they needed help to keep the cabins from falling apart at the seams. And all Delaney needed was Wyatt's signature to get that help on its way.

Delaney's mind was working in overdrive again.

"Maisie, is Pete Williams still the manager at the meat-processing plant?"

Maisie nodded. "Yep. He was just in a couple of days ago after hunting with some of his friends."

"And does he still keep a couple of cows in that tiny pasture beside the plant?"

"Far as I know, darlin'. Why?"

"Call Pete and see if we can use one of his walk-ins at the processing plant. Tell him he can turn those skinny cows out to fatten up in the clearing we'd planned to turn into the sports field. That will give us time to figure out the actual repair to our cooler."

"I can see your wheels turnin' when you do that, Del." Maisie laughed. "I'll call Pete." She moved through the swinging door that led out of the kitchen, and Delaney heard her open the door to the tiny office that took up the back corner of the main dining room.

Delaney turned back to Wyatt, expecting him to be happy now that the fridge problem was at least on its way to being solved. Instead, his face was even grimmer than when they'd first come in.

"Wyatt, don't worry. We'll figure this out. We always do."

"*You* always do," Wyatt replied softly. "But I'm not sure how much longer we can keep going like this."

Now. Tell him now, her conscience screamed. *He's worrying when the solution to everything is sitting in your purse.*

"Wyatt, I have something to tell you."

He seemed to snap out of his fog, but he didn't seem to have heard her.

"Del, let's go back to the office. We need to talk." His tone was so serious that Delaney's breath caught. The dread was back, and it rendered her silent as she walked through the door he held for her again on their way out of the Bean Pot. Delaney looked for Maisie, but she wasn't in sight. Their ride back was also spent in silence, and it wasn't an easy silence.

Worrying her lower lip, Delaney pulled her phone from her back pocket and sent a text to Ursula.

Can you grab the manila envelope out of my purse and put it up on the front desk? I need to grab it when I come in.

A few minutes passed with no response. Seeing that she'd missed a call from Bridget's mom, Kimberly, Delaney typed out a quick message that gave Rachel permission to spend the night and asked Kim to call when she got tired of *Lovestruck High* so Delaney could come pick her daughter up. Kim texted back before Ursula responded.

No problem. The sad thing is, I'm kind of getting invested in the show. Crazy, right?

Ursula's reply came in immediately after.

When did you get these? You didn't tell me they came already! Have you told Wyatt yet?

They passed the cabins and the second plot of tent sites. Wyatt was still stonily silent. Delaney shot back one more text to Ursula and then pocketed her phone.

Not yet. We'll talk later.

A few moments later, Wyatt put the truck in park right outside the front steps of the office and came around to open Delaney's door. Ursula, to her credit, was pretending to work when they walked in, but Delaney could see her yoga mat unrolled on the floor behind the front desk. She could sure use some of Ursula's Zen right about now. Grateful to see the manila envelope resting right at the edge of the worn Formica counter, Delaney managed to snag it surreptitiously as she and Wyatt passed. Wyatt went into his office first, rounding his desk and bumping his mouse to wake his computer up from sleep mode.

"Come in, Del. Close the door."

Delaney closed the door softly, peering around the edge to see Ursula craning over the desk to watch, her eyes wide. Wyatt *never* closed his office door. He prided himself on being the kind of boss whose door was always open—literally and figuratively. Turning back toward the room, Delaney sank into the lone chair that faced Wyatt's desk.

"There's no easy way to say this," Wyatt started. He was talking to her, but he wasn't looking at her.

His blue eyes were fixed on his desk—no, on a thin stack of papers on his desk. Delaney didn't have to search hard to see the top sheet was letterhead from the bank.

"You can tell me anything," Delaney said softly.

"Del," he replied, his voice shaking slightly, "My errand this morning—I was at the bank." He stopped speaking abruptly and cleared his throat. "We may have to close. For good."

She knew the sudden smile that she felt growing on her face would confuse him—after all, it wasn't the typical response when someone was told they were losing their job. "Wyatt, no, you're wrong." Reaching out, she slapped the manila envelope onto his desk. "We're not going anywhere yet."

CHAPTER 4

"So, you see, after Rachel and I binge-watched two whole seasons, I got to thinking about how much the renovations we'd been kicking around were going to cost. And then I had this crazy idea to submit the Pines as candidate for an episode, and—"

"Wait, wait, wait." Wyatt held up a hand to stop the excited flow of words pouring out of Delaney following her big reveal. "You're telling me that you volunteered the campground as a...a...a filming location for this TV show without telling me?"

Delaney winced, the words she'd been about to say dying on her lips. Wyatt stared at her with an expectant expression. Delaney thought about the speech she constantly gave Rachel, the "honesty is the best policy" one. She might as well lay it all out and let Wyatt decide with all the facts known.

"Yes. No. Sort of. It's a reality TV show, so the Pines is the *subject* of the show, not just the place they film it. And *you* weren't just out running some trivial errand this morning, Wyatt Andrews, so hear me out. Then you can explain to me what you've been keeping to yourself."

His eyebrows nearly hit his hairline. She rushed on before he could say anything else. "I haven't really promised anything. I just auditioned the campground, and they decided they were interested. I just got our foot in the door. The final decision is completely, one hundred percent, up to you."

Wyatt didn't respond. He just picked up the packet Delaney had tossed onto his desk, opened it, slid the release forms out, and scanned them. In the moments he spent flipping the pages, Delaney tried to keep her own eyes off the bank papers now set to one side of his desk. She wanted details of what the bank had told him, but she thought he'd be more inclined to share those if he saw a light ahead.

Instead of staring at him as he read, she looked around Wyatt's office with fresh eyes, his words from earlier ringing in her ears. The dark paneling was the same dark faux wood that had graced this room for as long as Delaney could remember. It was the same paneling that was in the cabins. Some people might find the popcorn ceiling and brass-hardware fan outdated, even tacky, but everything about this room made Delaney feel like she was home.

We may have to close. For good.

That just wasn't an option. Many things in Delaney's life had changed since she'd first set foot on the shores of Lake Fairwood, but the Pines—and Wyatt—never really had. Sure, they'd grown up, they'd had lives that a few times had taken them away from Fairwood, but they'd always ended up back here, where they had a foundation.

Her own thoughts sparked an unpleasant memory that Delaney had to struggle to push away. Anytime thoughts of her ex-husband came up, she had to re-mind herself that what had happened was for the best and that staying in Fairwood had given her—and Ra-chel—the best possible support network. *Don't think of Jacob. Stay focused on what's important.*

"And what, exactly, would they be doing here?" Wy-att asked carefully as he set the release forms aside. She fought a smile and tried to keep the flutter of hope she felt in her chest at bay.

"The host, Alexandra Brent-Collingsworth, is a business wiz. She comes into businesses that aren't doing their best"—she avoided the word *failing*—"and she overhauls them. She invests capital, oversees renovations, and relaunches the business, new and improved."

Delaney thought about the episodes she'd watched, wondering briefly what Wyatt might think of the beau-tiful, perfectly-poised Alexandra. The petite host of *The ABC's of Business*—Delaney guessed the woman was quite a bit shorter than her own 5'9"—was definitely not the rustic, homespun type. Alex was always made-up and styled, where Delaney always wore her dark hair in a simple ponytail and thought that mascara was something destined to melt off in the summer heat. Delaney did admit she'd often envied– just a little–the woman's glamorous persona, which was so opposite of her own casual style.

Wyatt's voice broke into Delaney's thoughts. He ap-peared skeptical. "So what's the catch?"

"No catch. They get to film here. It's a way to make their show economically. People vie for the chance to be on it. Think of the value of just the time on televi-sion, Wyatt. It's free national advertising."

She knew that Wyatt cherished the Pines, knew that he believed in the place, so she bristled slightly at his wariness. He was willing to change the campground with the updates they'd been discussing, but he was hesitating when she offered him a way to accomplish that without involving the bank, which had obviously given him bad news this morning.

"What are you worried about? It might help me understand what's going on in your head if you let me in a little."

He sighed deeply and stood, pacing while he raked a hand through hair that always looked a bit tousled, to her anyway. There was still a worry in the depths of his blue eyes, tension in his broad shoulders, but both were starting to ease. "I'm a little freaked out about having a whole television crew here, honestly."

She pursed her lips and rolled her eyes. "Baloney. You're the biggest movie buff I know. Wouldn't you love to see how it's done?"

Wyatt scoffed. "Classic cinema is not reality TV. I'm not the subject of *Casablanca*."

"Keep talking," she said, crossing her arms over her chest, watching him continue his nervous circuit back and forth across the room. He stopped by the edge of his desk, tapping two fingers on the desktop nervously.

"I'm just not one to air my dirty laundry to the whole world. My folks, and their folks before them, they built this place up. They made it the place we remember from childhood. I don't know if I want to broadcast to the whole world that I'm the one who's letting it fail."

Sympathy panged her heart. It had hit her hard when Wyatt's folks had passed. Carol and Bill had been like a second set of parents to her, had even given her the management job here when she'd had to go back to work after her divorce. Their accident had left a void in a lot of lives, and in Wyatt's most of all.

Delaney stood, walked over to Wyatt, and captured one of his hands in both of hers. It wasn't something she normally did—she did it impulsively, fueled by the need to soothe the hurt in his eyes. Delaney scrutinized the face of the man in front of her and saw clearly the grieving son he still was. Her voice was gentle when she spoke.

"I understand what you're saying. I miss them, too. And I know you would never do anything disrespectful of their memory. I'm not trying to pressure you either way in your decision about the show. I'm sorry for not asking you first. No matter what you decide, you haven't failed. You aren't the reason the Pines is in trouble. Your folks would have recognized that, too. But if we don't do *something*, it will be our fault in the end for just sitting here, and everything they've built *will* be gone."

She started to draw her hands away, but he caught one of them and laced his fingers with hers. She felt the little glimmer of hope in her heart, sparked by the thought that he'd consider her plan, turn into something warm and affectionate that she had no business feeling for her best friend.

Forget *The ABC's of Business*. She should be appearing on Rachel's new reality obsession, *Lovestruck High*. Delaney shook off the feeling, hoping it hadn't shown in the way she'd looked at Wyatt, and focused on the conversation.

"Are we still good?" she ventured hesitantly.

He narrowed his eyes at her. "I don't know yet. That was awfully sneaky of you, Friday. I feel like you ought to make it up to me. Double batch of those butterscotch oatmeal cookies?"

She pretended to consider his terms. "Deal," she finally relented.

He squeezed her hand. "I understand why you didn't tell me. I'm not a guy who asks for help easily—I know that. But you were right to take the chance. Even if we turn it down, we never would have had the option if it weren't for you. So thank you."

"And Rachel, and Ursula, and Maisie, and Slater," Delaney added.

Wyatt's mouth dropped open. "All of you were in on it? Mutiny!" But he was starting to smile, and she ventured a question.

"So, what's happened to make you so sure we're close to closing?"

Wyatt unclasped their hands, and Delaney felt an illogical rush of disappointment. He leaned over and scooted the location release forms aside, reaching for the bank papers she'd been eyeing earlier. He handed them to her.

"I was down at the bank this morning to try and take out a business loan for the site renovations, the upgrades, everything we've been looking at," he explained. "But the bank won't extend the funds to us without collateral. A substantial amount of collateral."

Delaney started flipping pages. "What do they want?"

"The Pines."

Delaney thought a moment about what that could

mean. "So, like, a mortgage on the Pines? Couldn't we handle that?"

"Not with numbers like these. The land and facilities being paid for—plus the business we do at the Bean Pot—seem to be the only things keeping us solvent."

Delaney ran some of the numbers quickly through her head and immediately saw the dilemma.

"Barely, you mean." The full weight of what he was explaining hit her. With the bank, they'd risk losing the Pines. At least now they were all still together, though barely afloat.

He nodded, and a soft knock came at the door of his office. Ursula opened the door and stuck her head around a moment later. She cut Delaney a significant look when she saw the two of them standing close; Delaney chose to ignore it.

"Hi. Sorry to interrupt, but you have a call on line two, Wyatt."

Wyatt scowled at Ursula. "Good morning to you, too, accomplice."

Ursula looked confused. Delaney waved away Wyatt's attempt at grouchiness. "I told him about the show. He's personally affronted that we all care so much about him and his business."

Ursula replied, a bit archly, "Well, young man, you'll have to get used it. We may be sneaky, but we're family."

"Yes, and as you are my aunt, I feel doubly betrayed by you. I'm keeping all of the cookies that Del now owes me. No cookies for the staff," he insisted, making a fist and thumping it lightly on his desk. "Clear out the safe. Oh, wait, it's empty. Cookies go in the safe!"

He picked up the handset of the phone that sat on his desk.

"I'll bake double," Delaney stage-whispered to Ursula, giggling at Wyatt's theatrics.

"Butterscotch oatmeal?" Ursula asked hopefully. Delaney nodded.

"Line two!" Ursula reminded Wyatt cheerfully, turning and breezing out of the office. Delaney stood before Wyatt could punch the line that would connect the person on hold. Feeling the pull of her responsibilities around the property—and the urge to scoot back over to the Bean Pot and confide in Maisie—Delaney started to inch toward the door.

"I'm going to make my rounds of the campgrounds. I'll have my cell phone, but you know how well those work around here, so get me on my walkie. Holler if you need me?"

Wyatt held up a hand. "Stay for a couple of minutes. Let me see who this is, and then we can decide together about the show."

She sank back down into the chair while he put the handset to his ear and pushed the flashing red button.

"Wyatt here." He listened to the caller for a brief moment. "Hey, Pete! Yes, it was actually Maisie who left that message."

More murmuring from Pete. Delaney waited impatiently, knowing the outcome of the call would either relieve some of their stress or add to it.

"Uh-huh. I see. Are you sure? Yes, that's plenty. I really appreciate it. I'll let Maisie know. Yes."

Wyatt hung up and offered Delaney a high five. "You were right again, Friday. Pete needed a place to turn out those skinny cows. He's bringing them over late this afternoon, and he says Maisie can use an entire rack in one of the industrial coolers there. I can stay and help him unload the cows. Think you can, too? Do you have to go get Rachel?"

Delaney high-fived Wyatt. "Great! I don't have to pick up Rachel. She's spending the night at a friend's."

Wyatt picked up the location release forms and looked at the stack, and then at Delaney.

He seemed reluctant as he grabbed a pen from the cup on his desk. "I feel stuck, Del. I know you're right. We can't sit here and do nothing. But are we ready to risk changing things?"

He was staring intensely at her. She felt her throat constrict slightly. It was almost—almost—as though he weren't speaking solely about the Pines. Or was it just her imagination?

"You never know unless you take some kind of chance, right?" she squeaked.

He nodded, a slow smile spreading on his face. She held her breath. What was he going to say next?

He tapped the end of the pen on his desk and leaned forward, his eyes never leaving hers. "Where do I have to sign these things?"

The spell was broken. Ah, well. At least he was agreeing to—wait, what?

Delaney jumped up from her chair. "Really? What about being nervous about hosting a TV crew?"

Wyatt was flipping through the pages of the document on his desk, scribbling his signature as he went. He put on his best Cary Grant and said, "Nerves? That's what I have you for. We're a team. That's what we are."

Delaney tossed down the sheaf of bank documents

she hadn't even remembered that she was holding and threw her arms around Wyatt. Laughing, he returned her hug. She closed her eyes and sank into the embrace, joy at the possibilities of his decision flooding her. She wasn't even ashamed that her eyes seemed to be misting a little, and he didn't seem to mind that the hug was awkward—Delaney standing while he was sitting.

"Thank you, Wyatt. Thank you for taking the chance."

He squeezed her tight, his reply making her even happier. "Del, thanks for giving me the chance."

CHAPTER 5

Over the next several weeks, in preparation for their upcoming visitors, the Cabins in the Pines turned into a whirlwind of activity. Every member of the staff pitched in to make the best first impression possible. All of them hustled to try and get ready for the "*ABC's* invasion," as Wyatt had teasingly taken to calling it.

Slater and Wyatt cleared brush that had been overdue for removal—way overdue. Delaney had spent days cleaning and airing out the cabins. Maisie purged every chipped coffee cup and faded dinner plate at the Bean Pot and spent long hours scrubbing, degreasing, and even repairing rips in the patio screens at the restaurant.

Ursula cleaned the front office from top to bottom, even chasing a possum family out from underneath the front porch—which Wyatt had been glad Duke hadn't been around for. Even Delaney's daughter, Rachel, pitched in by helping Wyatt fill in the major potholes in the road to the Bean Pot. Wyatt patiently showed Rachel how to measure and mix the patch material, and then they each took a pothole to fill as joint practice. Rachel—much like her mother, Wyatt thought warmly—took what she'd learned and did a better job than he did. This led to some good-natured ribbing from Rachel, with Wyatt mock-threatening to douse her with his bucket of water.

Before they knew it, the entire month between Wyatt's signing of the location release forms and the day the film crew was scheduled to arrive had passed. Now, on the morning of the crew's arrival, instead of his normal alarm, Wyatt woke up to the persistent sounds of a very loud and clunky vacuum cleaner.

He tried to ignore the invading hum, but the sound got alternately louder and softer as whoever was wielding it pushed it back and forth, disorienting him enough that he couldn't fall back asleep. He pulled the blanket over his head, hoping to block out some of the noise.

"Come back later," Wyatt mumbled.

Who the heck is that? And why are they cleaning so early? he thought groggily. Two short, sharp, very loud barks made him sit straight up in bed—which made him realize he wasn't in his own bed. Groaning, Wyatt swung his feet to the floor, scrubbing his hands over his eyes and scrunching his toes in the throw rug that sat in front of his office couch. He couldn't believe he'd fallen asleep here.

Wyatt noticed the blanket that had been covering him. He reached out and ran a hand over the soft, Southwestern-patterned throw. Where had he seen this blanket before? Duke sat at the end of the couch, wagging his tail happily.

"Come here, boy. Good dog." When Wyatt held out his open palms, Duke rushed to his owner, jumping up and licking at Wyatt's face.

Outside of Wyatt's half-closed office door, the vacuum cleaner stopped running. He heard the sound of the cord being rolled up and the creaky supply closet door being opened and shut, signaling the end of his wakeup call. He stood, grabbed his phone off of his desk where it had been charging, and checked the time.

Wyatt groaned when he saw it was barely 6:00 a.m. He scowled at Duke.

"You certainly look ready for the day. Wish I was."

Wyatt rose slowly and shuffled out of the office, Duke bounding ahead of him. Out in reception, Wyatt heard Delaney greet the dog. He found himself smiling at the fact that Delaney was already here, even though it seemed as if she'd barely left the grounds all week. In fact, she and Rachel had been staying in one of the cabins in order to avoid the drive time Delaney usually had between their house, clear across town, and the Pines. The few times she'd left had been to run errands, retrieve supplies, or shuttle Rachel somewhere or other.

"Good morning," he said as he came out of the hallway and into the reception area.

She looked up from her spot, kneeling next to Duke, and gave Wyatt a sheepish smile. "Hi. I didn't mean to wake you."

"That's okay. I can't believe you're up and working so early." He glanced around reception, which gleamed. It appeared as though she hadn't just vacuumed, but also dusted, polished, and even re-cleaned the windows. "Wow. You didn't have to do all of this."

As she stood, Wyatt noticed her hair was half down instead of in its usual ponytail, and she'd put on makeup. Whatever she'd done had made her warm brown eyes stand out even more. Her hairstyle and the hints of blush and lip color were soft and natural, and though he'd always thought that Delaney was beautiful, the little touches made him much more aware of it. He thought briefly to how they had held hands back in his office, just before he'd signed the papers for the show. The memory made him stutter slightly as he complimented her.

"Y-you look great. The camera's going to love you." Those words slipped out so easily—*love you*. Wyatt was saved from further contemplation by Delaney's light laugh.

"Thanks. You, on the other hand..." she teased.

He caught sight of his rumpled shirt and ran a hand through his hair, which he was sure was probably frightening. "Yeah. This is bad."

"I think you still have clothes here from the mud run last month, and there are new camp shirts in the cabinet just over there. You want to change?"

"Definitely."

While Delaney went behind the front desk and started hauling old record boxes out from the storage closet, Wyatt grabbed the clean clothes and the toothbrush he kept in his desk. He changed in the bathroom just off the hallway outside his office. He washed his face, brushed his teeth, and emerged feeling much more awake. Not so awake that he didn't immediately think of coffee, though.

He returned to his office to stash his toothbrush and put on his boots. As he sat on the couch to tie his boot laces, his eyes fell on the blanket he'd left draped over the arm of the sofa. He tied his boots, folded the blanket neatly and took it out to reception with him.

Delaney was just opening an ancient-looking record box when he returned, and when she lifted the lid, a cloud of dust rose into the air. She waved it away, sputtering.

"What's in those, anyway?" Wyatt asked, leaning on the reception counter. The boxes were vaguely familiar, and he felt a momentary wave of sadness when he realized they might contain something of his parents'.

"I don't know," Delaney said, shrugging. "But they've been taking up half the supply closet for years. I wanted to clear them out so I could put the office supplies away. It'll be neater for—"

"*The ABC's Invasion?*" Wyatt interrupted in his best spooky sci-fi voice. She shot him a look.

"Yes. This is part of why I'm here so early. But I didn't know you'd stayed the whole night."

Wyatt affected a put-upon face. "*Someone's* been working me to the bone, so I just passed out back there. But she was also nice enough to toss a blanket over me last night, so at least there's that." He held up the blanket.

Delaney laughed, dusted her hands off, and crossed to take it from him, setting it under Ursula's desk. *That* was where he'd seen it! It was the emergency blanket Ursula kept there for the cold winters in the drafty front office. Their heating system wasn't exactly state-of-the-art. Although the blanket was thin, his aunt swore it had been blessed with elemental energy and it kept her perfectly warm.

"You were pretty out last night," Delaney said. "I was only up here for five minutes, I swear, trying to find that set of keys to cabin two. I walked back there, and you were snoring."

"I do not snore," he protested. "Must have been Duke."

Duke, hearing his name, jumped up from where he'd settled behind the front desk. Delaney bent down and scratched behind his ears. "Uh-huh. Duke, do you snore, buddy?" Duke leaned into her, gazing up at her adoringly. "No? I believe you."

Wyatt watched them with amusement, finding himself staring, too. Something about the way Delaney's smile reached her eyes, the way tendrils of her soft, deep brown hair framed her face, made him look at her just a little longer than normal. He cleared his throat and clapped his hands together.

"So, where's Rachel?"

Delaney straightened. "She's down at the Bean Pot with Maisie and Slater. Need coffee?"

"Boy, do I," Wyatt said, stretching. Duke ran a few circles around him, barking. Delaney put the lid back on the box she'd been sorting through and came out into the waiting area. Wyatt held the front door for her, but it was Duke who took advantage of the opportunity first. He took off out the front door, his ears flattened and his hind legs kicking up dirt.

Delaney peered out the door after him, and then she turned to Wyatt. "Should we just let him run?"

Wyatt nodded. "He knows his way. It's where the food's at."

They both jogged down the weathered wooden steps, and Wyatt reveled in the morning. The day would soon warm up, chasing away the hint of cool dampness, but right now it was the perfect weather to wake up to.

The crisp green canopy of trees above them filtered the early light. There were slow signs of the forest waking up, and the low carpet of moss and wildflowers on either side of the camp road glistened with cool dew. The air was fresh, and the campground was quiet—maybe the last bit of quiet they would get for a while. As they hit the parking lot, Ursula pulled up in her pastel pink Volkswagen Beetle. The pink should have clashed with her fiery red hair, but it didn't—it just fit. She rolled down her window as they neared her.

"Hey, you two! Where you headed?"

"The Bean Pot. Mr. Dedication here slept in his office, so we're going to fill him up with coffee and bacon so I can get more work out of him," Delaney explained brightly. Wyatt could only shake his head, grinning.

Ursula wagged a finger in their direction. "Don't stay too long. Remember those TV people will be here at eight."

"We won't, Ursula. Promise. You want anything?" Wyatt asked.

"Nope. I'll head in, in case they show up early." Ursula clambered out of her car in a flurry of batik print and beads.

Delaney pointed to Wyatt's truck with a questioning look, and he nodded, fishing out his keys. It would be faster if they drove, even though the walk to the kitchen wasn't all that long and part of him wanted to savor the morning just a little longer. He jogged to Delaney's side to open her door, and once she'd hopped up into the cab of the truck, he dug out his phone and checked the time again. It was 6:30 a.m. T-minus one and a half hours until invasion.

Whistling the theme song to an alien show he remembered from when he was younger, Wyatt rounded the back of the pickup, trying to steel himself for the day.

Coffee wasn't enough to prepare Wyatt for what greeted him, Delaney, Rachel, and Slater when they pulled back up to the office an hour later. The crew had indeed arrived early. Two large black vans sat outside the small log building, and strangers were milling around like a hive of busy bees. Wyatt stopped just at the edge of where the camp road met the parking lot, and he and every one of his passengers stared at the spectacle descending on the office of the Cabins in the Pines.

"Wow," Delaney said, her eyes wide.

"How many people do they need to film a reality TV show?" Rachel wondered aloud, sounding as awed as Wyatt felt at the size of the crew, which appeared to be made up of about three dozen people.

"Well, filming outdoors like this, there are a lot more variables, takes a lot more prep. It's not like they shoot in a perfectly controlled indoor studio like *Lovestruck High*," Slater explained.

Wyatt, Delaney, and Rachel all turned to gape at him.

"What?" Slater said, flicking his hair out of his eyes. "It's easy to get hooked on. The drama, you know?"

Duke started barking excitedly out of the half-open back window of the truck cab, and Rachel had to hold him to keep him from jumping against the glass. Wyatt sneaked a glance over at Delaney, who was still staring at the office.

"Well, I've got things to do," she said, reaching for her door handle. "I trust you can—"

Without looking at her, Wyatt reached out and grabbed her hand, halting her exit momentarily. "Oh, no you don't. You can't desert me now, Friday."

She patted his hand, smiling reassuringly. "Don't worry, Wyatt. Just some last-minute checks to make sure we're ready. You go in, introduce yourself, see if Ursula needs you. You'll be fine."

Wyatt could feel himself staring like a deer in headlights at the crew pouring out of their vehicles. A man got out of one of the vans and moved to stand just at the bottom of the office steps. He was short, older, intimidating, and dressed unwisely for summer in all black—slacks, a long-sleeved shirt, and a dark charcoal newsboy hat. He was obviously in charge, barking orders at the milling crew.

"Man, I thought we'd never find this place!" he exclaimed. "Let's start with some exteriors! I'm gonna need that rock moved, and can we do something about that tree?"

"Hey," Wyatt groused to no one in particular. "I like that tree." Wyatt felt as bulldozed as that tree was likely about to be.

"Do you think Alexandra Brent-Collingsworth is in there?" Rachel asked, sounding starstruck.

"Come on," Delaney urged. "We won't know if we don't go in, and we can't spend all day in here."

Wyatt put the truck back into drive and pulled up alongside the vans, but not so close that he'd impede their ability to keep unloading case after case of equipment. Everyone spilled out of the truck, and Duke made himself a general, affable nuisance to the crew, many of whom paused and kneeled to give the dog a quick scratch or pet. Duke liked the invaders just fine, it seemed to Wyatt. *Traitor.*

They all stopped short of the stairs, and Rachel hoisted her bag over her shoulder as she asked Delaney, "Mom, can I go in?"

"Sure, honey, but ask Ursula to let you plug your laptop in behind reception and try not to get trampled."

Rachel didn't have to be told twice. She zoomed up the stairs and disappeared inside. Slater clapped Wyatt on the back and hefted the toolbox he was carrying. "Right. I'm just going to go do, y'know, my work stuff. Good luck, man." Wyatt had never seen the guy disappear so fast.

"Just you and me now, Friday," Wyatt said, taking a deep breath. Smiling affectionately, she reached up and fussed with his hair, and he absently repeated the motion, smoothing his hand over the same spot she'd just fixed.

The guy in the newsboy hat finally noticed them. He marched up to them, all business, without a hint of a smile on his face.

"You Wyatt Andrews?" he asked bluntly.

"That's me," Wyatt said, holding out a hand. The man eyed it for a moment, then reluctantly shook it. "And this is my right-hand gal, Delaney."

Delaney offered her hand and, this time, the man swept it up immediately. "Oh. Why, hello. I'm sorry we're late. This place is off the beaten path. We really got turned around back there at the bypass."

"No problem," Delaney replied sweetly. "You're definitely not the first."

The man flipped her hand over and kissed her knuckles. "Norman Gilmore, director, at your service."

Wyatt felt immediately uncomfortable and cut in as Delaney giggled. He took a step toward Delaney, putting an arm around her. The sudden surge of possessiveness gave him pause, but he brushed it off as he spoke. "Thanks, Norm. You're actually early, so..."

Norman released Delaney's hand, much to Wyatt's relief.

"Yes, yes," Norman said, waving a hand in the direction of the office, "but from what I've seen so far, even early would be late here. Listen, sorry for the chaos, but we're on a tight schedule. Can we go somewhere and talk?"

"Sure," Wyatt said. "My office?"

"Works for me," Norman said gruffly. Then, without waiting for either of them, the man turned and marched toward the office.

Delaney poked Wyatt. Realizing his arm was still around her, he stepped away, breaking contact. "Sorry," he said.

"I wasn't complaining," she replied, something sparking in her eyes.

Wyatt realized he hadn't minded having his arm around her, either—and the thought made a slow warmth creep into his chest. As crazy as it was, he let the warmth sit there and expand a bit. Delaney wasn't his, at least not in any romantic sense. She was his best friend, his right-hand woman, and that was all.

Is that really all?

He was jolted from his thoughts by another gentle poke from Delaney. "C'mon, boss. Our public awaits."

Moments later, they were in Wyatt's office with the door closed. Wyatt would have laughed had anyone told him he'd be closing his door twice in one month. A new record. Wyatt gave Delaney the chair behind his desk and motioned Norman to sit in the chair that faced it. Standing, Wyatt crossed his arms over his chest and listened as Norman launched into his rundown.

"You received the introductory emails, right? And you talked to the network people?"

"I did," Delaney said.

"Great," Norman continued. "Then you've got an idea about all this. To start, we'll set up here and take establishing shots, take a camera around the place to get some exteriors, that kind of thing. All of that can be done without involving either of you. But the interviews…"

Norman looked around Wyatt's office, appraising the space.

"Yes, here might be the best place for that. This room will work great on camera. We'll set up right over there." He pointed to a corner. "But that means we'll be coming in and out of here often."

Wyatt's head was spinning. He gripped the back of the chair where Delaney sat, and she reached up to pat his hand.

Norman continued. "So we can do the first on-camera interviews starting this afternoon. The questions will be given to you ahead of time. You know…tell us about the history of the business, what's wrong with it, why it's tanking."

Wyatt felt suddenly defensive. "Nothing's wrong with this place, actually."

Norman seemed to consider Wyatt's words. "Well, I'll tell you what, buddy. That all depends on what Alexandra thinks when she gets here. I've seen the network set up an episode, then Alexandra arrives and hates the place. You know what happens then? We pack up and leave."

Wyatt's tone was carefully controlled, but frustrated. "My family has built a great place here. We need some upgrades and maybe some new amenities, that's all."

Suddenly, Norman made a horrified face. "Upgrades? Amenities? Uh...you guys have indoor plumbing, right?"

Wyatt shook his head and rolled his eyes. A sharp reply was just at the tip of his tongue when Delaney sat forward.

"Yes, we have plumbing," she explained evenly. "He means an online reservation system, WiFi, cable, that kind of stuff."

Norman relaxed visibly, nodding his head.

"Okay. Whew. That's a relief. Because of the rushed schedule, we were relying a lot—maybe too much—on your audition tape, and we didn't get a chance to send out a scout. I was just worried that..." Norman laughed. "Sorry. Of course, you do. You're rustic, but you're not *that* rustic, right?"

Wyatt tried to take slow, deep breaths to calm his rising anxiety. He was grateful that Delaney had interjected when she had.

"So, like I was saying, here's what we're going to be doing, and here's what we're going to need from you." Norman began rattling off another laundry list of setups, tasks, and appearances that would be required of the two of them over the course of filming.

Wyatt felt the knot in his stomach returning. Just then, thankfully, the door to the office popped open—

no knock—and stopped Norman's rushed speech. A woman who Wyatt assumed was part of the crew bustled in. Leaning over by Norman, she cupped a hand over his ear and whispered dramatically. Tension quickly filled the air.

Now what? Wyatt wondered.

Norman cleared his throat, waving to dismiss the crew member. "Mr. Andrews, Ms. Phillips, Alexandra is almost here. Are you ready to meet her?"

Wyatt looked at Delaney. He gave her a nervous, crooked smile.

"Showtime," he said.

CHAPTER 6

"I feel like a ping-pong ball today," Delaney whispered dramatically.

From her easy, familiar morning with Wyatt to the chaos of the crew of *The ABC's of Business* descending, to now standing outside again in the steadily increasing heat of the day, waiting expectantly for the star of the show to arrive, she was starting to get a headache.

Wyatt stood next to her, hands in his pockets, rocking impatiently on his heels. To the casual observer, he might not seem too put out by the pandemonium unfolding around them, but Delaney could read the subtle tells that said he was stressed, too.

What if she hates it here? Delaney fretted. *What if she packs up and leaves?*

"Now, when Alexandra arrives, we'll need your office for about an hour so we can talk filming," Norman informed Wyatt. "You understand. We'll let you know if we need you after."

Delaney bristled at his tone but stayed silent. She could tell Wyatt wasn't fond of Norman, and neither was she, but the whole scenario was so overwhelming—and it had been her idea—so she tried to keep a cheerful, positive mindset about the whole fiasco. She'd never been involved in a TV show before. Maybe things would settle down once everything was set up.

The only ones who seemed to be ecstatic about the process so far were Rachel and Duke. The former was hanging out on the front porch behind them, watching the crew run a maze of electrical components in and around the office. The latter was bouncing around those workers, who, to their credit, stopped more often than not to show him a little love.

Delaney craned to see Rachel, who seemed settled into the rocking chair she sat in, with a big glass of lemonade beside her, her laptop on her lap, and her phone balanced precariously on the arm of the chair.

"Honey," Delaney said, "don't you want to go run around camp? Do outside stuff?"

Rachel shook her head. "I am outside. This is outside stuff."

It was Delaney's turn to roll her eyes. She supposed Rachel deserved a break after all the help she'd given cleaning up before the show's arrival, but they'd have to talk about spending some of her summer break outside in the actual summer.

The crunch of tires on gravel drew Delaney's attention, and she turned her head back to see a long, sleek, black luxury car pull up. The driver got out, but Norman rushed to the rear door and beat the man to the door handle.

"Allow me," Norman fawned as he popped open the rear door and held out a hand. One very expensive shoe came into view, and then the other. Their heels sunk slightly into the dirt of the parking lot as the woman they were attached to glided out of the backseat. Delaney had never glided anywhere, much less been able to exit a vehicle without looking like, well, she was climbing out of a vehicle.

Alexandra Brent-Collingsworth was slim, petite, and utterly gorgeous. She was even more dazzling in person than she'd been on TV. She appeared about ten years older than Delaney's thirty-three, with blonde hair cut in a stylish, chin-length bob and striking features that were accented expertly by just the right amount of makeup. She wore a skirt suit that was just a shade brighter than navy—colorful but still understated. She smiled politely at Norman as he guided her clear of the car door and shut it.

"You didn't tell me she looked like that," Wyatt whispered to Delaney. She had to tamp down on a not-so-teeny-weeny spike of jealousy.

"Well, you should have watched the show sometime in the last *month*," she shot back.

"*Touché,*" he conceded.

Delaney watched as Alexandra carefully walked the short distance between the car and where they stood, Norman trailing her closely the whole way. Behind them, another man exited the car from the other side, dragging several pieces of luggage with him, unassisted. Delaney frowned, but her attention was quickly drawn back to the woman nearing them.

When Alexandra reached them, she held her hand out toward Delaney first.

"Alexandra," she said simply. "You must be Ms. Phillips."

When Delaney took her hand, Alexandra's handshake wasn't limp or weak, but firm and professional. Delaney liked that. She felt a little embarrassed at her momentary jealousy. In person, Alexandra's cultured British accent wasn't as intimidating as it seemed onscreen sometimes. To Delaney, it was actually very soft and inviting.

Alexandra continued. "I absolutely loved your audition video. It showed the place off nicely. I'm anticipating the full tour—you know, without all of this mess around." She waved a well-manicured hand at the bedlam going on around them.

"Please call me Delaney. And thank you, I'm happy to show you around whenever you'd like," Delaney replied, cracking a smile. Her stress was easing a bit at Alexandra's easy demeanor, which seemed at odds with her no-nonsense appearance. "And this is Wyatt Andrews, the owner of the Pines."

Delaney stepped back so Wyatt could shake hands with her.

"Ms. Brent-Collingsworth, thank you for coming," Wyatt said sincerely.

"Mr. Andrews, thank you for having us. I love it when I can show my viewers a real family business like yours succeeding again. And, please, call me Alex, both of you."

Wyatt nodded, acquiescing. "Wyatt, then," he replied in kind.

Norman tried to cut in as he hovered behind Alexandra. "Uh, Alexandra, if I could get a quick meeting, I have a few things I'd like to—"

She held up a hand, silencing him. The man who Delaney had noticed at the car had reached them, and she turned to him instead of responding to Norman. "This is our production assistant, Charles," she explained to Delaney and Wyatt.

"Hey," came a muffled voice from behind a stack of luggage.

"Wyatt," Alexandra said, laying her hand on Wyatt's arm momentarily, "could you please show Charles where I'll be staying? He can see to my luggage and getting my room set up."

"Sure," Wyatt said, craning to see around the luggage. "You need some help there?" he asked Charles.

"Sure, that would be great," the voice replied. Wyatt relieved the man of a few bags, and the youthful face of a thin, slightly bookish man appeared. His glasses were askew. He adjusted the spectacles and gave Wyatt a grateful smile. "Thanks, man."

Norm spoke up again. "So, Alex, about that meeting?"

Alex turned on her heel. "Actually, right now, I'd love to take Delaney up on her offer of a tour. When Wyatt's done showing Charles my room, do you think you could be a dear, Norm, and start Wyatt's first one-on-one while we girls have a gander around the place? Maybe have your second shoot some establishing shots and exteriors?"

Norm sputtered, seeming as though he wanted to protest Alex's directions, but he recovered quickly. "Absolutely, Alexandra."

Lifting his chin toward Wyatt, he puffed up slightly. "I'll see you in your office in fifteen minutes, Mr. Andrews."

With that, Norm strode off, barking a few instructions to the outside crew on his way back into the office.

Delaney glanced surreptitiously over her shoulder to see if Rachel was watching all of this. Although

Rachel appeared to be engrossed in her phone, from where Delaney stood it looked like she was faking so she could gawk at what was unfolding right in front of her.

Delaney caught her eye and winked. Rachel made what Delaney had recently come to label as her "OMG" face. It was all Delaney could do not to burst out laughing.

Wyatt nodded at his truck. "You can put the luggage in the bed, Charles. I'll drive us over to the cabins." Charles swung himself and the remaining luggage in the direction of Wyatt's truck with Wyatt following him. Momentarily, the truck started up and the men were off to the cabins.

"Well," Alex said. "Now that we're alone, save the many, *many* people milling around your land to set all of this up, why don't you show me the Cabins in the Pines?"

Delaney smiled. "You got it. Let me grab the keys to the golf cart. I'll be right back."

As she jogged up the steps past Rachel and into the office, Delaney felt her optimism rising again. Alex seemed pretty normal, and, well...*nice.* Ursula was in a pretzel-like configuration on the floor behind the reception desk, and Delaney did a double take as she passed her on the way to the drawer where they kept the keys.

"Urs, what are you doing?" Delaney said, wide-eyed. "Did you fall? Are you hurt?"

Ursula unfolded and resumed a non-pretzel posture. She clicked her tongue lightly. "No, no, dear. That was tortoise pose, very good for core strength and stress relief."

Delaney grabbed the keys she was after and tossed them up slightly before snatching them from the air. "Well, I think you can relax a little. Alexandra's here, and she seems surprisingly normal. I'm showing her around in the cart."

Ursula moved into another stretch that hurt Delaney just witnessing it. "That's good, dear. Rachel going with you?"

"I would prefer that she stay here with you. Is that okay?"

"Of course," Ursula replied from somewhere in the middle of her pose. "I will try to pry her away from her technology and teach her to balance her chakras."

Delaney scoffed. "Good luck."

Back outside, Delaney asked Rachel to move back inside so she could be near Ursula and so the film crew wouldn't be stumbling over her or her gadgets. Rachel, with an overexaggerated sigh, picked up her things. Delaney kissed her forehead and dashed back down the steps. Alex stood there, looking as though the increasing summer sun wasn't affecting her one bit.

"Ready?" Delaney asked.

"Lead the way," Alex replied with a smile.

Moments later, they were bumping along the camp road in the only golf cart that existed at the Pines. Like a lot of things on-site, it wasn't new, it wasn't shiny, but it had been around for years and Delaney loved it. Though the ride wasn't a smooth one, Delaney was thankful they had patched up what they could. The camp road in the golf cart had previously been more akin to a ride on the rapids than a relaxing cruise down a scenic forest trail.

"And these are the tent sites. They used to be very popular with backpackers. We've got a lot of trails and climbs around—some on the property, some just a short hike away."

"Used to be?" Alex asked, her tone neutral. Delaney reminded herself that Alex was here to help, and she fought her urge to defend the predicament the Pines was in right now.

"Well, we've lost a lot of clientele to the bypass. And we're not online, so unless you know we're here, it's hard to find us."

"I see," said Alexandra, and Delaney detected a genuine note of sympathy in her voice as she continued. "It's a shame. It's so beautiful here. I know plenty of people who would kill to get out of the city for a retreat here."

Delaney watched the lush, tranquil scenery fly past as they drove down the camp road toward the lake. "Actually, the Pines was once a famous honeymoon spot and getaway back in the 1940s and '50s. Lots of couples would get married back in the city and come out here for a little peace and quiet. We've hosted a few weddings here, too."

"Is this where you and Wyatt got married?" Alex asked.

Delaney sputtered. "Oh! Oh, no, we're not—I mean, not that there'd be anything wrong with that. He's just... we're just..."

"Friends?" Alex prompted, laughing lightly. "I'm sorry to have assumed."

"Yes, friends," Delaney said, recovering. "And don't

be sorry. I've known Wyatt since we were little. Rachel's father and I divorced years ago. Jacob took a big-time job in the city and probably goes on retreats like the one you mentioned with his new wife."

Alex looked chagrined. "I know a lot of men like that. They usually wear very expensive suits but spend Christmas alone. So that was your daughter back there? It must be hard raising a daughter and trying to keep everything together here."

Delaney took a moment to answer, her thoughts sidetracked by Alexandra's question about her relationship with Wyatt. Wyatt dated, Delaney knew that, but he always confided to her when things fizzled out after a few dates that no one ever felt like a forever fit. Delaney took a soft right turn at the lake access road, bringing her mind back to Alex's question.

"It can be a juggle, but this town, this place, brought me a lot of happiness as a child, and Wyatt and his parents really saved me after my divorce. They—and he—cared for Rachel and me when I was at my lowest. Now I want to return the favor. I want to take care of the Pines the way Carol and Bill would have wanted. But I know I can't do it on my own. And Wyatt's stubborn, but he wants to preserve the legacy, too."

"So, Wyatt's parents retired?" Alex had taken a small notebook from somewhere and was jotting down notes.

Delaney paused. "No, they passed away a couple of years ago. Car accident."

Alex paused, too, her pen hovering over her notebook. "I see. I'm sorry to hear that." She clicked her pen closed and tucked it and her notebook back inside her suit jacket.

Silence fell as they drove up to the lakeshore and parked. They sat for a moment, staring out over the sparkling water. The slightest of breezes made the surface of Lake Fairwood ripple just enough to catch the sunlight and explode into a wide, glittering spectacle. Delaney took a deep breath as memories of Carol and Bill came flooding back. She swung a leg out to get out of the golf cart but was stopped by Alex's hand on her arm.

"You're a good friend," Alex said sincerely. "Wyatt's lucky to have you."

"Thank you," Delaney said, blushing slightly. Despite her upper-crust appearance and her no-nonsense persona on TV, Alexandra was surprisingly easy to talk to. They both got out of the golf cart, and Delaney led the way to one of the lake jetties. Alex made the trip slightly awkwardly in her high heels. They stepped up onto the pier and walked to the end, staring out across the water.

"We'll get some fabulous shots here. This view alone was worth the trip."

"It's stunning," Delaney agreed.

She thought about Wyatt back at the office dealing with Norman, and of Norman trying to interview Wyatt. They had to be mixing like oil and water. Delaney wondered what other difficulties lay ahead in the filming.

As if Alex were reading her mind, the older woman spoke up.

"Our schedule is going to be very hectic while we're here. I'm sure Norman already told you some of the details. You've seen the show, of course?"

Delaney nodded.

"Well, I'm not sure if he told you that, sometimes,

for dramatic effect, we'll have to, you know, exaggerate the problems around here a bit."

You won't have to exaggerate much, Delaney thought, thinking of the leaky bathroom, the creaky walk-in cooler, and the dozens of other little issues that had popped up around camp. But Delaney recalled the episodes she and Rachel had seen, remembered the dramatic scenes right before the show would cut to commercial.

"I love the show, but I kind of thought all that was real. Some of it was *exaggerated*?"

"Tut, tut," Alex admonished. "It's nothing more than a little movie magic, my dear. The lawyers and accountants will arrive this afternoon to comb through the financials, but I almost don't care what they say. I'm mad about this place already. We're going to make it shine like the day it opened."

Delaney felt a surge of hope. "Really?"

"Absolutely. You know," Alex said, turning to face Delaney, "it's a hard world out there for us women. We have to stick together. You did the right thing, inviting me out here."

"Yes, I think so," Delaney said with more confidence than she'd felt just a few hours ago.

The two women looked out over the lake again, and Delaney felt a huge weight begin to lift from her shoulders. It seemed as though the Pines was going to be all right.

Alex clasped her hands together, turning back toward the golf cart. "Well, let's get going, then. I want to see the whole place, right down to the washrooms. I think it's time to get started bringing the Cabins in the Pines back to life."

CHAPTER 7

A few hours later, Wyatt was grateful to be out of the hot seat. He'd had no idea that the list of questions he'd be asked during his interview would feel so invasive—or bring up so many mixed feelings. By the time Norman was done asking, asking again, and then asking with different emphasis, Wyatt's head was pounding. He'd never been happier to get out of his own office.

Collapsing into the second chair behind the reception desk, Wyatt sagged dramatically. "Remind me why we're doing this?"

Ursula, who was shredding paper noisily at the desk, rolled her eyes at him and shook her head. "Please. You'll get no sympathy from me. You know that Delaney's been out doing all of her work, working *around* all this nonsense? And Maisie's got a crowd down at the Bean Pot, mostly lookie-loos from town, trying to get a peek at the circus. Oh, that reminds me, Slater took your truck. He had to run over to Pete's to get backup supplies from the cooler there."

Wyatt noticed that Ursula was sorting through one of the old record boxes Delaney had cleared out of storage. "Find anything in those yet?" he asked.

"Nope. Unless you're interested in the receipts your dad kept for toilet paper and pens. Want to lend a hand?"

Wyatt smiled despite the small, sad reminder. "I'm good. You're doing great work. Did you tell Del that Rachel went down to the Bean Pot to get lunch?"

"Yep," Ursula replied, feeding more scrap paper into the shredder. "Got her on her walkie. She's down at cabin six. Now that Slater has that bathroom all fixed, Del's painting it. Looks like we'll need it, too, for the crew."

Wyatt hopped up out of the chair and gave Ursula a kiss on the cheek. "Thanks, Urs. I'll go down and see if I can lend *her* a hand. The walk might do me good."

He hadn't even made it out from behind reception when the door to his office opened and Norman's voice carried into the lobby. "Mr. Andrews?"

"Yes?" Wyatt asked hesitantly, wincing. Ursula paused in her shredding.

"Don't go anywhere. We're almost set up for filming Alexandra's arrival, so we'll need you in about ten."

"Didn't she already arrive?" Ursula whispered.

Wyatt shrugged and made a confused face at Ursula.

"Okay!" Wyatt yelled back down the hall. Norman didn't reply, just closed the office door with a firm *click*.

Wyatt sank back down into the chair he'd just vacated. It was almost noon, and reminding Ursula about Rachel and the Bean Pot reminded Wyatt that he was getting hungry. He wanted to talk to Delaney, see what Alexandra had said on their camp tour. It actually felt a little strange to him to not just be able to radio her and meet for lunch. He didn't like the feeling.

True to Norman's prediction, ten minutes later, Wyatt's hair had been rearranged for the third time— a feat, considering his crew cut—he had a boom mic hovering over him, and he was being coached on what to say when Alexandra "arrived" at the Pines. He stood outside, in almost the exact spot he and Delaney had stood this morning. He felt that same strange feeling, standing here without her, something he couldn't quite place.

"Roll it!"

The filming went by in a blur. He was acutely aware of the two cameras set up surrounding the black sedan that Alexandra pulled up in. Wyatt's palms were sweaty when he reached out to shake Alexandra's hand. He did what they'd told him to, making small talk with Alex, thumbnailing the reason they'd asked her to come and help with the Pines, and holding the door open for her as the camera followed them from the parking lot to the office.

"My, this place is in the middle of nowhere, isn't it? How long since this building's been painted? What's this décor—early '70s chic?" Wyatt's ears burned when Alexandra's words came out clipped and critical. He was shocked at her sudden change in personality—a change that had happened after the cameras started rolling.

They'd made it into the lobby and reception area. Wyatt was expecting to see Ursula at her post, shredding. Instead, she'd taken that exact moment to take a yoga break. Wyatt, Alexandra, and the whole crew behind them stopped at the reception desk. Ursula, oblivious, completed a swan-like stretch that Wyatt was pretty sure he'd never been limber enough to complete, even in his younger, football-playing days.

Wyatt cleared his throat, but Ursula didn't hear him. Behind them, the cameras still rolled. Alex reached out and ran a finger over the counter, appeared to inspect her finger for dust, then tapped the bell that sat on the front desk twice, sharply. Ursula stood up, startled.

"Oh, I thought you folks were going to be outside for a while." Ursula reached over and lifted a bowl that was wafting wisps of smoke and began waving it around the reception desk. Alex covered her nose and coughed.

"What is *that*?" Alex asked, face bearing an expression of horror.

"Sage," Ursula explained. "It clears bad energy."

"Ursula," Wyatt said, perhaps a little more sternly than was necessary, "can we put that out?"

Ursula suddenly spotted the cameras over Wyatt's shoulder, went a little pale, and simply nodded, carrying the bowl off past the cameras and out the front door.

"Not a very traditional greeting for your guests," Alex commented.

"Yeah. Sorry about that. It won't happen again," Wyatt mumbled. He felt both embarrassed and guilty. Ursula's little rituals were part of the character of the Pines. He actually loved hearing her meditation music waft down the hall and into his office early in the morning. But under the microscope of the cameras, he found himself apologizing.

Just then, Slater burst through the back door, calling out, "Hey, anybody around? I'm headed out to the kitchen, thought I'd see if anyone wants to come.

And I fixed that gnarly clog in the family bathrooms. It wasn't easy, but I..." Slater skidded to a stop when he realized he'd just walked into a room full of people—one of them hoisting a camera. He wasn't exactly camera-ready, wearing a pair of stained coveralls that had seen better days.

"Oh, hey everyone." Slater seemed to notice Alexandra last. Recognition dawned on his face, and he leaned forward, holding out a hand toward her. "Wow! You're the famous lady. I don't think we've met. Slater."

Alex recoiled from Slater's extended hand. Slater's hand hung in the air for a moment, and then he withdrew it, wiping it on his coveralls. Wyatt could tell he was embarrassed.

Wyatt jumped in, scrambling for words. "Slater, I don't think—I mean, Alex, you don't have to—"

He felt Alex's hand on his arm. "Oh, don't worry about it, Wyatt," she said sweetly, tucking her short blond bob behind one ear and fluttering her lashes. "We're here to help the image of your business. Come on. Which way to your office?"

Wyatt knew she knew where his office was. She was just playing for the cameras. *Jeez*, he thought, *this alone could get exhausting—always pretending.* And her implication rankled him a little. His crew wasn't bad for the image of the Pines. He wanted to protest, but he was nervously cognizant that they were still being filmed.

"Just down this hallway," he said, putting a hand on Alex's back. "Open door at the end." He gestured, *After you.*

Alexandra smiled and nodded, then started down the hall. Wyatt followed, throwing a look back over his shoulder, expecting to see Ursula coming back in. Instead, he saw Slater, who was glaring at Alexandra with annoyance—and Delaney, standing quietly by the door, her arms crossed over her chest and her eyes full of disappointment.

Uh-oh. The expression on her face said it all.

Delaney was starting to get a bad feeling again. She's seen *The ABC's of Business*, so she knew Alexandra's onscreen persona didn't exactly jibe with the softer, more personable side Delaney had seen on their camp tour. But something about how the cameras had caught Ursula doing something so...so...*Ursula*—a little kooky, yet endearing—and twisted it into something negative made Delaney uneasy. And Wyatt had just seemed frozen.

The office was full of the crew, and Slater had slipped out the back door before Delaney could talk to him, so she backed out the door and closed it quietly behind her. Once she was back out in the summer sun, she was grateful for the warmth and fresh air. It helped clear her head. She walked around the office, searching for Ursula, but she didn't see her anywhere. Her VW was still in the lot, parked next to Delaney's car, so Delaney knew she hadn't left work.

Slater was climbing into Wyatt's truck just as Delaney rounded the corner of the office and hit the camp road toward the Bean Pot. He rolled down his widow and leaned out.

"Where you headed, and why are you frowning?"

Delaney's walkie-talkie crackled, and she reached down and switched it off, not wanting Wyatt to try and reach her—not until she'd found Ursula and talked to her. Jogging around the back of the pickup, she popped the passenger's door and climbed in. She peered over the backseat and into the bed of the truck. A collection of cardboard boxes sat stacked in the back.

Answering Slater's first question but ignoring his second, Delaney said, "I'm headed to the kitchen. You?"

Slater shook his thumb toward the bed of the truck as Delaney fastened her seat belt. "Me, too," he said. "Maisie ran out of eggs this morning, and she was guessing she'd be out of burgers. I made a run to Pete's."

"That's great," Delaney replied distractedly, still stewing over what she'd seen inside. What was she more upset about, Alex's behavior toward Ursula and Slater, Wyatt's not standing up for them, or the sight of Wyatt's hand on Alex's back?

"So, show's going well. Alex seems nice," Slater joked.

Delaney didn't respond, just snorted indelicately and stared out the window as they drove.

"Something happen before I came into the office, Del?" Slater asked.

"Yeah," she said, avoiding any elaboration. "But maybe I'm just letting it get to me too much. I need to talk to Ursula. I'm hoping we'll find her at the Bean Pot."

Slater thankfully let it go without further question. They were at the kitchen within a few minutes, and Delaney and Slater both stared at the abundance of cars in the gravel lot adjacent to the restaurant.

"Well, it could be that Maisie's about to put both of us to work," Slater observed.

They parked, and Delaney climbed out of the truck. Rachel burst out of the restaurant, wheat-colored braids flying, a food-stained apron tied around her waist, and a huge smile on her face. "Mom!" she shouted, skidding to a stop by the tailgate of the truck. Delaney stifled a laugh at her daughter's overexuberance.

"Mom, Maisie's letting me take orders and deliver food to the tables! I'm writing everything down exactly like the customers say it. It's so fun. And I'm even getting tips!" Rachel reached into the front pocket of her apron and came out with a neat stack of folded bills. Delaney pressed her lips together to keep a giggle in check and nodded, impressed.

"Wow, honey. And not a phone, laptop, or television in sight."

Rachel rolled her eyes.

"Oh, but an eye roll. Well, at least *that's* still the same," Delaney added, reaching out and tugging on one of Rachel's braids. "Great job, honey. I'm sure Maisie appreciates the help, and I'm proud of you for pitching in. You want to help me and Slater unload these supplies?"

From inside the Bean Pot, a faint, "Order up!" could be heard.

"Oops. Sorry, Mom. Gotta go. That's me." With another impish grin, Rachel was off, disappearing into the screened-in porch and back inside the restaurant.

"Looks like it's just us, boss," Slater said. "Shall we?"

Delaney grabbed a box of burger patties from the

back of the pickup and motioned with her free hand to Slater. "After you, kind sir."

The moment they stepped inside the restaurant, Delaney wondered if this was a situation where she could back out quietly as she'd done at the office. But Slater was behind her, so she reluctantly stepped into the dining room.

Every table was full, as were the dozen barstools that were fixed to the concrete floor and lined up beneath the front counter. Maisie, easily spotted because of the sparkly rhinestone headband in her blonde hair, was zooming between the kitchen and the counter, refilling drinks and dropping off plates.

Rachel came through the swinging double doors balancing four burger baskets, yelling, "Coming out hot!" Delaney couldn't hold in her laughter.

Tables were filled with mostly familiar faces and a few patrons dressed all in black who Delaney thought must have been part of the filming crew.

Delaney noticed Charles, Alexandra's assistant, squeezed onto the stool at the far end of the counter. Maisie glanced over, saw Delaney and Slater, and motioned them toward the kitchen.

"You go ahead," Delaney shouted over the din of the packed restaurant. "I'll be right there."

Slater nodded. "I'll grab the rest of the stuff from the truck."

Delaney tightened her grip on the box she was carrying and carefully weaved her way through the crowded dining room to where Charles was sitting. As she neared, she noticed he was peering shyly over his glasses, watching Maisie as she flitted around like a friendly, French-fry-bearing hummingbird.

"Hi!" Delaney said. "How's your lunch?"

He jumped slightly, as though she'd startled him. "Me? What? Oh, yes. It's great, thank you."

"You're welcome. We like to make sure everyone's happy. It's a very friendly place here."

"Yes, she is, isn't she?" Charles sighed, a sappy smile on his lips. Realizing what he'd said, he sat up straighter and corrected himself. "*It* is. Definitely a nice change from the city."

Delaney shook her head, amused. "I was actually coming over to make sure the room was okay for Alexandra. I cleaned it myself this morning, put in fresh towels, and opened all the windows."

Charles took a bite of a fry and nodded, chewing. "It's perfect. We travel a lot with the show and Alex is very particular, but everything in her cabin looks great. I know she'll love it."

"Good," Delaney said. "Let us know if Alex or the crew need anything. If *you* need anything."

Charles smiled again, this time warmly at Delaney. "Thank you. It really is lovely here."

Delaney couldn't help but notice that his gaze had returned to Maisie as he'd spoken.

How sweet, Delaney thought as she turned to pick her way back to the kitchen. Charles seemed like a nice guy. Delaney wondered how long the crew would be here and if the nerdy Charles had any chance of a date with the vivacious Maisie, or if he would ever have the courage to ask.

You're one to talk. How long have you kept these new feelings for Wyatt a secret?

It had always been easy for them to be around each other. In the past few years, it had become more than easy—it had become *important*. He had slipped seamlessly into Delaney and Rachel's life, helping in a million little ways Delaney had started to notice—especially the ones that involved her daughter. Wyatt patiently helped Rachel with schoolwork, taught her to drive the camp golf cart, and—to Rachel's extreme delight— even built the swimming deck that floated in the water near his house last summer, expressly at the request of Rachel and her friends.

Delaney felt more for Wyatt than mere friendship, but she had no idea if he felt the same way. And she would never have the courage to find out.

Trying to redirect her thoughts, Delaney made it back to the relative quiet of the kitchen. Sitting at a prep table on a spare stool and munching on a sandwich, sat Ursula. Delaney dropped her box of burgers on a nearby counter and rushed to her friend.

"Urs! Are you okay? I saw what happened at the office. You didn't do anything wrong, no matter what it seemed like—"

Ursula wiped her mouth with a napkin and waved away Delaney's emphatic words. "Honey, honey, calm down. I didn't take any of that seriously. Really? I didn't get to be this Zen by letting little bumps in the road like that get me down. Besides, I hoofed it down here just in time to catch an extra tuna melt that got made by mistake."

"Win-win," Slater piped up, hauling in the last of the supplies from the truck. Ursula popped a fry into her mouth, grinning. Slater reached over and stole a fry. Delaney was relieved.

"Oh, thank goodness. You're family. You know Wyatt loves you."

"I know, dear. But, despite the fact that this place really needs the boost that this show's going to give us, I'd like to say for the record that that woman, Alex, has some pretty unhappy energy."

"It's the first day. It's stressful for everybody, I'm sure," Delaney offered. Ursula lifted the basket of French fries toward Delaney, but Delaney declined. "Nope, got to get back to cabin six and do a second coat of paint in that bathroom in a few minutes. Thanks, though." Delaney gave the other woman a kiss on the cheek.

"Later, Slater!" she called.

"Bye, Del!" Slater called from inside the walk-in cooler.

Back out in the dining room, Delaney was relieved to see some of the crowd had eased, and the small group of people who had been waiting for seats had cleared. Everyone had a seat. Rachel and Maisie were still circulating, but the pace didn't seem as frantic. Delaney checked with Maisie to make sure she couldn't use an extra hand, and Maisie shooed her away.

"Just don't take Rachel back quite yet. That girl's the best darned worker this place has seen since you and I worked summers here in high school."

"She may be as hardworking as we were, but we had way bigger hair," Delaney quipped. "Because we were cool."

"I think my hair's cool now," Maisie replied, gesturing to her summer-appropriate pixie cut. It suited her, highlighting her high cheekbones and green eyes.

"I think someone else here thinks so, too," Delaney said, tilting her head toward Charles.

"He's cute, right?" Maisie said, giggling. "In a quiet way."

"Yes, he is. Not my type, though. You go get 'em, girl."

Off of Maisie's laughter, Delaney made her exit, making a quick drive-by to kiss Rachel on the cheek. Rachel scrunched her nose up but didn't wipe the kiss off, which was something. As Delaney passed Wyatt's truck on her way to cabin six, she ran her fingers over the warm metal side panel, thinking uneasy thoughts.

Had inviting Alexandra here been a mistake?

CHAPTER 8

Delaney managed to get her mind off the events of the day as she began the second coat of paint in cabin six's freshly repaired bathroom. The back-and-forth of the brush was soothing, and soon she was lost in her work and even humming as she coated the wall in pale mint green. After she finished, she took her paint tray and brushes outside to rinse them.

As she approached the water spigot on the corner of the cabin, she noticed that next door, parked outside of cabin five, was Alex's dark sedan and one of the crew vans.

Hmm. They must have finished filming up at the office. As she rinsed out her paint brushes and tray and left them to dry, she saw several crew members exit the cabin, get in the van, and drive off toward the Bean Pot. Alex's car remained.

Feeling like this was a good opportunity to ask Alex what she planned to do with that accidental footage of Ursula, and wanting to catch her alone, Delaney jogged the short distance between cabins and stepped quietly up the steps of cabin five.

Those steps used to creak, she thought. *Slater must have fixed them.*

The door was open to the cabin, and only the screen was shut. Delaney raised her knuckles to knock on the doorframe, but her hand froze in mid-air when she heard voices inside. Not just Alex's voice, but *two* voices.

"Ready when you are, Alex." It was Norman. Delaney could just barely make out the shapes of people inside.

"Roll tape anytime," Alex responded in her smooth, cultured accent.

They were filming? Delaney quickly stepped to the side of the door, not wanting to interrupt or mess up whatever work they were doing.

"Rolling," Norman called.

A few silent seconds passed, and then Delaney's stomach started to sour at the moments that unfolded after. Alex's fancy high heels clicked on the well-worn tile floor as she made her way around the small, one-room cabin.

"Look at this! More of this sad, dated décor. This bedspread, these curtains! No wonder guests keep away. It's like being in a time machine."

Delaney's anger flared. If the Pines was a time machine, she'd gladly get in.

Alex continued. "And that fan. It's *covered* in dust."

It is not! Delaney knew she'd scrubbed every inch of the six cabins in preparation for the show's arrival—and that process was the same as her normal cleaning routine, regardless of whether it was a TV star staying in a cabin or not.

"Come over here," Alex called, sounding a bit further

from the door. Delaney pictured her gesturing to the camera to follow as she click-click-clicked around the cabin. The camera often followed Alex closely, mimicking the audience following her, through the more dramatic moments of the show. What more would she find to complain about?

"Oh, my goodness! Is that—is that a *dead mouse*?" Alex's shrill, accusatory voice made Delaney's breath catch. Was that possible? Between her fastidious cleaning of the cabins, Duke, and a few feral camp cats, the Pines had never had an issue with mice. She wondered if she should step in, but she held back. Was this just part of the show, as Alex had explained at the lake? Was this something they'd have to endure to reach the happy ending of their episode?

"Well, this is just disgusting. We really should have a talk with the management. If this is the kind of experience people are having, it's no wonder this place is failing."

That was just about enough. Delaney grasped the handle of the screen door and yanked. Thankfully, it was unlocked, so she didn't end up embarrassing herself—any more than she was about to.

"Is there a problem?" she asked, stepping inside, making sure to keep her voice even and calm. "I thought I heard someone call for management."

Inside, Norman, Alex, and a single cameraman froze when Delaney stepped in. Their heads swiveled in her direction. Alex held up a small, brown mouse by the tail. One glance told Delaney that the poor little creature was, indeed, dead.

A hard look passed over Alex's face, though it was only there for a split second before she composed herself. The camera was still filming, and when the cameraman gestured to Alex, seemingly asking if he should stop filming, she shook her head.

"Miss Phillips, so glad you popped in. I found this"— she held the mouse away from herself, holding the tail between two perfectly painted fingernails—"in my room. Is this what your guests have to put up with?"

Delaney stepped forward and took the mouse from Alex, not bothering to be timid with her grasp. She opened her cupped hand to examine the small, furry creature. "Well," Delaney said, "it's not impossible for this guy to have gotten into one of the cabins since we're in the woods, but I can tell you that growing up around this exact land has made me pretty much an expert on all of the local wildlife species."

"Oh?" Alex looked at her strangely, as if to say, *Where are you going with this?*

"Yep. This is more like a fancy mouse, not a wild one."

"What's a *fancy mouse*?" Alex asked.

Delaney tilted her head as though she were thinking. Then she explained patiently, "A fancy mouse is the kind you buy from a pet store. They're bred to be pets. Or, in the case of this guy, since he's ice cold, probably the kind of mouse that gets sold frozen for snake food."

Alex's mouth dropped open. She motioned for the cameraman to stop filming.

"But don't worry," Delaney said, turning, "I'll get rid of this for you. How strange that it was in your cabin. Maybe you should check your luggage for snakes."

Not bothering to wait for a reaction, Delaney turned, dropped the mouse into the small wastebasket by the front door, and bumped the screen door open with her hip. She nearly ran into Wyatt, who stood right outside.

"Hey!" he said, stepping back slightly when Delaney came barreling out of the cabin.

"Wyatt! Hey." She turned her head to make sure that neither Alex or Norm were following her. Hushed voices were murmuring inside, but no one came out the door behind her. Delaney still shook with adrenaline from the confrontation with Alex. Would it all be on camera?

Grabbing Wyatt's shirt sleeve with the hand that hadn't touched a dead mouse—she shuddered at the memory as her momentary bravado faded—she tugged him down the stairs and away from cabin five.

"Everything okay?" he asked, squinting at her as he allowed her to pull him along. "I tried to get you on your walkie-talkie earlier, but you didn't answer."

Shoot. She'd forgotten that she'd turned her walkie-talkie off. She released his sleeve and clicked it back on. "Yes, everything's fine. I just, uh, I want you to see how six's bathroom repair came out. Looks really nice. Come on."

"Okay..." he said, eyeing her suspiciously. He followed her inside and stood by silently while she washed her hands twice in the hottest water she could stand—without asking her what had happened. He just stood there, leaning in the doorway, watching her carefully.

"Bathroom looks good," he observed.

"Thanks." When the silence between them stretched, Delaney knew she wouldn't last under Wyatt's questioning gaze. She'd just opened her mouth to spill the story of what had happened with Alexandra when Wyatt started talking at the same time.

"I went to five to talk to Alex about Ur—" she started.

"Listen, Del, about Ursula—" Their words jumbled together, and they both broke off, laughing.

"Everything's okay with Ursula. I saw her eating lunch when Slater and I went to drop supplies off with Maisie," Delaney explained.

Wyatt's contrition was clear in his tone. "Good. I felt like a jerk. We just barreled in there. It's not like she did anything wrong."

"I know, and she knows. And I just had another weird incident in five with Alexandra. Do you think we... Are *you* still okay with the show being here?"

Wyatt nodded. "Yeah. You know, I was nervous at first, and there seems to have been some bumps here at the start, but we've been through worse, right?"

Wyatt reached out and squeezed her shoulder, his hand sliding down to her elbow. "Look, I'm sure it's just first-day hiccups. The restaurant's been hopping all day. Rachel's having a blast, right?"

Delaney nodded, almost sighing at the warmth of his hand on her elbow. Standing in the cabin, suddenly aware that they were alone, she wanted to lean into him, bury her cheek in the soft, faded fabric of his shirt, and just breathe for a few minutes with his arms wrapped around her. She struggled to dredge up all the reasons why she shouldn't: he was her friend, he was her boss, and there was the ever-present chance her world would change drastically if he didn't feel the same way. And she wouldn't do that to Rachel or to herself, not after the divorce had upset things before.

"It'll be better tomorrow," he assured her, his blue

eyes warm and concerned. "We have a real chance here, I think. A chance to save the Pines."

Delaney nodded again, not trusting herself to speak, lest she blurt out what she'd been thinking. Wyatt was probably right. And, thinking back to what she'd reminded herself of earlier, the show *was* punctuated with moments of high drama. Maybe those weren't reality at all. Had all those other people been as thrown off by the invading TV crew as Delaney felt right now?

"Anyway," Wyatt said, dropping his hand from her arm, "I skipped lunch. You care to come back to the kitchen with me for a bite?"

Delaney realized she hadn't eaten lunch yet either, despite feeling like she'd been zipping between the office, cabins, and kitchen all day. She nodded. At least the Bean Pot was far away from cabin five. Delaney wanted some time, and the adrenaline from that run-in, to pass.

She managed a quick turkey sandwich with Wyatt—served by a very proud Rachel—and then refocused on getting the rest of her work done for the day. Thankfully, the film crew had cleared out of the office and was off shooting on the property, so Delaney was able to return to reception and continue her project with the old record boxes. Ursula, back at the desk and answering phone calls that were now lighting up their heavy, old handset, waved as Delaney came in.

The rest of the afternoon went by quickly. Delaney managed to clear all but one record box, finding that everything they'd been keeping in the storage closet ended up being the leftovers of the meticulous receipt-keeping habit of Wyatt's dad, Bill. That wasn't necessarily a bad habit to have, Delaney knew, but the boxes were filled with decades-old slips bearing the proofs of purchase for things like inner tubes for the swimming pier that were likely long gone—lost relics of summers past, simple things that had probably been forgotten, even by the people who'd enjoyed them all those years ago. By the time she was done with all but one of the boxes, she was hot, sweaty, and covered in dust.

But the last box, the one at the very back of the closet, made all the tedious work of the first boxes worth it. When she opened the lid, instead of receipts, she found keepsakes that Bill had tucked away. She unloaded the box, handling the items carefully. There were photos that went all the way back to when the Pines first opened, and even a few menus from the Bean Pot from when it had opened shortly after. Further down in the box, Delaney found family pictures.

There were Bill and Carol, about the ages Delaney and Wyatt were now, with a small, smiling Wyatt standing in front of them. Delaney felt her eyes mist. She really missed Bill and Carol. Next was a picture of Wyatt swinging out over the lake on a tire.

"Whatcha got there? More receipts?" Ursula's voice cut in on Delaney's daydreaming.

Delaney picked up the stack of photos she'd been sorting, handing them over to Ursula.

"No, actually, there's some really great stuff in here. I think Bill, or maybe Carol, must have boxed it all up."

Ursula sorted through the stack, making occasional oohs, aahs, and, once, letting out a small, sad sigh. "Wow. Look at this. You two are so cute together."

In the photo Ursula held out, a pigtailed, freckle-faced Delaney stood next to an equally freckled and sort of rumpled Wyatt. They had to have been about twelve in the photo, their arms slung around one another, each holding a s'more stick over a campfire.

Delaney's gaze was fixed on the fire and her flaming marshmallow. Wyatt's eyes were on Delaney, and his goofy, gap-toothed grin was full of the fierce affection they'd had for one another as children. She ran her fingers over the photo. If only she'd been able to capture that spark in her adult relationships. The slightly bitter memory of her divorce reared up. She'd loved Jacob, and she would always be grateful that their marriage had given her Rachel, but he had never been dedicated to them quite as much as he'd been dedicated to his work. And he'd never looked at her the way Wyatt was looking at her in this photo.

But you should never risk your friendship with Wyatt. The little inner voice was always present, warning her not to upset what was between them now. She cleared her throat and noticed Ursula watching her with a gleam in her eyes.

"It was a long time ago. We were kids."

Ursula carefully set aside the keepsakes she held and dusted her hands on her flowery skirt. "I just came to say I'm leaving. I did all the follow-up calls on the chamber members from Wyatt's meeting." Ursula squeezed Delaney's shoulder as she passed behind her. "It's been a long day. Get some rest, dear."

Delaney put her hand over Ursula's and squeezed back. "I will. I want to talk to Wyatt before he leaves, and I've got to go down to the kitchen and pry Rachel away, too."

"No need," came a cheerful voice. "I've already pried."

Wyatt and Rachel had come through the back door, and Delaney leaned over the reception counter to see them coming up the hallway. Wyatt was carrying Rachel piggyback, and Rachel was chewing on a long, red strip of licorice, grinning happily. Ursula waved at them both and called goodnight as she slipped out the front door.

When Wyatt and Rachel reached the front desk, Rachel hopped down from Wyatt's back and ran around to hug Delaney. She pulled back and wrestled a bag of licorice from her pocket. "Mom, want some? I bought it with my own tip money."

Delaney thought about lecturing Rachel about candy before dinner, but the pride on her daughter's face warmed Delaney's heart. Reaching into the bag, Delaney grabbed a piece. "Mmm. This is so good. Thank you! And great job today."

"What did you want to talk to me about? Wait, hey, is that us?" Wyatt said, reaching over to steal the photo that Delaney had been holding.

She swiped to try and get it back, but he'd already pulled it out of her reach. "Yes, it is," she said. "And look at you!" *He'd better not make fun of my braids.*

"Yikes, you're right," Wyatt said, chuckling. "Thank goodness I got braces. But look at *you*. Just as pretty back then as you are now."

Delaney felt herself blush. Wyatt tapped the photo gently on the desk before setting it down. Delaney had thought for a split second that he'd been about to take the photo with him, and the thought had made her heart soar. She cleared her throat. "Thank you for carting Rachel up here. Glad she stopped wearing those spurs."

"Yeesh," Rachel said, rolling her eyes. "I stopped wearing boots and spurs when I was seven."

"Lucky me," Wyatt said. "And no problem. I couldn't let my best waitress walk up here after she's tired out her poor feet working so hard all day."

Rachel beamed. "I'm your best waitress?"

"Probably my best employee, period," Wyatt stage-whispered. "But don't tell anyone."

Rachel nodded. Delaney's heart swelled watching them.

"I'm actually out for the night," Wyatt said. "I locked up the back already. You guys take off, too. Go relax. It's been a tough day."

"Mom, can we make spaghetti?"

Delaney grabbed her purse from under the desk and stood, hugging Rachel close. "Sure, honey."

Wyatt had moved to the front door and was holding it open. Delaney watched as Rachel bounded out the front door. With one last glance at the photo, Delaney slipped it back into the records box.

"Hey, you said you wanted to talk about something?" he asked.

"Oh," she said, suddenly remembering. She'd been planning to tell him more in-depth about what had happened with Alex at the cabin, maybe warn him in case the show was planning to show the Pines in a less-than-flattering light. "Just work stuff."

He shook his head at her. "No more work stuff. C'mon, Friday. Tomorrow's another day."

She thought about her misgivings about the show, about the dire situation the Pines was in. She didn't want to talk Wyatt out of what she'd already talked him *into*. If this was their chance to save the Pines, she had to grin and bear it.

"You're right."

She followed him out of the office, clicking the light off as they left, taking one last glance behind her as she locked and closed the door.

Tomorrow will be better.

CHAPTER 9

"**C**an you tilt your head, honey?"

A production assistant held a tiny earpiece out for Delaney to see. Delaney nodded and moved her head as the assistant slipped the device into place, adjusted it, and connected the wire running from it to the device on the back of her belt. The wire was easily hidden in her hair, which she'd left down today.

Delaney sat in Wyatt's desk chair, tapping her foot nervously on the worn carpet. In front of her was the camera for the "one-on-ones," as Norman had called them. Norman was standing behind the camera with the cameraman, speaking in low tones that ensured Delaney couldn't make out what they were saying.

Delaney watched as other members of the crew adjusted lights and fussed with large, white light reflectors. Another assistant was rearranging some of the office supplies and books around Wyatt's office. *Gotta look good for the cameras*, she guessed.

And speaking of, she'd never been more aware of her plain work attire. She'd worn her hair down today, but she still felt it was rather simple—not fashionable like Alex's blonde coif.

Rather than a microphone extended overhead, she had a small, nearly invisible microphone attached to her collar, and a wire was run behind her to a bulky battery clipped to her belt.

"How's that feel?" the assistant asked.

Delaney shrugged noncommittally.

The assistant smiled. "Well, I've gotten it in place and connected. You can adjust it in your ear. Just be careful of the wires."

"Okay. Thanks." And with that, the assistant moved away from her, leaving her at the calm center of the production hurricane swirling around her.

As out of place as she felt in this situation, at least she hadn't experienced any awkwardness when she'd arrived at work this morning. Norman had been pleasant, even chatty when Delaney had arrived. Alexandra was nowhere to be seen, but Norman had explained that she'd be with Wyatt for the morning with a small crew of their own. Ursula had actually beat Delaney in, which was a surprise considering all Delaney had to do for her commute was take the golf cart from cabin one to the office.

Rachel had insisted on helping out at the Bean Pot again, but Delaney had only allowed it for half the day, on the condition that the girl go outside and do something fun with her afternoon. With a kiss and a promise to get outside, Rachel had zoomed inside the restaurant, leaving Delaney shaking her head. What kid actually *liked* to work during their summer break?

Luckily—or perhaps unluckily, since it made the Pines seem even more desperate—there were no new check-ins that morning, so there wasn't much for Delaney to do other than wait for Norman and the

lone cameraman to set up, adjust, and otherwise prepare to interview her. The time spent sitting in front
of the camera made her hyperaware not only of her
own appearance, but also of her surroundings, and as
much as she had convinced herself that she'd soldier
through her misgivings, they still nagged at the back
of her mind as she surveyed the room.

The décor *was* dated. The dark wood paneling
wasn't what anyone would call modern, for sure. And
maybe the tops of the file cabinets in here were a little
dusty. But was that all the world would see of the
Pines? Would anyone see what Delaney and Wyatt,
what the rest of the staff, saw?

She heard someone clear their throat. Her eyes
snapped up to see Norman and the cameraman staring at her.

"Are you ready, Miss Phillips?" Norman asked.

Focus, Delaney.

"Um, yes. I'm so sorry. I was just daydreaming."

"Easy to do in a peaceful place like this," Norman
said, surprisingly kindly.

Delaney sat up straighter and arranged the hem
of her shirt. Norman stepped forward and shifted a
paperweight on Wyatt's desk slightly to the left. He
stepped back, appraised Delaney and the desk, and
seemed satisfied.

"Okay, so, we'll start with the softball questions.
You know, how you came to work here, how long you've
been here, what you do here, that kind of thing."

She could do that. She smiled, thinking about how
to tell the story of Carol and Bill's previous manager,
who'd eloped with his girlfriend to Las Vegas on the
spur of the moment and decided to stay, leaving the

couple without a property manager just as Delaney had found herself in need of a job. Up until a few years ago, they'd still gotten the occasional card from the old manager, often accompanied by a picture of glittery showgirls, or a shot of him, his wife, and their son on some breathtaking desert hike. Everyone had loved Carol and Bill.

"Then we'll move onto the tougher stuff. Those will be the last questions we do before we wrap. It's easier that way."

Uh oh.

"Tougher stuff? Like what?"

"You've seen the show, right? Our last questions will be the ones the audience really want answered, the ones that give us that, that...*drama* they tune in for."

Delaney's uneasiness was back. She felt her eyebrows scrunch together. "Do I get to see the questions beforehand?"

Norman waved a hand as if to dismiss her concerns. "We're aiming for the most authentic reaction possible, the realest emotion. You'll be fine. Just answer like *you*. Didn't Wyatt tell you about what we did yesterday morning? His one-on-one went fabulously."

Wyatt hadn't talked with Delaney about his interview, but with the mess that yesterday had been, she wasn't surprised. And it stood to reason that if it had gone well, there really wouldn't be much to gossip about. If Wyatt could do it, so could she. What was the worst they could ask?

"Okay. Yep, that's understandable. Let's do this."

Norm explained, "I'm going to step outside the door

so my voice won't be heard on camera. You won't see me, but you'll be able to hear me."

Delaney nodded her understanding. Norm gave a few murmured, last-minute instructions to the cameraman, and then left the office, closing the door. A moment later, quietly, the cameraman said, "Rolling."

Delaney didn't know what to do with her hands, so she rested them in her lap. She willed herself to relax. Norm's voice came through the tiny earpiece. Though she'd known this would happen, it still startled her.

"You've lived in Fairwood your whole life, right, Miss Phillips? Can you tell us about that? How about your history with the Cabins in the Pines?"

Those were easy questions.

"Yes, I was born and raised here, just like Wyatt. My parents still live here. Even though we took other trips, my family still spent many, many summer vacations here while I was growing up. It was a magical place. We'd all wander through the trees, I'd play hide-and-seek with my sister, Wyatt, and our friends. We'd swim in the lake until the grown-ups had to come and haul us out. Then, at night, all the families would sit around the bonfire, roasting marshmallows and looking at the stars. The sounds of crickets in the air, the fireflies, falling asleep in a hammock..."

Delaney got a little lost in her memories, feeling her nervousness ease as she remembered how wonderful it had been here. "The Pines wasn't far from home, but it was always a wonderful, family-centered getaway that filled my childhood with special memories."

"Good, Delaney. Great, actually. Exactly what we're going for." Norm's voice in her ear was encouraging.

She found herself smiling easily, leaning back in her chair slightly.

"You've known Wyatt since you were both children. What else can you tell us about growing up together?"

"Growing up? He was the same way, so attached to this place. Much more responsible now than when he was twelve, though. He was always cooking up some scheme. We used to get into some trouble."

Delaney found herself laughing, forgetting the camera was there. She recounted the story of the summer when she and Wyatt had decided to climb up and knock down a beehive they'd found. Delaney had been reluctant at first, but Wyatt had convinced her that the hive was a treasure trove of honey, just waiting to be raided for all the sugary goodness they could want.

Delaney had a serious sweet tooth she knew he'd been exploiting. But being the better tree climber between the two of them, she'd quickly clambered up the tree in question. Walking stick in hand, she jabbed the beehive once, hard enough that, surprisingly, it had fallen on the first try.

To their horror, it hadn't been a beehive at all, but a hornet's nest. When it had hit the ground, they'd been in the path of a very angry group of hornets. If she thought back, she could almost feel those first stings.

"I've never gotten out of a tree so fast. In fact, I climbed down so quickly I sprained my ankle on the last jump down. That still didn't stop me—us—from running as fast as we could right into the lake, fully dressed. We were screaming like banshees. And we scared the tar out of all of the guests who were down at the pier that day. Thank goodness neither of us are allergic to hornets. We got a lot of itchy stings and a very stern lecture on respecting nature, though. And we gave any kind of nest a wide berth after that."

The cameraman was smiling. Norman's voice sounded in her ear again.

"And now that Wyatt is your boss, does that ever cause problems, since you've known each other for so long?"

The answer came as naturally to Delaney's lips as breathing. "Actually, no. If anything, it makes us a better team. We understand each other. We know everything there is to know about each other. And Wyatt is a great boss. He really cares about everybody here—not just the guests, but the staff. He thinks of everyone as family."

"Awesome. Now, speaking of family, Wyatt doesn't really have one of his own, right? He's not married?"

Where is this going? Delaney hesitated but then said, "No, he's not married."

"So are the two of you romantically involved?"

Whoa. That was getting *very* personal. She was suddenly reminded of how Alex had probed about her relationship with Wyatt yesterday, and Norman's question gave Delaney similar pause. Would viewers want to know that? Would Wyatt want her to talk about that—and, well, what was there really to talk about?

"No, we're actually not. I don't see how that's relevant to the business, though."

"We'll use the single-mother angle. Just had to ask to make sure. I mean, it's got to be hard, successfully running a business and doing the parent thing on your own."

The single-mother angle? What the heck was that? Delaney's discomfort ratcheted up a few degrees. "I'm sorry, but none of this has anything to do with how we do our jobs. Did you ask Wyatt any of these kinds of questions?"

"We have the same type of questions for everyone we interview, generally," Norm replied matter-of-factly. The cameraman looked a little embarrassed.

"Really? And what did he say about your questions?" She felt heat rise into her face, and she struggled to keep her voice even.

"That's something you'll have to wait for airtime to see for yourself," came the reply. "Now, you have a daughter, I believe."

"I do," Delaney responded coolly.

"How old is she?"

"She's eleven."

"Aww, that's such a great age. Very tween, right?"

Delaney smiled. "Yes, it is."

"What's her name?" Norman asked.

"Rachel."

"Rachel," Norman said, "I love that name—Rachel. You know, I was wondering. That's such a pivotal time in a girl's life. Do you feel your daughter suffers at all with you having to spend so much time here at the Cabins in the Pines?"

Anger flared, hot and heavy. She felt her face heat as her throat tightened, restricting her from responding—which might have been a blessing at the moment. *How dare he?*

She reached up, yanked the little earpiece out of her ear and tossed it on the desk. She unclipped the tiny microphone from her collar and unwound the wire from behind her, unfastening the battery pack and placing it on the desktop in front of her next to the earbud.

"I'm done with questions for now."

She stood and marched to the office door, yanking it open and charging out. That was getting to be a habit of hers these past two days, fleeing rooms. There was no Wyatt on the other side of the office door as there had been at cabin five yesterday, though. Delaney took a few deep breaths as she strode past Norman, whose face reflected his surprise—to say the least.

"Miss Phillips? Excuse me, Miss Phillips?"

She didn't stop, and she didn't want to walk past Ursula at the front desk and have to explain herself later, so she opted for the back door. Once outside, she clicked on her walkie-talkie, which she had turned off during her interview, to try and radio Wyatt.

There was no answer to her call. Well, she knew he was on the property somewhere, and the campground was only so big. She reached for the keys to the golf cart.

The summer sun was definitely heating up, and Wyatt squinted as he watched the filming crew pan around Alexandra, who was seated in one of the picnic ramadas as she talked with one of their few guests.

The guest—a man—was obviously charmed by the beautiful reality show host, and based on her fashionable dress, her perfectly applied makeup, and her impeccable poise, Wyatt could see why he would be—if the man had been, in fact, one of the actual guests of the Pines. When Alexandra had brought in the man and Charles had introduced him to Wyatt, it had been with the explanation that the show often used actors to portray "real experiences."

Wyatt listened as the conversation unfolded, the cameras silently filming. The pair discussed the faux guest's stay at the campground, and he repeated many of the glowing comments Wyatt had heard from their guests in the past. It put Wyatt at ease, at least a little, that people would hear some good about the Pines on the show.

Aside from the sun in his eyes, it wasn't shaping up to be such a bad day. Duke was dozing in the soft, thick layer of pine needles that covered the ground at Wyatt's feet. Wyatt found himself wondering how Delaney's interview was going and if it was going to turn out as uncomfortable as his had been. His walkie-talkie had died in the heat, or he would have radioed her some encouraging words before she'd been subjected to the hot seat.

He hadn't minded reminiscing about his younger days at the Pines, but when they'd gotten to questions about how he'd taken over for his parents, the interview had gotten hard. Wyatt hoped she was doing okay. He felt like he'd hardly seen her these past two days.

The sound of tires braking hard on gravel made Wyatt turn his head. Delaney had skidded to a stop several yards away. He took one look at her, and he was on his feet, headed her way. Duke jumped up, suddenly alert, and bounded after Wyatt.

Delaney's face was flushed, and she looked seriously out of sorts.

"Del," Wyatt said, slowing next to the golf cart, "are you okay?"

Duke jumped into the backseat of the golf cart and launched himself half over the front seat, licking Delaney's face.

She reached up to pet Duke, craning her neck to avoid getting completely slobbered on. She peered around Wyatt, narrowing her eyes at the scene being filmed.

"No. I did my 'interview.'" She said it while she made air quotes. "And it was more like an ambush."

She was huffing slightly, and he was taken aback to realize that Delaney was *mad*. That was something he rarely saw. A sudden, fierce feeling of protectiveness came over him.

"Oh, Friday. Mine wasn't exactly easy, either. You want to get out of here and talk about it?"

Her eyes darted from the scene to Wyatt, then back again. "You don't have to stay here?"

"I own the place, remember? Let me let Charles know, and I'll be right back."

"Okay, thanks," she said, sounding relieved.

Wyatt jogged over and got the attention of Alex's assistant. He told Charles he was going to make a round through the property with Delaney, and asked Charles to let Alex know.

"I'll let her know. But, according to this schedule"—Charles checked a clipboard he held—"Alex has a meeting with you in forty-five minutes to discuss financials. Then there's another scene to film that involves both you and Miss Phillips. So, can you meet us back at the office in forty-five minutes?"

Wyatt agreed, then jogged back to Delaney. He swung into the passenger's seat of the golf cart, relaying the schedule Charles had just laid out. She didn't waste any time scooting them away from the film crew, out into the cooler, darker, denser part of the forest.

"Financials? What does that mean?" she asked, tying her hair back into a ponytail as she spoke. Wyatt found himself missing the sight of her hair falling, loose and dark, over her shoulders.

"I'm not quite sure. You're the expert on the show."

"Well, the only two segments they ever have about money are when Alexandra makes an offer for the business or when she excoriates the business owner for handling money poorly."

Wyatt grimaced. "Well, luckily, we've always been good with the money we have. So maybe it's the former?"

"I hope so," she replied.

"Drive down and park by the lake. It'll be quiet there. We can talk."

She nodded but didn't say anything. The dappled light filtering down through the canopy of trees flashed over her face, highlighting her worried expression.

What happened during that interview? he wondered.

CHAPTER 10

After a restorative half-hour break at the lake, during which Delaney vented about her interview, told Wyatt all about the mouse in cabin five, and ate two of the three granola bars—coincidentally, her favorite kind—that he'd somehow, mysteriously had in his pockets, Delaney was feeling better.

The sun was bright, reflecting off of the water, and it made Delaney squint as she and Wyatt walked along the shoreline. They weren't really going anywhere, just doing a slow back-and-forth along the small stretch of lakeside that belonged to the campground. Delaney relaxed in the warm air, breathing in the smell of the trees and the damp, grassy scent of the reeds that grew in the dense lake. A family of geese swam lazily in the water, the adults honking and the cluster of yellow-gray goslings tweeting cheerfully behind them.

Wyatt didn't laugh at her when she told him about the awkward relationship question and the questions about Rachel. He didn't make any assumptions about her discomfort at the questions. He'd just sympathized with her and made her describe—in detail—Norman's shocked expression when she'd stomped out. Then, he'd tried to replicate it until she was giggling.

Sitting on the pier, their feet dangling just an inch above the water, Duke napping again between them, they took turns skipping rocks across the wind-rippled surface of the lake. Every breeze that blew across the water was a small, welcome relief from the summer heat.

"I feel so silly," she said. "I mean, this is how the show is, and I knew that before they showed up. But I don't want anyone to get the wrong idea about this place."

"Definitely not," Wyatt agreed, his face solemn. "I would never want anyone to know that I can't tell a beehive from a hornet's nest, either. I mean, I own a forest full of, y'know, *nature*."

She shoved him playfully. "Stop it. It's disconcerting. Like they're just looking for something dramatic or a sob story to play off of. They could have asked anything relevant, and they had to ask if I felt like Rachel was suffering because of the time I spend here?"

Wyatt put on his best falsetto. "I would never prioritize my job over my child. Never, America. Especially since I work for a man who can't identify a beehive."

She laughed so hard she had to hold her sides, and he put an arm around her shoulders to steady her. There was a suspended moment where she held her breath at the embrace, until Duke yipped in protest when he was squeezed between them. Stumbling up, disturbed from his nap, Duke trotted to the golf cart and jumped up into it, doing a few circles before settling on the floorboard in the back.

"Don't fall in the lake, Friday. We've only got ten minutes before we have to be up at the office."

Delaney made a face. "Do I have to?"

"Yup. You brought all of this craziness down on our heads, and now you must participate."

Wyatt stood and offered her a hand. She accepted, and when he pulled her up, they were close—really close. She felt her heart do a little flutter in her chest.

"And thank you for bringing this craziness down on our heads. You've given us a chance."

Her heart did another little dance at the phrase *given us a chance*, but the moment passed quickly, and Wyatt didn't seem to have noticed. She hoped, at least, that she hadn't blushed when he'd said it. Maybe she *should* take a chance on Wyatt, on something more than what they had now. After the show, business would be more stable, there would be less stress. If she just waited to confess her feelings until after filming, when life wasn't falling apart around them, they might have a chance to make a new life—together. Delaney thought about this as they made the drive back up to the office.

The crew van was just arriving from the ramada, and Alex climbed out of the passenger's side. She was followed by Charles, who exited from the driver's seat. Alex saw them first, and Delaney braced for an icy greeting. She hadn't really had any interaction with Alex since the mouse incident, and Norm must have told Alex about the interview debacle by now. But Delaney was surprised when Alex walked right up to her and pulled her into a hug.

"Delaney! I'm so sorry about that awkward interview this morning. I know you must have been caught off guard."

Over Alex's shoulder, Delaney's eyes met Wyatt's. He made a surprised face, shrugging.

Alex pulled away, grasping Delaney by the shoulders. "The crew has to take a break before the next scene, so we have time to talk. Come, let's go inside. I want you both in on this meeting. No cameras."

"Okay," Delaney said, a little dumbfounded at Alex's greeting. They all filed inside the office, and this time, as promised, there were no cameras. Wyatt pulled a chair in from the front desk and sat down next to Delaney while Alex took Wyatt's chair.

"Listen," Alex started, "I'm sorry about the interview. We're really trying to build the female demographic of the show. I just thought our audience might identify with your life—you know, the struggle of being a working mom who's also taking care of her kid on her own. Even if we would have been playing it up a bit, it really wasn't meant to make you uncomfortable."

Delaney considered her response before she said, "I just don't see how it has any bearing on whether or not you help us revive the camp."

"It doesn't," Alex said bluntly. "I already love this place, and I already know what it needs. I went through your books with a fine-tooth comb. I usually have a ton of criticism for struggling business owners when it comes to the financials, but, really, you guys run a tight ship here on the money side of things."

It was Wyatt's turn to speak up. "So why the drama? Why the mouse?" He crossed his arms over his chest.

Alex waved her hands as she spoke. "It's what the people want to see. A little conflict! A little redemption! What am I going to tell them, that this picture-perfect place is spotless, run by Gary Cooper in plaid and his childhood best friend who's *also* managing to be the world's best mom, and the only reason it's failing is that people have forgotten about it? Who would watch that?"

Wyatt and Delaney exchanged an uncertain glance. Delaney felt a slow sense of embarrassment creep up on her. "I guess you're right."

"Of course, I am. I've done this a million times. But, listen, I understand it's all foreign to you. I'm just asking you to roll with it and trust me. Once the place is improved, once the offer is on the table, I think you'll both find this was all worth it."

Delaney was elated at the mention of an offer. It was exactly what they needed. She felt flooded with relief at the prospect.

"Del?" Wyatt said, questioning. She knew he wanted her opinion before he acquiesced to Alex's request.

"Thanks for talking with us. I think we can do that," Delaney replied.

Alex's smile was instant and genuine. "I'm so glad. And, again, I am deeply sorry about the bad first impression." She looked chagrined.

Delaney shook her head. "Don't worry about it. I think we can all go forward feeling a little better now. What's a little reality-bending between friends, right?"

"Speaking of," Alex said. "They might be ready to head down to the kitchen to film our next scene. I think we're getting everyone in this one. Let me just go check on Charles and see if he and Norman have sorted everything out."

With that, Alex stood, gave them both another beaming smile, and left them in the wake of her expensive perfume.

Wyatt knew exactly how Delaney had felt when she'd told him the show's first day at the Pines had left her feeling like a Ping-Pong ball. He felt the exact same way as they arrived at the Bean Pot. So far today, he'd gone from the office, to the cabins when Slater had radioed another minor emergency, to the ramadas to film some improvised camp-touring with Alex, to the lake with Delaney, *back* to the office, and now out to the kitchen. His head was swimming, and not in the summer-fun kind of way.

Wyatt was glad Delaney had talked to him, and he was glad they'd talked to Alex. Delaney seemed more relaxed, and he, in turn, felt better. He made a mental note to watch a few episodes of *The ABC's of Business* tonight. Maybe he'd ask Delaney and Rachel if they wanted to come over. Or maybe they would all have had enough of the show by the time evening came. Hopefully, things would run more smoothly from here on out.

Maisie seemed to have been told about the upcoming scene, because the parking lot to the Bean Pot was roped off, blocking outside cars from coming in. Inside, barely any of the seats were filled. Wyatt spotted Rachel spinning slowly on one of the counter stools, and when she saw Wyatt and Delaney enter, she hopped down and ran over.

"Guys! This is so cool. They're about to set up cameras in here!"

Wyatt grinned at Rachel's enthusiasm. Rachel reminded him so strongly of Delaney at her age. Same freckles, same wide, friendly smile. Her nose even turned up slightly on the end like Delaney's. Wyatt stifled the spike of resentment that flared up in him at the thought of Delaney's ex. How anyone could just up and leave Rachel—or Del—was beyond Wyatt. Reaching out an arm, he hooked Rachel under his elbow, pulling her in for a big hug.

"What? Cameras? I don't see any cameras." With her face smooshed into Wyatt's shirt, he knew Rachel couldn't, either. "Where?"

She shrieked and giggled, flailing. "You are such a nerd! And you smell like Duke."

He let go and pretended to be offended. "What? You've always loved my hugs." He sniffed his shirt. "I won't tell Duke you said that. It'll offend him."

Delaney was shaking her head. "You two."

But, again, Wyatt was relieved to see her smile had returned. Maisie came out of the kitchen with Slater. They were followed by Charles, who was studiously checking things off on his clipboard. Delaney waved, and the trio came across the dining room to join Wyatt, Delaney, and Rachel, making their way around the audio-visual equipment being set up.

"Seems like this whole production is nothing more than standing around waiting for stuff to be put up or taken down," Maisie commented when they'd made it over. Wyatt had just been thinking the same thing, and he grinned.

"Well, that's about half of it, yes," Charles said, pushing his slipping glasses up his nose. "Another quarter is filming," he added.

"And the last quarter?" Slater asked.

"Getting coffee, mostly," Charles quipped.

Maisie grinned at Charles. "Speaking of, I wasn't

sure how long we'd all be here, but I set up fresh coffee and lemonade in the kitchen."

"Ooh, lemonade?" Rachel perked up.

"Yep," Maisie replied. She lowered her voice to a loud whisper. "And I think there's some ice cream back there, too."

Rachel didn't need to be hinted to twice. She zipped back through the swinging door to the kitchen.

Slater regarded the remaining group. "Well, I'm sure that you four have stuff to talk about. I'm just going to…"

"Go get ice cream?" Delaney said, busting him.

With an innocent look, whistling nonchalantly, Slater turned on his heel and sauntered toward the kitchen. "Actually, I just have to go do that thing in the kitchen that I forgot about," he explained.

Charles tapped his pen on his clipboard and addressed Wyatt, Delaney, and Maisie. "So, we all know—myself included—that this place is fantastic. But for the purposes of this scene, things will need to go wrong."

Maisie's nose scrunched up and a suspicious expression flitted across her face. "What do you mean, go wrong?"

A British accent answered the question. "He means we'll be showing the viewer what a worst-case scenario day would be like here, that's all."

Wyatt hadn't noticed Alexandra come in. Charles, who had seemed relaxed and chummy with Slater and Maisie when they'd come from the kitchen, suddenly straightened and grew quiet.

Maisie frowned at Alex, and Wyatt could see a spark

of fire in Maisie's eyes as she said, "So folks are going to think we can't handle a little lunch crowd?"

Uh oh. Wyatt hadn't had the chance to talk to any of the other staff about the talk he and Delaney had had with Alex. But before he could think to intervene, Alex answered.

"Not at all. We'll film contrasting footage later showing the resilience of the staff, showing how everyone bands together to pull off a successful shift, really giving viewers the true view of how the Pines operates and how resilient it and its people are, even under pressure."

"Oh," Maisie said, "well, that makes sense. I think I could get on board with that."

"And," Alex said, "it will give everyone a chance to stretch their acting muscles a little. Consider it like the play you'd put on every year at summer camp."

Maisie smiled wistfully. "Oh, yeah. We actually used to host a summer camp here. Stopped a few years back."

When my parents died, Wyatt realized. So many little things they'd started had fallen by the wayside after their deaths.

"And, not to brag, but I was Juliet in *Romeo and Juliet* my sophomore year," Maisie continued.

"I bet you were great," Charles interjected shyly.

Alex shot him a withering glare that silenced him, even as Maisie giggled in response.

"I was, thank you," Maisie drawled, blushing at his compliment.

Wyatt glanced over at Delaney, who was already grinning at him—a very silly grin. He gave her a questioning look, but she just suppressed her smile and shook her head at him. What was that smile about?

"Shall we get started?" Alex suggested, gesturing with a sweeping hand to the restaurant, which looked to Wyatt a pretty sad setup if they were supposed to be busy.

"Is this meant to be the rush?" Wyatt asked.

"No, no," Alex explained as they all walked back toward the kitchen, Alex leading the way. "We have, umm, about..." She was searching for something, and she snapped her fingers twice, sharply.

Charles, who had been at the back of the group with Maisie, hustled up at the sound.

"Twenty," he said. "We have twenty more patrons scheduled to come in. They're out back right now, being prepped by another production assistant," he supplied.

"Is anything to do with this reality show real?" Wyatt whispered to Delaney.

She gave him a reassuring pat on the arm. "Yes. The renovations and the offer at the end," she explained.

"Ah, yes," he said, as if suddenly remembering.

Back in the kitchen, they found Rachel and Slater with two spoons, scooping what looked to be second helpings out of a party-sized tub of ice cream. Rachel gestured with her spoon to a nearby stack of bowls and extra spoons. "We knew you all couldn't resist."

Wyatt didn't put up a fight. He grabbed a spoon and bowl and helped himself. Alex and Charles surveyed a sheet on Charles's clipboard, and Wyatt heard them speak in TV language that sounded like Greek to him. Wyatt took a bite of ice cream, sighing happily. At least something around here was still the same. This home-made ice cream tasted exactly the way it had since the Bean Pot had opened.

Charles flipped another page up on his clipboard. "Ok, Pines people. It looks like we need everyone for this except Slater."

"Sweet," Slater said, and then, as he noticed a few disgruntled faces, "Oops. I mean, no offense. I was just hoping to hit some of the bike trails this afternoon. If you don't need me, Del."

"Wyatt?" Delaney asked, deferring to him. "Here, you think about it. I'll take this." She reached over and stole his remaining ice cream and his spoon, ignoring his affronted expression and digging in.

Wyatt remembered Delaney telling him she'd only let Rachel wait tables during the breakfast shift this morning on the condition that Rachel wouldn't hole up with her electronics afterward.

"Sure thing. Take the afternoon off, Slater. On one condition—take Rachel with you riding. You can get one of the spare bikes from storage."

Slater didn't seem fazed at all. "Double sweet! You ready to learn how to rip up some dirt, kid?"

Rachel high-fived Slater. "Yes! That sounds awesome!"

Delaney smiled at her daughter's excitement. *The magic of the Pines*, she thought.

"Oh, Alexaaaaaaandra!"

The singsong voice carried all the way back to the kitchen from the dining room. Alex and Charles looked up from where they'd once again become engrossed in the clipboard. Alex hustled toward the kitchen door.

"Ok, everyone, I'll go out and chat with Norman, verify the setup, and then we'll come back and bring you all out as needed." She didn't wait for a response before disappearing, leaving another wave of flowery scent in her wake.

"C'mon, let's get out of here," Slater said to Rachel.

She hopped up, full of excitement. "Can we jump off some stuff?"

Delaney coughed through a bite of Wyatt's ice cream. Recovering, she held up a cautioning hand. "Just low stuff. Like, really low. How about just go over some slight bumps?"

Wyatt, who had been about to cheer Rachel on, curbed his response. He put on his best serious face. "Your mom's right. Responsibly low things."

Rachel rolled her eyes at Wyatt. "Seriously? You're supposed to be on my side."

"I'm always on your side. The non-concussive side," Wyatt replied with a grin.

Rachel hugged Wyatt, kissed her mom on the cheek, and she and Slater left, followed by Delaney's last-minute reminder to wear their helmets.

"You're such a great mom," Wyatt said, the words rolling easily from thought to speech.

Delaney turned back to face him. "Oh, thank you. That's very sweet of you to say," she said, her face surprised, her cheeks coloring.

"Well, it's true. You always have her back. You're always there for her. You're her rock. Just like you're mine."

The subtle claim in his last words actually made him pause. He hoped that hadn't come out wrong. Wait, how *had* he meant it? His eyes locked with Delaney's. Her cheeks were still flushed. Delaney saved him from a moment of uncomfortable self-reflection when she pointed to Maisie and Charles, who had stepped over to a nearby steel prep table. Charles said something that made Maisie laugh.

"What do you think of that?" Delaney whispered, leaning in close to him. "They were awfully friendly yesterday, too."

Wyatt looked over at Delaney, at her wide, expressive brown eyes, at the wisps of hair that fell around her temples. He tried to see the giggly little girl he'd been inseparable from—but with her standing so close, all he could see was the beautiful woman she'd become.

What is going on with me?

"I, uh..." He tried to subtly watch the flirty pair, but he was too nervous about being caught staring. He was inwardly glad Delaney hadn't caught him staring at *her*. "I don't know. She's laughing, right? Maybe she just thinks he's funny."

Delaney rolled her eyes at him. "No, that's not all. She laughed and then put her hand on his arm. That combo definitely means she's interested."

"It does?"

Delaney nodded toward the back of the kitchen. "Yes, it does. C'mon, let's go put this ice cream up. We can take some trays of lemonade to the people waiting out back, give these two some time alone."

Delaney gathered up the dirty bowls and spoons, and Wyatt closed up the ice cream and hefted the heavy container. He was shaking his head as he followed Delaney toward their single working cooler.

"Really, Friday?" he whispered to her.

Her laughter was equally subdued as she tried to open the cooler quietly. "Wyatt Andrews, you can be *so* clueless."

CHAPTER 11

"Well, this is a disaster," Delaney observed dryly. Just an hour or two later, there were tables full of unhappy patrons, the kitchen was backed up on food orders, and there was even a broken plate or two on the floor. She and Wyatt stood against the wall just to the right of the back entrance to the Bean Pot, watching all the chaos unfold.

"So why are you smiling?" Wyatt asked, nudging her with his shoulder.

She looked over at him, shooting back, "Why aren't you out there helping your staff, boss?"

"You know Alex told us to stay out of the way."

Delaney nodded, trying to stay behind the camera nearest her to avoid being caught in the current shot. Alex was walking through the Bean Pot, speaking to guests, soothing tempers as she made her way toward the back of the restaurant. Inside the kitchen, Delaney knew there was another camera set up. She and Wyatt had been shooed out of the kitchen earlier so the crew could set up. But it was just as they were picking up their trays of lemonade, so they hadn't minded.

Outside with the extras—actors paid to simply fill a scene, Delaney had learned—she and Wyatt had passed around drinks, chatted about the production, and even asked them what they thought of the Pines; what they liked, what might be improved. It did Delaney's heart good to hear from the group an echo of exactly what she and Wyatt had wanted to accomplish with the renovations—just a few more small conveniences and some updating, but the rest was paradise.

She knew she was watching the scene unfold with a goofy smile on her face. She felt better about the show's presence than she had before they'd both talked to Alex. When, or if, she had any doubts from here on out, she'd hold onto the idea that the Pines had a chance now. And, honestly, the pretend parts of the show were actually kind of fun. She wasn't sure if she would admit this to anyone, but they might even be more fun than the boring, true parts.

Alex reached Maisie, who was running around behind the counter. Maisie's apron was askew, and she was frowning slightly. Alex put a reassuring hand on Maisie's shoulder and drew the younger woman to the side to talk to her. Maisie was nodding, trying to appear brave as Alex spoke, but Delaney could see Maisie's lower lip quiver even from across the room.

"Is she supposed to cry?" Wyatt asked, sounding surprised.

"That's not what I heard Alex asking her to do earlier. Must be something extra she's throwing in," Delaney guessed. "You know what they say in *Romeo and Juliet*, 'Venus smiles not in a house of tears.' Maybe Maisie's mourning the interruption of her summer romance."

Suddenly remembering her doubts about Alex after the mouse incident, Delaney caught Maisie's eye just to be sure her friend was faking. Maisie put a hand over her heart and hammed up a sob, her theatrics doing nothing to disguise the sparkle of amusement in her eyes. Maybe not everyone would have caught it, but Delaney did, and she smiled in response.

"Alex did kind of snap at Charles for getting distracted with Maisie," Wyatt recalled. And then he stopped, uncertain of what he'd just heard. He turned to Delaney. "Wait. Did you just quote Shakespeare?"

Delaney barely smothered a smile as she continued to watch the action of the scene. "Yes. Maisie was in *Romeo and Juliet*, remember? And maybe you don't know *everything* about me, boss. When I was away at college, I took a whole class on Shakespeare. Fell in love."

Wyatt tilted his head, stifling his own grin at this surprise. "No. Maybe I *don't*. Shakespeare, huh? What other secrets are you keeping?"

Delaney concentrated on keeping her laugh casual, grateful he couldn't read her thoughts at that exact moment. "Oh, tons of secrets. Now, shhhh. You're going to get us into trouble."

Still smiling, Wyatt turned back to the scene, and they both watched as Alex gripped Maisie by the shoulders and drew her in for a strong hug.

"The plot thickens," Wyatt whispered, fluttering a hand near his lips. Alex pulled away and began speaking to Maisie with an earnest look on her face.

"What do you think Alex is saying?" Delaney whispered back.

"I've got this. I read lips," Wyatt said cockily.

"Oh, you do? Since when?" Delaney narrowed her eyes at him, wondering where he was going with this.

For as long as she'd known him, she had never known him to read lips. That would have been a handy skill to have when they were kids.

"Since...always," he finished lamely.

"Let's just move closer," Delaney suggested.

Wyatt sighed with great exaggeration and uncrossed his arms from over his chest. "No, oh ye of little faith. Let me give this a shot." He rolled his shoulders like a baseball pitcher coming up to the mound. He took a deep breath. He cracked his knuckles.

"Any day now," Delaney said. "She'll be back in the kitchen soon, and your powers will be ineffective."

Wyatt held up a hand. "Shhh. I need complete silence."

Delaney was pretty sure she'd never rolled her eyes so hard in her life.

"She's saying, 'Don't worry, dear, everything will be okay. Hush, hush, I'm here now, and you don't have to toil alone under the poor management of that inept Mr. Andrews anymore.'" Wyatt seriously might've had the worst British accent in history.

Delaney put up a hand to cover her mouth and hide her laughter, but she was sure Wyatt could see her shoulders shaking. He continued, undeterred by the fact that a few people were staring at them now.

Not dropping the accent, he continued. "Also, I'm sorry I broke up that little rendezvous between you and the dashing Charles. Please, do forgive me. I did that in haste, before I tasted the peach pie you make here from scratch. I now give the union my complete, enthusiastic blessing.'"

Delaney couldn't control it any longer. She laughed so loudly that more heads turned. Norman's eagle-eyed gaze lasered in on them from the other side of the dining room.

Wyatt whispered, "Busted."

Delaney swallowed her merriment and sobered quickly. The whole room was now staring at them.

"Uhh, sorry. Umm, excuse us," Delaney squeaked. She grabbed for Wyatt's hand and pulled him quickly out the back door. Once outside, they both burst into laughter.

Duke, who had been digging in the dirt by the parking lot, rushed over to weave around Wyatt and Delaney, barking.

"You are a bad influence," Delaney accused, shaking a finger at Wyatt. But there was no force behind the accusation, only the same glee that had been there when he'd gotten them into many, many scrapes as kids. He swiped at his eyes, taking deep breaths, trying to compose himself.

"You asked what they were saying," he said. "I was just trying to help."

She was so glad he was having fun. For the past year or so, Wyatt hadn't been the carefree, happy-go-lucky guy she'd grown up with. The tragedy of his parents' passing and the added stress of his responsibilities at the Pines had had a more profound effect on him than she'd realized before. Now, as she saw the old Wyatt, the difference was crystal clear. She felt a momentary sensation of guilt—if they were best friends, why hadn't she noticed how everything had been weighing on him?

Since the area behind the restaurant was empty now that all the extras were inside, they spent the next few minutes sitting outside in the sunshine, taking in the sights and sounds of the thick, verdant woods surrounding them. They didn't talk, but Delaney knew that, with Wyatt, she didn't always have to. Duke chased squirrels until his tongue hung out of his mouth, then trotted over to find his water dish.

The screen door at their backs squeaked open, and Charles stepped out, walking a few steps toward them as he checked off something on his clipboard.

"Mr. Andrews, we're ready for you now," he said.

Wyatt stood and leaned over to Delaney. "I bet you got me in trouble," he said with mock seriousness.

"Go inside," she said. "Face the consequences of your actions."

With another boyish grin, Wyatt went inside. Charles, instead of following behind him, walked over and sat down beside Delaney on the picnic bench.

"He seems like he's in a good mood," Charles observed.

"Yes," Delaney agreed, "I actually think the show is giving him something positive to look forward to."

"Well, there's a lot of that around here," Charles said. "Doesn't seem like you need much positivity from us."

Delaney nodded, reflecting on the strong, solid—if a bit ragtag—family they'd all created here. "Are you taking a break? You want some lemonade? Coffee? I put out a few extra packets of brown sugar for you."

"Just a short one. The next scene is just Wyatt and Alex, and Norm doesn't like me around for the smaller scenes. How did you know I use brown sugar in my coffee?" Charles asked, a look of surprise on his face.

"Maisie told me," Delaney admitted, watching him

for a reaction. "But it's not the only thing she noticed about you."

Charles blushed adorably behind his thick-rimmed glasses. "Yeah, well, don't mention it to Alex. I don't want her noticing that Maisie is noticing me."

Delaney winced slightly. "Sorry about that. I'm sure no one meant to get you in trouble."

"Nah, I know."

Duke, sensing that someone new with the potential to pet him had arrived, came over from where he had been lying on the deck near his water bowl. He put his front paws up on the bench between them and put his head in Charles's lap. Charles, to Delaney's surprise, put down his clipboard and started scratching Duke's ears.

"You know," he said, looking around the woods that swayed and sighed with a warm breeze that suddenly kicked up, "I went to summer camp for all of middle school. It was a place up north, a lot like this one. Fishing, hiking, swimming, getting dirty. My first year, I was terrified to go because I'd always lived in the city. But my parents made me. I wasn't happy about it, but I went."

Delaney didn't interrupt, just propped her chin in her hand and nodded, watching Charles pet Duke. The wind wafted steadily but gently around them, and Charles seemed to be lost in memories.

"But after the first day, I wished I could stay forever. My parents both worked a lot, and we never did much as a family. Add in growing up in an apartment in a concrete jungle surrounded by thousands of people who live right on top of each other but never speak, and I was a lonely kid. The excitement of camp, being surrounded by people, running around with other kids, and just the space of the outdoors... Man, it was heaven to me."

Delaney smiled. "That's lovely. I'm glad you had that."

"This place takes me right back, and I know it must do the same for a lot of other people."

Duke, satisfied that every inch of his ears had been properly scratched, hopped down from the bench and trotted off.

A comfortable silence fell between Charles and Delaney. She watched the woods, which might seem like a still-life to some—but not to her. It wasn't just the wind moving through the trees, either. Birds rustled and hopped in the branches above their heads. Squirrels chittered and chased each other through the pines. Several yards away, at the edge of the clearing behind the diner, something red-orange flashed in the brush. Delaney guessed it was the mama red fox Maisie had been trying to keep from the garbage bins at night.

Delaney smiled, content to study the woods and wait. Charles appeared very serious for a moment, and then he turned to Delaney and pushed his slipping glasses up the bridge of his nose. "Miss Phillips—"

"Delaney, please," she interjected.

"Delaney," he repeated. "I've seen Alexandra when she doesn't like a place. She likes it here. In fact, I've already got construction orders in place for the renovations she's planning, and I think you'll be very pleased. I know the show seems intrusive, and the scenes being partly set up seems a little false. But I also know that, in the end, things will work out for you and Wyatt. Not because of us, but because of the two of you."

Her brain interpreted that a little differently than Charles had probably meant it, and Delaney had to remind herself, again, that she had to focus on the Pines and set aside whatever she'd been feeling for Wyatt lately.

"Thank you, I—wait, renovations?" Delaney remembered the list of ideal improvements she'd submitted to the show when she'd sent in her audition tape. The list had seemed major to her then—all the cable wiring to run, the WiFi network to set up, the computer system and getting the Pines online, updating the cabins—but to the show, and now that Delaney thought of the huge-scale changes she'd seen Alex pull off in other episodes, the things on Delaney's wish list were probably small potatoes.

Charles nodded. "Oh, yes. Though the list here doesn't seem like a lot. Probably something we can get done in a day."

Another production assistant stuck her head out the back door of the Bean Pot.

"Charles, Miss Phillips is next," the woman said brightly—too brightly, Delaney thought, for a woman dressed head-to-toe in black on a summer day. Charles picked up his clipboard and stood, Delaney followed.

When she and Charles slipped back inside, Delaney saw that many of the extras had left. There were a few stragglers in the dining room still, and Maisie was chatting among them. A few of the cameras were being taken down. Wyatt and Alex stood at the front counter.

Delaney did a double take at the sight. Alex was standing close to Wyatt—intimately close. Since he had about six inches of height on the other woman,

Alex had to tilt her head back to look up at him, and she was laughing. Delaney watched as Alex lifted a perfectly manicured hand and laid it on Wyatt's forearm—and then left it there.

Delaney felt a sudden, irritating spike of jealousy. This was the second time she'd seen Alex touch Wyatt in a flirtatious way. The first time, when the embarrassing incident with Ursula had happened, Delaney had brushed it off as a fluke. But now, Delaney had some serious suspicions about the beautiful Alex's intentions.

But he doesn't seem to mind. Wyatt certainly wasn't trying to slip away from her touch.

Charles stopped short next to Delaney, glancing up from his clipboard. He didn't say anything when he saw Wyatt and Alex, but he urged Delaney forward. "Let's get started. Alexandra!"

Alex and Wyatt looked over and spotted Delaney and Charles. Alex made no move to lower her hand from Wyatt's arm. But Wyatt stepped back quickly as they approached, putting distance between himself and Alex.

Delaney took a slow, calming breath. There was no reason for her to act weird about what she'd just seen, and there was no reason for Wyatt to feel guilty for enjoying Alex's flirting. The TV show, straight from the big city, had brought people to the Pines who were different than the people he was around on a daily basis. Alex, in particular, was exotic, cultured, and beautiful—all very attractive traits.

"Delaney," Alex greeted her. "Wyatt was just telling me you used to work here at the restaurant when you were a teenager."

Was that what they'd been laughing about?

"I did," she said hesitantly. "Maisie and I both, actually, long before I became the property manager and she started running the Bean Pot."

"I was just telling Alex about how I always used to try and talk you out of going to work so we could hang out, but you'd never be convinced to call in fake sick," Wyatt explained.

Delaney shook her head, smiling, trying to keep her voice light. "The more this show reminds me of what a miscreant you were, the more I wonder where Alex even saw the potential."

"Oh, I think there's a lot here with potential," Alex replied.

Wyatt seemed oblivious to Alex's implication, but Delaney didn't miss where Alex's gaze had gone. She decided that, rather than hanging out and waiting to see what other cheesy lines Alex might try, she would get her afternoon's obligation over with so she could go make her campground rounds and have a chance to shake off the queasy feeling in her stomach.

"Did you need me for something?" Delaney asked, hoping her voice didn't convey her vexation.

"Oh, yes," Alex said, waving a hand as though trying to pluck a reminder out of the air. "Charles, what is it we need Delaney for?"

Charles flipped pages. "The get-the-reluctant-manager-on-board scene. Delaney digs her heels in against change, you convince her that in order for the business to move forward, things have to change from the way they always have been."

"That's it. Where's Norman? Get that single camera

ready. Norman? Norman!" Alex pursed her lips, looking displeased.

Delaney was taking so many calming breaths today that she might as well be going through Ursula's morning meditation routine. Norman appeared, obsequiously escorting Alex out from behind the counter.

"Ursula radioed from the office," Wyatt said to Delaney. "She thinks we may have a party booking from that chamber meeting. I have to go back up and call the customer. You going to be okay here?"

"You go do what you have to, and I'll go do what I have to," Delaney said, waving him off. "I'll be fine."

In order for the business to move forward, things have to change from the way they always have been. Was that true? Was it true beyond the updates to camp? Was it true between Delaney and Wyatt? She was starting to feel like the line between reality TV and reality was getting a little blurred.

CHAPTER 12

"And we did jump stuff, but Slater would only let me jump really small stuff, like you said—until I get my technique down. And, oh, Mom, did you know that there are campgrounds that have *built-in* bike and skate parks? How cool would that be? I mean, not that I don't like the trails, those are cool, but Slater said if we had a more even surface, he could teach me some really sweet moves."

Walking back along the path to their cabin, Delaney's tired brain semi-tuned out on her daughter's stream of words. Delaney was bone-tired. It took all the strength she could muster to make the trek back to cabin one at the end of her day. She regretted leaving her car parked at the cabin this morning, rather than driving it to the office.

The saving grace of the journey was Rachel. Delaney's daughter skipped beside her as they walked back to the cabin in the fading twilight, happily recounting her afternoon of mountain biking with Slater.

By the time Delaney had finished her scene with Alex and done her camp rounds to check on the guests, Rachel and Slater had returned, saving Delaney from having to go back up to the office and see Wyatt—well, really, saving Delaney from thinking about what she was *feeling* for Wyatt.

Instead, she'd spent over an hour at the lake with Slater and Rachel, rounding up a half-dozen empty kayaks that had been pushed out into the lake by some local troublemakers. When she'd returned to the office to finish up for the day, Wyatt's office was dark. Delaney was thankful for the respite, too tired to analyze her confusion.

Rachel must have noticed that she'd tuned out because she bumped Delaney with her shoulder. "Mom?"

"That sounds good, honey," Delaney responded woodenly. Her mind kept wandering back to Alex's hand on Wyatt's arm, how he'd smiled down at Alex, how he hadn't stepped away from the glamorous star until Delaney had come in. Filming her scene with Alex after the incident hadn't been awkward. In fact, Delaney had thought it was the easiest thing they'd done so far.

"And then, after riding bikes, Slater told me that real extreme sports enthusiasts shave their heads for aerodynamics. I thought it sounded like a great idea, but I told him I'd have to ask you. Do you think I could shave my head? And what about my eyebrows? Those, too?"

"Mmm-hmm, sweetheart. Yep."

Rachel stopped in the middle of the trail. "Mom, seriously?"

Delaney stopped, too, turning toward Rachel. She squinted in the dying light, trying to make out the girl's expression. "What? Sorry. You're right. I wasn't listening. I'm just really beat from today. Hauling in all those kayaks, I can't believe you aren't exhausted."

"I'm not," Rachel insisted. "But I'm sorry you're so beat. What about that new season of *The ABC's of Business* back at the cabin, and maybe we order a pizza with everything on it?"

That sounded like heaven to Delaney. Well, the pizza part, anyway. Watching any more of the perfect, blonde Alex parading around looking dazzling didn't sound too appealing. But the only other things they could watch were slightly fuzzy local channels or the multiple seasons of *Lovestruck High* Rachel had brought with her. Delaney guessed it would have to be *ABC's* for tonight.

"Deal," Delaney said, pulling Rachel in close to her side. They walked like that, their arms slung around one another, down the darkening camp road toward their cabin. Fireflies blinked like tiny magic lanterns in the air, flashing for a millisecond before fading into the crispness of the cooling forest. When they got near the cabin, Delaney could see hers wasn't the only vehicle parked near the front porch.

"What's Wyatt doing here?" Rachel asked.

"I don't know," Delaney admitted.

Was something wrong? Her heart leapt into her throat at the thought of the last time Wyatt had paid her a late-night visit. She'd been cleaning cabin one instead of crashing in it, and it had been the night of his parents' accident. He'd been shaking like a leaf, too devastated to drive to the hospital alone. She quickened her pace as they neared the cabin.

The tailgate of the truck was down, and Wyatt and Duke were sitting on it. Wyatt was holding a gigantic pizza box.

"Hey," Delaney said cautiously, searching his face

for any signs that something was amiss. "What are you doing here?"

"Well," Wyatt said, "I got halfway home and realized that the three of us have hardly seen each other since the show got here. I know you both have been working really hard, and I thought you might like a break from having to cook."

"So you brought us pizza?" Rachel pretended to be offended.

"I can't cook," Wyatt admitted.

"He can't cook," Delaney blurted out simultaneously.

"That explains why we always order out at your house," Rachel said, taking the pizza box from Wyatt. Duke sat up at attention when Rachel lifted the lid. "Everything, yes! Thank you, Wyatt!"

"Yes, thank you, Wyatt." Delaney noticed he was still in his work clothes. Her heart warmed at the notion that he'd just turned around and come back at the thought of them. "You'll join us, of course?"

"I wasn't going to invite myself, but if you'd like the company..." He trailed off as he stood up. Duke launched himself off the tailgate, sprinting up the cabin steps after Rachel.

Rachel called back over her shoulder. "C'mon, Mom. C'mon, Wyatt. Before it gets cold."

Delaney tipped her head toward the cabin, addressing Wyatt. "You're always welcome. But I have to warn you, the entertainment choices tonight are local weather, the newest season of *The ABC's of Business*, or a whole lot of *Lovestruck High*."

Wyatt took Delaney's keys when she offered them and unlocked the door, letting Rachel and Duke inside. He held the screen door for Delaney but made a face. "What the heck is *Lovestruck High*?"

"It's a reality show set in a high school. You don't want to go there."

He shrugged and followed Delaney inside. "Maybe I do. Is it any good?"

"You still haven't watched *The ABC's of Business*. I think you should do some studying up."

"We'll see. Maybe I don't want the ending spoiled," he joked.

Inside the tiny cabin, Rachel and Wyatt flopped down onto the soft, well-worn leather sofa while Delaney put pizza on plates and poured them all glasses of tea. As she carried everything over to the sitting area, she smiled at the assault Wyatt was bravely trying to survive. Rachel was holding her precious *Lovestruck High: Season One* box set out for him to see.

"And this is Scott. He's like the jock, but he also writes love poetry to the nerdy girl, Faye. He never gives it to her, though. He's too worried about what his friends will think. Isn't that rotten *and so romantic*?" Rachel sighed, then took her plate as Delaney held it out.

Wyatt looked over at Delaney, panic in his eyes as she passed him his pizza. "Uh, sorry, kiddo, your mom says I have to watch *The ABC's of Business*. Maybe we'll watch yours some other time."

Delaney shook her head at him. *You are unreal*, she mouthed.

"Here, Rach, hold my plate. I'll load up the DVD," Delaney said, attempting to soothe the sting of losing hours of dreamboat quarterback-poet viewing. Once everything was queued up, Delaney settled on the couch, Rachel between her and Wyatt, and pressed play.

As they ate and watched, Delaney snuck glances at Wyatt. She tried to gauge his reaction to Alexandra, see if his eyes regained the warm, interested glow she'd seen when Alex had been flirting with him this afternoon. There was nothing but his calm, normal expression. And that strong jaw. And that always-slightly-messy hair. She tried not to sigh.

Two episodes later, with all the pizza gone and Rachel and Duke fast asleep between them, Wyatt caught her studying him when he glanced over during the end credits.

"What's up?" he whispered over Rachel's head.

"Nothing. This is nice," she replied. And it was. No cameras, no strangers, no made-up drama. Just the four of them and the night sounds of the woods coming through the window screens.

"It is," he agreed. He looked at her for a long moment.

"Do I have pizza on my face or something?"

"What? No. Why?"

"Because you're staring at me," she explained, amused.

"Oh. Sorry. Can we... Do you want to go outside and talk?" Why did she always get nervous when he asked that? He reached down and grabbed her hand. Her heart lurched in—what was it, anticipation or fear?

Why did she always get nervous when he asked that? Delaney thought back to how touchy Alex had been with Wyatt. She was just coming to terms with the chaos the show had brought to the Pines. She didn't want to have any other bombs dropped on her, like Wyatt telling her he was interested in Alex.

"Sure," she agreed. He nodded, seeming relieved, and dropped her hand.

They stood, each careful not to wake Rachel. Delaney laid her gently back on the couch and covered her with a blanket. Then she followed Wyatt out onto the cabin porch where they leaned against the front railing. He didn't look concerned about anything; his posture was relaxed, his face serene.

The day sounds of the woods had been replaced by the evening orchestra. Delaney heard the chirp of crickets, the occasional hoot of an owl—all lit by the seemingly synchronized flashing of fireflies, blinking among the trees beyond the warm glow of the lighted porch. When Wyatt didn't start the conversation, Delaney grew even more anxious.

"Everything okay?" she asked, her nerves jangling despite her observations—or maybe that was just her teeth chattering. With nightfall, the temperature had dropped quickly, and what was normally a warm summer breeze had turned a bit chilly. His face suddenly registered concern.

"Hang on," he said, jogging out to his truck and returning with a jacket. He settled it over her shoulders, pulling it closed in front. She grasped at the edges of the jacket and wiggled her arms into the sleeves, donning it the right way despite it being a number of sizes too big for her. It smelled like wood smoke and pine and Wyatt's cologne, and she resisted the urge to bury her face in the leather and breathe in.

"Better?" he asked.

"Much. But you're making me really nervous, so can you just tell me what you really came out here for?"

He grinned, reaching into his back pocket. "Tell me how you really feel, Friday. Don't mince words," he said, chuckling. He pulled out a piece of paper and unfolded it, handing it to her.

"What's this?" she asked, even as she reached for it.

"Something Alex gave me today. Well, Charles gave it to me, but she went over it with me right before my scene. I wanted to show it to you when you came into the Bean Pot, but there were a lot of people around, and I wanted the chance to talk to you about it alone. Y'know, those people aren't part of our real lives."

Delaney clung to the warmth that his last words sparked in her. She scanned the paper. It was an outline of what looked to be construction projects, a sequence of completion, and a budget to go along with it. Delaney's eyes almost popped out of her head at the total. "This is way bigger than the list I sent the show for ideal renovations." She started ticking off items out loud. "Cable, yes, WiFi, yes, repainting the cabins, yes. But all this other stuff? Who asked for this?"

"No one asked for it. It was all Alex's idea. Check out the signature at the bottom," Wyatt urged.

Delaney scanned past a dozen other small—but needed—updates, until her eyes landed on the scrawl at the bottom of the page. Alexandra Brent-Collingsworth.

"Alex approved all of this?"

Delaney couldn't believe it. It was all she'd hoped for—and more. Her entire list was here, approved, right down to the new computer system and the website that would allow guests to book with the Pines online. But there were myriad other things: paving the camp road and the parking lot of the restaurant, fixing the second walk-in cooler, adding a cookout space down near the lake so the receptions they'd hoped to host could prepare food right at the lakeshore.

Delaney felt tears start to fill her eyes, and she felt petty for having been jealous over Alex's flirtations with Wyatt. At the same time, a little voice in her head piped up that maybe all of this going the extra mile was because Alex *was* interested in Wyatt. Delaney lifted a hand to her lips, but a small, gasping sob escaped anyway.

Wyatt's eyes filled with worry, and he stepped forward to cup his hands over her elbows. "Oh, Del, I'm sorry. I didn't mean to upset you. If there's something on there you don't want done, just say the word. This is as much your business as it is mine."

She threw her arms around him and clung, squeezing tight. "No, no! I'm not upset. This is wonderful. More than I could have hoped for. Thank you for bringing this."

"I couldn't wait until tomorrow to tell you. You've been working so hard."

His arms came around her, and he held her for long, sweet moments. Delaney had gone from worrying about the Pines to worrying about the interloping show, from her own confusion about her feelings for Wyatt to a jealousy over Alex that made her certain she was falling for him. And tonight, with all of them together as though they were a real family and knowing that Wyatt had rushed back to share this news with her instead of waiting for tomorrow... Well, it made her wonder if she might be able to tell him he'd become more than just her friend.

She slowly pulled away from the hug, and his

hands slid away from her back to rest on her sides just as slowly. They regarded each other like that, just an arm's distance away, for another minute.

"You know," Wyatt said, reaching up to brush a wisp of hair away from her face, "Jacob was a fool to let you guys go."

Delaney felt her heart become a little more his. In the moonlight, Wyatt's eyes were deep and intense, and she let her gaze lock with his. Her heartbeat seemed to pick up. "I think so, too, but thanks for saying it."

She picked at a loose button on his shirt, focusing on the frayed thread instead of looking up at Wyatt. "You know, I wasn't that sad when he left, to be honest—not sad for me, anyway. He'd been in the process of leaving for years, being gone so much for work. But Rachel, he broke her heart, too, and that's what I regret the most."

She felt tears well up again, but this time, they weren't tears of joy. She swiped at her eyes, and he drew her back against him again.

"Shhh, it's okay. Hey, listen to me. You're the strongest, kindest, most dependable person I know. You fix everything—the fallout from Jacob's screw-up, the Pines every single day with that genius brain of yours. Heck, you've even kept me on the straight and narrow over the years."

"The semi-straight and moderately narrow, you mean," she said, pulling away to look at him again, managing to laugh through her tears. "You were kind of a mischief maker when you were a teenager."

"That's true. Trust me, Friday. I've had my moments of doubt lately. But the show seems like it's going to come through for us. And you did that, too. You should be proud. I'm proud."

She nodded, sniffling. Silence fell between them. His arms were still around her, and the silence stretched, deepened. She found herself swaying toward him. His head dipped closer for the briefest of moments. She held her breath, staring up at him. The next moment could answer all of her most secret questions.

Then, as though thinking better of the move, Wyatt straightened and stepped away. He checked his watch, the face glowing when he pushed a button on the side. "It's late, Del, and I know you're exhausted. I'll see you tomorrow, okay?"

Her disappointment nearly stole her voice. She nodded again, cleared her throat, and said, "Duke's still asleep in there. Is it okay if I let him stay and just bring him to the office in the morning?"

"Sure," Wyatt agreed. He leaned in to give her a soft kiss on the cheek. "Goodnight," he whispered.

The touch of his lips and the husky rasp in his voice caused every fine little hair from the back of Delaney's neck to her forearms to stand up. A pleasant little thrill went up her spine. Without another word between them, he jogged down the cabin steps and climbed into his truck.

He was gone before Delaney realized she hadn't broached the subject of Alex's flirting at all. She looked down at the renovation plans, which she still held in her hand. Nothing was settled, and she was still just as confused as ever.

"M-mom?" Rachel's groggy voice cut into Delaney's thoughts.

"Coming, honey," she called, putting the paper into the pocket of Wyatt's jacket and turning to go back inside.

CHAPTER 13

The next morning, Delaney sat in bed, enjoying the warmth of the summer sun as it streamed through the open curtains. She sipped her coffee while she waited for Rachel to wake up. It was still very early, so Delaney was in no rush. Duke, who had opted for Delaney's bed rather than the high loft over the kitchenette where Rachel was sleeping, cocked his head as Delaney's cell phone rang.

"Well, isn't that a rarity. A call that isn't on a walkie-talkie." Delaney was fully aware that she was talking to a dog, but she wasn't embarrassed in the least. She'd always found Duke to be an excellent listener. She picked her phone up off the nightstand, and she swiped to answer it when she saw whose number it was.

"Hey, Maisie, what's up?" Delaney tried to keep her voice low to avoid waking Rachel.

"Del, honey, we've got a problem."

Delaney was shocked at the loudness of Maisie's voice. She pulled her phone away from her ear and turned the in-call volume down several notches. "Yikes. Why are you talking so loud?"

"Oh, I'm not. You're just used to the shoddy cell

reception we've had out here for years. You know how you've been fighting to get the phone company to put up a cell tower on the property?"

"Yeah," Delaney said slowly.

"Well, darlin', it's a Christmas miracle. I come in this morning, and there's one practically in the back-yard of the Bean Pot. Darned thing's disguised as a pine tree, too."

Delaney was not quite awake enough for this. "I'm sorry. Did you say it was disguised as a *pine tree*?"

"That's the honest truth. Phone sounds great now, huh?"

Delaney squinted, trying to make sense of Maisie's purpose. "So, the problem is what, now?"

"Oh! Oh, Ursula's here. She's real upset about the office. The show's kicked her out of there and started taking apart the front desk. Wyatt was in here a bit ago for breakfast, but he took off super early with Slater to mend the fence in the back field. You know, the one where Pete's cows are? Seems the crane they used to hoist up that cell tower did a number on the fence, and some of the cows got out."

"Did anybody call to tell them?" Delaney asked.

"The cows?" Maisie asked. "Honey, you better get down here for some coffee."

"No, Maisie. Not the cows. Wyatt and Slater. Do they know the show's tearing up the office?" Delaney was climbing out of bed as she talked, rummaging in the small dresser next to the bed to find clean shorts and a Pines tee. Once she found them, she carried them with her to the small bathroom and placed them on the sink.

"I tried," Maisie explained, "but neither are answering their cell phones, and neither of the fools took walkie-talkies. Said it would be a quick repair."

Delaney cranked on the shower. She closed the curtain to let the water heat up. Turning, she ran a hand through her messy hair and stared at her bed-rumpled reflection in the mirror.

"So, what should we do?" Maisie's voice held a note of desperation.

Delaney sighed and rubbed the bridge of her nose. "Okay. Just sit tight. I'll drop by there first, bring Rachel. Do you mind making her breakfast and letting her hang out there while I sort out the office situation?"

"I'd be glad if you did, and I'd be happy to have Rachel."

"Thanks. I'll be there in fifteen minutes."

"Bless you, sugar," Maisie said, sounding relieved.

Delaney hung up, put her phone on the counter, and leaned out the bathroom door.

"Rachel, time to get up!" she hollered.

Delaney and Rachel made it to the Bean Pot in exactly fifteen minutes. After taking Duke around back to his overflowing breakfast bowl, they walked into the fairly full dining room. There was a breakfast crowd of regulars Delaney recognized and none of the mayhem that had descended on the place yesterday was in sight. Maisie was walking the floor, filling coffees and checking on tables. Everything seemed perfectly fine to Delaney.

Maisie spotted them and angled her head toward the counter. There, sitting next to a beleaguered-seeming Charles, was a weeping Ursula. He was holding a tissue box, patting her on the back, and seemed completely out of his depths. Delaney made eye contact with Charles, who waved weakly.

Rachel gasped. "Mom, Ursula is *crying.*"

"I know, honey. She's upset about some changes at the office. This has been a hard week for all of us. Let's go see if we can cheer her up."

When Rachel and Delaney got to the counter, Charles stood and offered Rachel his seat. Ursula lifted her head as Rachel sat down next to her. The older woman dabbed at her eyes with a tissue and then blew her nose loudly. "Oh, Rachel, dear, hello. I'm so sorry. I'm a mess. Excuse me."

Rachel rubbed Ursula's back. Delaney threw an arm around Ursula and hugged her. Maisie slid behind the counter and poured fresh coffee into Charles's mug, placed a fresh tea bag and cup of hot water in front of Ursula, and handed Rachel a menu.

"Orange juice?" Maisie asked.

"Coffee?" Rachel countered.

Delaney shook her head. "Orange juice is fine."

Ursula blew her nose again. "Oh, girls, I'm so sorry. I just came in this morning, and my chair is gone, my yoga mat is gone—"

"They're starting the remodel of the office," Charles explained gently, adjusting his glasses. "Sometimes, the crew isn't as thoughtful as they should be. I'll talk to them, Ursula, I promise."

"Thoughtful?" Ursula shook her fist. "They…they broke my Namaste mug!"

The group collectively grimaced. Delaney switched into problem-solving mode. "Okay, well, the good thing about it is that the office will be so much better when they're done. But I'm sorry you got ousted like that. I really had no warning about it, or I would have told you."

Ursula nodded. "I know. I know."

"But"—Delaney was looking around the Bean Pot, reconfiguring in her head—"what do you need to get your work done today?"

Maisie went to get Rachel's juice while Ursula dried her eyes on one last tissue. Ursula lapsed into silence for a moment, thinking. "I need a phone line, the old computer, and the pink and purple flowered folder from the front desk. It has all my notes from those chamber calls I've been making.

"If I had those things, I could answer calls, check out anyone who's leaving today, check in anyone who shows up, and keep working on filling the campground with summer parties. But check-out is at ten, and check-ins can happen anytime."

Delaney checked her phone screen. It was just now 7:30. She scanned the dining room again. Suddenly, her eyes landed on a solution, one that was tucked off by itself by the door to the kitchen, an alcove too cramped for more than the raggedy two-seater booth that currently occupied it.

"There," she said, nodding toward the space.

Maisie returned with a glass filled to the brim with freshly squeezed OJ. She set it down carefully in front of Rachel and popped a straw into the glass.

"That booth? No one sits there. You're welcome to it," Maisie offered. "Doesn't look very comfortable for working, though."

"Charles," Delaney said, turning to him with a plan forming, "you have guys who can run all sorts of electrical and audio, right?"

"Yes, ma'am," Charles replied.

"Can you get someone to come in here and run a phone line extension from there"—Delaney pointed to a phone outlet a yard or so away from the booth they'd all been discussing—"to there?" Delaney indicated the booth.

Charles nodded. "Yes, that'd be easy, actually. Is that all?"

"And how about borrowing one of those heavy-duty extension cords and some of that tape... What's it called? The kind that would keep everybody from tripping over the cord if we taped it down?"

"Gaffer's tape, yes," Charles was starting to sound excited. "I see where you're going with this."

Rachel, Ursula, and Maisie watched Delaney and Charles with widening smiles on their faces.

"And how about a hand carrying that old booth out?" Delaney finished.

Charles picked up his cell phone and brandished it with an expression of purpose on his face. "Let me call up to the office. I'll have them come down and measure that space. They can cut the old countertop from the front desk to size, and we'll set it on some wall brackets. It won't be fancy, but it'll work."

Ursula was beaming. "Oh, thank you. That makes me feel so much better."

Charles grinned back at the group. When his eyes reached Maisie, they smiled a little differently at one another, and Delaney didn't miss it. Charles tapped a few times on his phone screen and then excused himself. As he walked out, Delaney heard him start to talk to whomever was on the other side of the call.

"Hey, it's Charles. Listen, I need two guys from the

office demolition to come down to the restaurant. And here's what I need them to bring…"

Delaney, satisfied that the plan was in good hands, turned back to the counter. "Maisie, can I get a *large* coffee and a cinnamon roll to go? I've got to go down and see if Slater and Wyatt are finished at the back field."

"You got it, hon. Rachel? How 'bout you? Decide what you'd like?"

Rachel ordered French toast, scrambled eggs, bacon, and fruit salad. Delaney's mouth watered at the thought, but all she really had time for was the warm cinnamon roll that Maisie passed her a few minutes later. With thanks, she also accepted the tall travel cup of coffee Maisie handed across the counter. Delaney took a long, slow sip. It was perfect, just the right amount of cream and sugar. But there was something else…

"Is this…is there brown sugar in this?" Delaney asked.

"New Bean Pot secret recipe," Maisie said, winking. "Isn't it good?"

"It's great, actually." And it was. Delaney was pleasantly surprised.

With a hug for Maisie and Ursula and a kiss for Rachel, Delaney was on her way. When she left the restaurant, she circled around to the back, even though she was parked out front. She stood for a moment, sipping her delicious coffee, staring up at the new cell tower now erected just at the edge of the clearing behind the Bean Pot. It was so real, with its bark-brown trunk and faux pine branches, that she thought the squirrels and birds might even be fooled.

"Huh," she said, awed. "I'll be darned. It does look *exactly* like a pine tree."

Wyatt and Slater were not at the back field. Delaney tried to call both of them on their cell phones again but had the same result as Maisie had. She climbed back in her car and drove back up to the office. When she neared, she could see both Wyatt's truck and Slater's old Jeep parked out front.

As she neared the front door, it swung open, and Slater came walking out, hefting over his shoulder a length of the old front counter that had served as the reception desk.

"Whoa!" Delaney ducked just in time to avoid being taken out by the pale-pink Formica.

"Hey, Del! Charles called. I'm just heading down to the old Bean. I'm going to install the temp workspace for Ursula. I want to make sure it gets done right for her."

"That's sweet, Slater, thanks," Delaney said.

"No prob, boss. Some of the guys already left with the computer and wiring supplies. We should have her up and running in less than an hour. Oh, and I'll take her chair, too."

Delaney felt a swell of pride. Slater was a stand-up guy. The entire staff here was like family. She could see it in the way they all banded together around one of their own when there was upheaval. And not just this office displacement. Last month Slater had gone clear across town to help Ursula when her VW had suffered a blowout on the highway. There was Delaney's divorce, Wyatt's parents ... the list of how this crew had helped one another was nearly endless and constantly growing. Heck, they'd all stuck with each other for years, despite the decline in business.

"Is Wyatt inside?" Delaney yelled to Slater, who was hefting the desktop into the open back of his Jeep.

"Yup," Slater confirmed. "He's in his office, clearing stuff out."

Time to tackle the next set of challenges, Delaney thought, swinging the door open to the office with a spring in her step. Even though she was dismayed that Ursula was upset, Delaney was happy the solution was forthcoming. She felt good, confident that she could handle anything else the day might throw at her.

She walked past the men at the front desk, who had dismantled much of the counter and almost all the cabinetry. Old, slightly yellowing wallpaper was being stripped off a back wall. When she passed the bathroom in the hallway, she peeked through the propped-open door to see the old wood paneling being carefully taken down.

With all the demolition going on and a half-dozen people working in the small office building, it was incredibly noisy. Delaney pushed open Wyatt's half-closed office door, shouting to be heard over the din.

"They're really hustling out there. Gosh, I can't wait to see—"

Delaney stopped abruptly at the scene that greeted her. She hadn't heard any noise coming down the hall, likely due to the level of construction chaos. But inside Wyatt's office, he wasn't alone. Alex was with him, and she was in Wyatt's arms, looking up at him with adoring eyes.

When Delaney burst in, the two sprang apart—or,

more accurately, Wyatt pushed away from Alex as though she were on fire. Stammering, he pointed to a ladder in front of Alex.

"We were just taking down pictures. She fell...off... uh...off the ladder."

Delaney's eyes went to Alex's feet, which were encased in expensive high heels. Those didn't seem to be the kind of shoes a woman climbed a ladder in. She looked back at Wyatt's beet-red face, then at Alex's perfectly-made-up expression, which was neutral. It was an expression designed, Delaney guessed, to allow Delaney to draw her own conclusion.

She waved off Wyatt's embarrassment, leveling her gaze so that it was locked with Alex's. Her tone dripped with faux-concern. "Oh no! Are you okay? I hope you aren't hurt."

"No. I'm fine, thank you." Alex's expression had changed from neutral to surprised. So, she'd been expecting Delaney to assume something. How had she known Delaney was on her way?

I don't know what game you're playing, Alexandra, Delaney thought, *but I'm not falling for it.*

"Great," she replied to Alex. "Now, let's talk about these renovations."

Delaney wouldn't let Alex sidetrack her. She'd get to the bottom of what was going on here later, when the Pines—and the future of everyone here—was secure.

CHAPTER 14

Delaney hadn't said a word to him in almost ten minutes. Wyatt wasn't sure if she was just concentrating on their work or if something else was going on. They were finishing up clearing out his office, carrying boxes to his truck. He'd started to say something to her a couple of times, only to pull himself back from explaining.

It had all happened so fast—he'd been holding the ladder and Alex's high heel had slipped as she'd climbed... He'd just caught her to prevent her from getting hurt. Why did he feel such a strong need to re-assure Delaney that it hadn't been anything romantic?

Speaking of romantic...

Wyatt recalled the previous night, standing on the porch with Delaney, that soft-focus moment where the crazy thought had entered his head to kiss her. Should he have?

No. Del was his best friend. They didn't feel that way about each other—did they?

Before Wyatt could broach the subject of the awkward scene with Alex, Charles showed up, trusty clipboard in hand, and gave them the rundown on what the next forty-eight hours would entail. Wyatt was relieved to find that he and Delaney wouldn't be needed for the remainder of the day. Maybe he could talk to her once they were alone.

An idea sparked in Wyatt's mind. He kept it to himself for now, listening to Charles brief them on what would be happening with the Pines while they were absent.

"Renovations will be in full swing for the rest of today and all of tomorrow," Charles recited. "Our crew will move out of the cabins and either camp in the tent areas or sleep in the crew RVs that are hooked up over at the RV campsites. Alex will be staying in town at the bed-and-breakfast."

"We have three yurts that you're all welcome to use, as well," Wyatt offered. "They have two sets of bunks each, and there are clean linens in the storage closets at cabin one."

Charles nodded. "Thanks, Wyatt. And speaking of that, Delaney, we'll need to get into cabin one tomorrow during the day for renovation. Do you mind moving your bags?"

Delaney shook her head. "No, I don't mind. No problem at all. Rachel wanted to go home and grab more DVDs anyway, and her friend Bridget has been dying to take her to the water park. I might as well just pack our suitcases and take everything home. If we only have a few days left of the show, I'll just move us back and make my regular drive."

"Ok, so that's settled." Charles made a few notes. Wyatt thought back to last night, to Delaney in his arms on the porch of cabin one. Now she'd be clear across town again. Why did that seem so far away?

"The film crew will be splitting up, some of them

taking exterior shots and filming the renovations, some of them taping scenes with only Alexandra." Charles looked at Delaney and said conspiratorially, "They won't be down at the restaurant at all, so Ursula shouldn't have anyone else bothering her. Renovations start there tomorrow."

Delaney smiled at Charles, and Wyatt felt slightly uneasy at the familiarity of the exchange.

"Anyway, I don't see either of you on this list. I'd say take a break, get away from work. We'll call you if we need anything during renovations. Otherwise, the next time we talk will be so I can let you know what time to show up for the big reveal. Alexandra may also call you to discuss the evening event that will happen that night."

"What evening event?" Wyatt and Delaney both spoke at the same time.

Charles screwed up his face. "You guys do that a lot?"

"Not since we were kids," Wyatt said, chuckling. "We used to do it so often that people thought it was some sort of prank."

Charles shook his head. "Interesting. The evening event is a...what should we call it—a party? You've seen the show, right?"

When they both nodded, he continued.

"After the renovation, there's always a chance to show off the progress the business has made. With restaurants, there's a grand reopening. Here, it's a little different. We have lots to show off, so Alex wanted to throw a party."

Wyatt and Delaney looked at one another, both with the same unsure expression.

"Okay, you guys are getting a little too cute," Charles said dryly. "Consider it like an open house. We'll have a big bonfire, the new pavilion at the lake, reopen the Bean Pot to serve for the night, have all the cabins available for people to walk through. That kind of thing."

Wyatt found himself excited by the idea of a party. To have the Pines filled with people again would be wonderful. Just like old times. "That sounds fun. So, we just have to show up?"

"Yep. We will be filming that night, so feel free to wear your summer best. I'll make a note to have Alex call you with more details. Now, you two, shoo!"

Delaney paused, and there was a spark of something in her eyes.

"Are you thinking what I'm thinking?" he asked, reaching into his pocket and fishing out his keys.

"You still have your rowboat?" Delaney asked. Her mood appeared to be easing—or maybe it was just his discomfort at being caught in a seemingly compromising position with Alex. Maybe they didn't need to talk about it. Delaney seemed fine now.

Wyatt nodded. "Let's ask the rest of the gang if they want to come along." He unclipped his walkie-talkie from his belt. Darn, he'd almost forgotten he had it on him still. "I'll radio Slater and see where he's at. He can help me grill."

She considered for a moment. "Maisie's bound to be done with the breakfast rush, and Ursula can wait on those calls to the chamber. I think we could all use a break."

Charles shook his head again. "You do know that no one else has a clue what you two are talking about."

Wyatt grinned and felt a slow, warm pride creep up into his chest. He liked understanding Delaney, and he liked how well she understood him. He looked over at Charles.

"That's okay," he said. "We know what we're saying."

Delaney took out her cell phone and tapped the screen a few times. "Hey, Maisie, you and Ursula want to come to the other side of the lake with us? We're clearing out to let the renovation crew do their thing, and we're going to drive around to Wyatt's place."

Delaney covered the ear opposite her phone as construction noise kicked up from inside the office. "Hang on one sec, Maisie." Delaney walked away to talk with Maisie away from the din, leaving Wyatt and Charles standing on the front porch of the office. Charles watched her walk away.

"I don't get it," Charles said.

Wyatt crossed his arms over his chest and returned the man's confused look. "Don't get what?"

"You and Miss Phillips have known each other almost your whole lives, and not only do you work together, but even when you get time off, you're going to spend it with each other."

"Yes," Wyatt said. "What's the big deal?"

"No big deal," Charles said, a hint of merriment in his voice. "But I remember when you did your one-on-one, you said you'd never consider a romantic relationship with Delaney."

Wyatt hadn't told Delaney when she'd vented to him about her awkward interview that Norman had asked him some of the same questions about her. At the time, Wyatt had been just as taken aback as she was, and he'd blurted out the safest thing he could think of.

"Well, I...uh... I wouldn't. She's my best friend. Why would I want to jeopardize that?" Wyatt looked out into the parking lot. Delaney was nowhere to be seen, and he didn't want her to overhear them talking about something so personal.

Charles shrugged. "It seems to me that you two are already in a relationship with each other. It's just that neither of you calls it that."

Wyatt stammered, "We're not. I mean, we wouldn't. She's great—amazing, actually. But I doubt she would—"

"Yes!" Delaney came out the screen door behind them, from inside the office. Wyatt's heart leapt into his throat. Charles froze.

"Where'd you come from?" Charles managed, trying to sound light but only managing, at least to Wyatt's ears, to sound guilty of something.

"Inside," Delaney said. "I wanted to see it one last time before we left. You know, a true 'before' picture. I took one with my phone, actually." She scrolled on her phone's screen, flipping it around to show them a picture of the torn-up interior of the office.

Wyatt and Charles both stood dumbly, both seeming to be waiting to see what she'd overheard.

She seemed oblivious to their discomfort. "But everyone said yes to the lake. I just need about ten minutes to pack up our stuff at cabin one, and you can meet me at the Bean Pot to pick up Rachel, Maisie, and Ursula. Does that sound okay?"

"Deal," Wyatt said. He hadn't realized he'd been

holding his breath until he let it out—and heard Charles do the same.

"What about Slater? What did he say?" She looked questioningly at Wyatt. He realized he hadn't even done as he'd intended.

"Actually, Charles and I have been talking, and I haven't even called Slater yet. I'll radio him on the way over. I think he's down at the cabins."

"Well, get a move on! Charles, you're welcome to join us," Delaney offered. "Maisie would be happy to have you there."

Wyatt was amused to see the other man's ears turn pink. Charles shook his head, declining politely. "Thanks, Delaney, but I have to stay. Every circus needs a ringleader."

"If you change your mind, the offer stands," Wyatt added, reaching out a hand. Charles shook hands with Wyatt, and Wyatt and Delaney descended the steps to the parking lot. The lot was being roped off. A large asphalt truck and a heavy-duty compacter sat to one side of the gravel lot.

"Would you look at that," Delaney said as they walked together toward their cars. "I guess things really are changing around here."

Wyatt felt another foreign tightening in his chest. Charles's words echoed in his head, and he thought about how he might have reacted had Delaney overheard their conversation. What if she had—and had been saying yes to him?

Ursula had actually been the hardest to convince to stop working. Delaney almost didn't blame her. With the breakfast crowd departed and the restaurant closed afterward so that the construction crew could begin updating, it was quiet out at the kitchen. Much quieter even than the office was on a normal day.

Maisie had opened a few windows to let the summer breeze in, and the scent of pine wafted in as Delaney came out to the dining room from the kitchen, carrying an industrial-sized box of stadium franks. She placed the box on the counter by the large tubs of potato salad, coleslaw, and the six peach pies Maisie had already piled there.

Delaney saw Ursula leaned back in her office chair at her new workstation, holding the phone to her ear and talking animatedly.

"Yes, I know. The show really has been drawing a lot of attention to the Pines. But trust me; we're still all about our love of local. We'd be delighted to host the fall festival this year."

Delaney saw her pause and then continue.

"Next week, we'll be back to normal, and you can take a tour to see the space we have to offer. What's that? Friday after next? That's just perfect. Thank you, Mr. Mayor. Talk to you soon!"

With satisfaction evident on her face, Ursula hung up the phone. She stood when she noticed Delaney walking over to give the woman a big hug. "Wow, Ursula, the mayor?"

"Well, he is on the chamber board, so his contact details were there from the meeting. And one of the things Wyatt underlined in his meeting notes was that there still wasn't a home for the fall festival. I know it's a ways off, but it couldn't hurt to try, right?"

"Definitely not. Great call."

Ursula looked proud of herself, and Delaney was proud of her. Heck, Delaney was proud of everyone—how they'd stuck out everything they'd all been through, and not just this past week.

Wyatt came out of the kitchen with another huge cardboard box. "I found the buns. How many people are we actually inviting now?"

"I'm not sure. Should we leave word with Charles that any of the film crew can come by for food?" Delaney asked.

Wyatt surveyed the mountain of items on the counter. "We'll need to. I don't think this will all keep if we have to be out of the kitchen for two days. Besides, the more, the merrier."

Rachel, Slater, and Maisie all came in through the front door.

"Let's go!" Slater whooped. "I got first dibs on diving off the swimming dock."

Wyatt carried the box of hot dog buns to Rachel, who turned to carry it out to Wyatt's truck, which was parked close to the front door for convenient loading. Slater and Maisie came to grab the pies and salads. Ursula made up the end of the parade, her bright, colorful skirt swirling as she followed the rest of the group outside.

Everyone was beaming. The beautiful day offered limitless possibilities, and the impromptu lake party seemed like the perfect way for all of them to shake off the stress of the show and reconnect, really spend some quality time together.

Once everyone was gone, Delaney stood in the empty restaurant, giving it one last glance. This would be the last time she'd see the faded, mint-green booths, the counter with its metal trim and the gold flecks in the surface, the stools that Rachel loved to spin on.

Wyatt, the only one left in the dining room with her, came up behind her and placed both of his hands gently on her shoulders. She reached up and placed one of her hands over one of his. They both stood like that for a moment, and Delaney loved that she didn't even have to speak.

"Come on, Friday," Wyatt said. Delaney registered the low, husky drop in his voice, and she felt her breath catch with emotion and tears fill her own eyes. She knew he was feeling the same things. Wyatt was thinking about the years here, and probably—most painfully—about his parents. He dropped his hands but caught one of hers in his.

"Let's get out of here," she agreed. As they walked out, still holding hands, the first of the crew arrived to clear out the dining room. Delaney wanted to look back, but she kept staring ahead. In the gravel lot, surrounding the group of cars that they'd all pile into for the trip to Wyatt's, waited the rest of the group.

When Delaney reached the cars, Ursula pulled her into a hug.

"My dear, my dear," Ursula said, her expression serene and motherly, "to say goodbye is to die a little."

Delaney pulled back from the hug and wiped her eyes, nodding. "Who said that, Gandhi?"

"Raymond Chandler, actually," Ursula replied. Then, off of Delaney's expression of mirth, the older woman said, "What? I love a good mystery every once in a while. A person can't live by the metaphysical alone."

Wyatt looked from his aunt to Delaney and smiled

at her. "I guess we're all learning things about each other."

The group laughed and dispersed, all chatting as they loaded into their vehicles and prepared to depart. Delaney watched Wyatt as he climbed into his truck. She wondered how he'd react if he learned how she felt about him. The notion that he might return her affections sent a thrill through her, and her stomach filled with butterflies.

She shook the notion off and adjusted her rearview mirror. She checked to make sure everyone was buckled in, put her car in gear, and drove forward.

CHAPTER 15

"Hey, Mom?" Rachel said out of the blue. "What are you thinking?"

Ursula, Maisie, Rachel, and Delaney had spent the latter part of the afternoon lounging on the three porch swings that hung from the heavy beams of the small, neat wraparound porch of Wyatt's cabin. The porch faced the peaceful shore of Lake Fairwood. Ursula read, Maisie knitted, and Delaney sat, Rachel's head in her lap, swinging back and forth in the drowsy summer air.

As they continued to swing, Delaney ran her fingers through her daughter's silky, flaxen hair, marveling at how much she'd grown in just the past year.

Delaney's hand stilled. "Oh, nothing, really. Why do you ask?"

Rachel smiled up at Delaney. "You're doing that thing you do when you're thinking about something sad. You get that little line between your eyebrows."

Delaney laughed lightly. "Ok, ok. I was just thinking about how you've grown. How you'll be a teenager before I know it. You'll want to go spend more time with your friends, go chase boys. Your old mom won't be cool anymore."

Rachel made a face. "Don't worry, Mom. You'll always be cool." Rachel nestled into Delaney.

"Yeah?" Delaney said, leaning down to kiss her daughter's forehead. When Rachel nodded, Delaney felt her heart warm.

"Of course. You've got an awesome job. You basically work on a big playground. And you get to hang out there all day with your best friend."

Delaney laughed out loud at that one and nodded. "It is that. And, you're right, I do."

They lapsed into silence. The day at the lake was one of the best days Delaney could remember having had for a long time. It was free of worries about money and the Pines, free of the pressures of schedules and the juggle that came with working and being a single mom. Delaney could relax and spend time with Rachel and their friends without having to race off to some disaster or fix some problem that had popped up at an inopportune moment. This was what summer was supposed to be like.

She'd always loved Wyatt's house. Only about a mile around the lake from where the Pines was, the modest cabin was situated right up near the water. A one-story clad in natural, weathered, rough-hewn boards with a strong foundation of stone, it boasted a cheerful lake-blue trim that made it seem welcoming. It was like a fairy-tale cottage, and it looked as though it might have actually grown out of the forest around it.

When the group had first arrived, Slater and Wyatt had rolled out Wyatt's grill into the backyard and made a big show of doing the cooking. After twenty minutes of trying to light the grill, Delaney and Maisie stepped in to fire up the charcoal, then let the guys take over with only a small amount of good-natured teasing.

Aside from Ursula, who'd settled on the porch to meditate but ended up napping with Duke in her lap, they'd all swam in Lake Fairwood until they were wrinkled. Slater taught Rachel to do a backflip off the swimming dock that floated a few yards out from the shoreline, much to Rachel's delight—and Delaney hadn't even had that much anxiety about it. Maybe just a little.

Then, it had been time for lunch. Dried and changed, all pleasantly exhausted, they'd all sat on the grassy slope that led to the lake and had eaten until they were near to bursting. Ursula, roused from her meditation, had joined them. Delaney had looked around at the faces of the people she loved, breathed in the fresh air, and sent up her gratitude for the day.

Wyatt had been skeptical that they'd be able to finish all of the food they'd brought from the Bean Pot. To their surprise, a group of construction workers and film crew from the Pines showed up just as they were finishing their own lunch.

They all pitched in to help feed the crew, who left with a hearty round of thanks and smiles on their faces. Delaney saw a bit of disappointment in Maisie's eyes when Charles wasn't among their guests, but it was fleeting, and her friend returned to her bubbly demeanor as compliments on the food were as plentiful as the food itself. Between everyone, they even managed to make all six of Maisie's peach pies disappear.

But with lunchtime over and plenty of the day left, there was still a lot of relaxing to do. And that was what they were all busily doing on Wyatt's porch.

Rachel reached up and tapped the middle of Delaney's forehead with her index finger. "You're doing it again."

Delaney swatted playfully at Rachel's hand. "Sorry, sorry. You're right. I should stop thinking. One more thing, then I'll stop. I promise."

Rachel let out a put-upon sigh. Delaney resumed stroking her hair.

"I do love my job, but I know things can get hectic. And I know it's not easy for you, not having your dad around. But you're the best thing that's ever happened to me. You know that?"

Rachel rolled her eyes. "You only say it to me every day." Her impish grin made Delaney tickle her in retribution.

"Oh, really? I'm so sorry that I love you so much. I'm sooooo sorry." Delaney didn't let up until Rachel hopped up, faux-affronted but grinning. Ursula and Maisie watched, smiling too.

Duke, unsure if there was fun to be had or danger about, bounced around the porch, even spinning a few times to check for danger in case it was the latter. Rachel sat back down next to her mom. Now, it was Rachel's face that was serious.

"I love you, too, Mom. And I know that when Dad left, it was *his* choice. And he's missing out. Because we're pretty awesome."

Delaney put an arm around her daughter, too touched to reply.

"You're darned right, you are." Delaney and Rachel turned to look in the direction of the voice. Wyatt stood at the top of the porch steps, holding a fishing rod. A moment later, Slater came bounding up the steps behind him, causing Wyatt to step up onto the porch and to the side.

Slater and Wyatt had gone fishing, but Delaney didn't see that they carried any of their catch.

"Thanks," Delaney said, putting on her best confused face. "Uhh, where are your fish?"

Slater rubbed the back of his neck, his shaggy hair falling into his eyes. "Guess they weren't biting today."

Delaney pulled a sympathetic face. "You got nothing?"

Wyatt set his fishing rod aside. "Nope, but I've got all the ingredients in the fridge to make my mom's beef stew. It's the only thing I can actually cook without fail. I'll even haul out the Dutch oven to make it on the shore."

Maisie leaned forward on her swing to see around Delaney. "That sounds great. Delaney and I will light the fire." She stared pointedly at Wyatt and Slater.

Delaney stood and pulled Rachel from the swing. "Can you get the folding wagon from the trunk of my car and bring some firewood from Wyatt's woodpile down to the shore?"

Rachel nodded and took off with Duke on her heels.

"I'll start prepping," Wyatt said. "Right after I wash up. All those worms and no fish." Sighing, he let himself into the house through the sliding door.

Delaney discovered that Ursula had fallen back asleep.

"Let's go start a fire, sister," Maisie said softly, being careful not to wake Ursula. She stood and linked arms with Delaney.

"Let's," Delaney repeated, nodding formally. The two women skipped down the porch steps.

Behind them, Delaney could hear Slater mutter-ing. "I can light a darned fire," he griped to no one in particular. "Wyatt was getting in my way."

Delaney grinned and kept her arm through Maisie's until they reached the round, stone firepit near the lakeshore. She remembered when Wyatt's dad had come out to help him build it, about five years ago, when Wyatt had first bought the cottage.

As the sun dipped low on the horizon, Delaney heard Rachel playing with Duke near the woodpile. Her daughter's laughter merged with the quieting day-time sounds of the woods and the rising cadence of crickets. A few minutes later, Rachel came barreling down to the shore with the firewood, and Maisie and Delaney had a blaze going in no time.

"Great job!" Wyatt called as he brought a metal tripod and a large, heavy Dutch oven down to the fire. "You guys are way better at that than we are. Don't tell Slater I said that."

When Wyatt set the pot down to set up the tripod, Delaney lifted the lid and was greeted by the scents of garlic and red wine. "This looks so good. I can't wait." Her mouth watered.

"Well, you have to—for a little while, at least." Wy-att hefted the pot onto the tripod hook and swung it over the fire. He set a heavy steel ladle on the edge of the firepit.

"Meanwhile," Wyatt said, digging out his wallet and opening it. He slipped out some money and waved it at Rachel. "How would you like to go get some stuff to make s'mores for after dinner?"

Rachel's eyes lit up. "Yes! I totally would."

Suddenly, the bills were gone from Wyatt's hand.

He looked momentarily surprised. Maisie waved them, her green eyes mischievous. "I'll take Rach to the store. That is, if that's okay with you, Del?"

Delaney shrugged. "Sure, that's fine with me. Rachel, you still got my keys?"

Rachel took Delaney's car keys from her pocket. "Yup. Right here. I'll take the wagon back up to the trunk, too."

Delaney watched Maisie and Rachel sprint up the hill toward the driveway. How her daughter could move that fast while pulling a wagon was beyond Delaney.

"I'm fairly sure Rachel never walks anywhere," Delaney observed. "She's pretty much always running."

"Like her mom," Wyatt teased. At Delaney's eye roll, he added, "Not that I don't appreciate it. I do, actually. I depend on it. But it was nice to slow down today, wasn't it?"

Delaney nodded, admitting, "Yes, it was. It was really nice."

Wyatt shoved his hands in his pockets and looked up toward the house. "Slater said he was going to use the garage to fix something on his bike, and Ursula will probably be asleep until dinner. This needs about an hour." He nodded toward the fire and the stew. "So, since it's been so nice to slow down, how about a walk?"

Delaney crossed her arms over her chest. She thought about the last time she'd been close to Wyatt in the twilight, back at the cabin, and taking a romantic walk with him around a picturesque lake wasn't going to do her wavering heart any good. It was getting way too hard to deny her feelings—she was even starting to wonder why she should hold back.

Because you've been hurt before, remember?

"I don't know, Wyatt..." She searched for an excuse but could only muster a few weak ones. "It's getting dark."

He reached behind his back and pulled a flashlight out of his back pocket. How had she not seen that before? She narrowed her eyes at him.

"It might get cold," she tried.

He reached into one of the pockets of his cargo shorts and pulled out a soft, neatly folded shawl. Darn it. He knew her so well. The grin on his face said he could tell he was getting through her defenses.

"C'mon, Friday. Just a walk to the inlet and back. It's the perfect amount of time for Maisie and Rachel to get to town and back with dessert."

He looked so eager in the fading light, so carefree, that she could see the boy she'd known in the handsome, broad-shouldered man standing next to her. And she was so afraid of breaking the spell that had been cast by this perfect day that she ignored the little voice telling her not to complicate things for herself. She reached out and took the shawl from him, wrapping it around her shoulders and tying it loosely in the front.

"Lead the way," she said. He offered her his arm, and she took it. It should have felt the exact same as when she'd taken Maisie's arm earlier—a gesture of friendship, with none of the sudden, breathless, heart-deep longing that came when he pulled her close to his side. But it didn't feel *platonic*—was that how Alex had described them? It felt like she was falling head over heels for Wyatt, despite her best efforts to the contrary.

Delaney tried her best to ignore her suddenly racing

heart and enjoy the sights, sounds, and smells of the woods as the twilight stretched. She had to get control of herself. She couldn't risk the solid friendship she and Wyatt shared for the chance that he'd return her budding feelings.

What if he didn't feel the same way? It would make things strange between them, and they might never be able to repair the awkwardness. And she had Rachel to think of. Rachel loved Wyatt, and Delaney wouldn't want to take away the closeness they had cultivated because she'd given in to a flutter of loneliness.

"You're quiet. Everything okay?" Wyatt asked.

The moon had risen, bright and full, in the sky—so bright, in fact, they didn't even need the flashlight Wyatt had brought. They'd reached the inlet, and she realized she hadn't spoken the whole way here. She scrambled to explain her silence without letting him in on her tumultuous thoughts.

"Yes, everything's fine. I was just thinking of the Pines and all the changes that must be going on over there."

Their walk had taken them nearer the Pines and, staring out over the flat surface of the water, Delaney could see the blazing floodlights the construction crew had set up on the shore near the camp's lake decks. The brightness of them obscured any detail on the shore, but she knew from what Charles had told them that the workers would be there late into the night.

"A lot of changes," Wyatt said, looking with her toward the camp. "But good ones, right?"

Delaney stared at the water for a moment, wondering where they would be if they hadn't gotten on *The ABC's of Business*. Would the Pines have had to close in a month...in two? Would she have had to find work in the next town over, be further away from Rachel her whole work week? And what about Wyatt—what would he have done? Seeing his family's legacy fade would've deeply affected him. And then there was Maisie and Ursula and Slater.

"It's a miracle, almost," she answered. She realized the last reason that she had to keep her feelings under wraps. The show.

The renovations were going forward, but the offer still hadn't been made that would pull them out of the financial depths they were in. Delaney couldn't do anything that might make Alexandra pull up stakes and leave the Pines before that oh-so-important offer. And Alexandra seemed to be taking a particular interest in Wyatt.

"Well, I fully believe in miracles," Wyatt said, his gaze on the water. "But I also believe you should take a little credit for this one."

His gaze slid over to her, and their eyes locked. His face was clear in the moonlight, and he was scrutinizing her with those kind, familiar blue eyes—the same eyes she'd known for so long. She let herself get lost in them for a brief, indulgent moment.

"Delaney," he said, his voice carrying the same warmth as his eyes. "There's something I've been meaning to tell you about my one-on-one interview."

"Yes?" She was too aware of the fact that her arm was still wrapped around his, and that his warm side was pressing against her.

"They asked me about you, too—about us, that is, and why we aren't together."

"Oh?" She wasn't exactly the queen of articulate

conversation at the moment. But she couldn't help her brevity. He had dipped his head slightly toward her, and she had somehow found herself turning toward him. "What did you... How did you answer?"

He dropped her hand from the crook of his arm, reaching up to rub at the hem of the shawl near her collar. "I told them you were my best friend, of course."

"Of course." She nodded, a little unsure of what she was agreeing to. She could smell his cologne—mixed with that same combination of wood smoke and Wyatt—and her brain was going a little fuzzy.

"We're best friends, right, Friday?" His head dipped lower. Those beautiful blue eyes were staring into hers.

"Definitely," she replied, almost whispering. Was he going to kiss her? She was half panicking and half thrilled, and despite her resolve to keep things simple between them she couldn't pull away. He eased so close that she could feel his breath fan against her lips.

"Wyatt! Delaneyyyyyyy!"

Slater's voice cut right through the buzz in Delaney's head. She pulled away from Wyatt abruptly, just as Slater rounded the bend in the trail that led to the inlet. Duke came crashing through the brush behind Slater.

"Hey, you two. Rachel and Maisie are back. You guys ready to eat?"

Delaney pulled the shawl closer around her shoulders, shivering at the loss of Wyatt's warmth. "Yeah," she said, hoping her voice wasn't as falsely cheery as it sounded to her own ears. "I'm actually starving."

"You coming?" she asked over her shoulder as she brushed past Wyatt, avoiding his gaze.

"You guys go ahead," Wyatt replied huskily. "I'll be right behind you."

Delaney didn't argue, and she didn't acknowledge Slater's curious gaze as they walked quickly back up the trail toward the house.

CHAPTER 16

I t had been a rough day off for Wyatt. Not the day of the cookout; no, that had been a day and a memory he'd fondly clung to for the twenty-four hours that had followed it. It was the day after he'd taken that walk with Delaney that had him so frustrated.

Swinging on one of the porch swings the next night, Wyatt reflected on what an idiot he'd been. He wasn't sure why he'd started to tell her about his interview, about the question he'd been asked. Maybe it had been his conversation with Charles at the office that had made Wyatt's mind race with questions of his own as he'd driven to the camp kitchen right after.

Maybe it had been Delaney's tearful face in the Bean Pot just before they'd left for his house. Standing in the restaurant with her, taking it in one last time, it had made him feel more connected to her. She would carry the same memory of the old restaurant—and of the people attached to it—as he would.

Or maybe it had been the way she'd looked in the moonlight on their walk—soft, beautiful, relaxed—that had made him want to tell her she meant the world to him. But he'd started out with the smooth, classically romantic, "I told them you were my best friend," and then he'd almost kissed her.

Because that wasn't confusing at all.

Wyatt had to admit he *was* confused. He didn't know what he felt. He'd never want to be without Delaney—or Rachel—but he hadn't been lying when he'd told Norman during his one-on-one that he wouldn't ever want to jeopardize what he had with Delaney now.

But he might've done just that. He could've blamed the fact that her phone was cutting straight to voice mail on the cruddy cell service around the lake, but the new tower Alex had had erected at the Pines had given him excellent cell reception at his house. And he had tried several times to call her during the course of the day.

Though she'd stayed through dinner last night, she'd been distant, and her goodbye when she and Rachel left had been wooden. He debated texting Delaney, but he didn't want to be intrusive. If she needed space, he'd give it to her.

He stared out across the darkened lake. He got lost in thought, so deeply that he actually jumped a little when his phone rang. He snatched it up from the seat of the swing, swiping to answer it before he even registered the caller ID.

"Hello?" he said, clearing his throat when his voice came out sounding overeager.

"Wyatt, it isn't too late to call, is it?" The voice on the other end wasn't unwelcome, but it wasn't the one he'd been hoping for.

Wyatt let out a breath. "Alex, no. It's fine. What can I do for you?"

"We're finishing up here with renovations, and everything looks smashing. I was wondering if you might want to come by tonight and have a peek at everything before tomorrow. You know, without a camera in your face."

Wyatt scrubbed a hand over his eyes. "Have you called Delaney yet?" He braced for Alex to say that she had, braced for the conformation that it was just his calls his best friend wasn't taking.

Alex hesitated for a moment before responding. "Actually, I did try her. Her phone cut straight to voice mail. I assumed you two would be together. Is she not with you?"

There was something in Alexandra's voice that gave Wyatt pause. He remembered Alex's little stunt with the ladder. Had she really called Delaney? He felt like she was digging here, trying to get Wyatt to admit to something—something she could use for the show? He would never sell Delaney out like that.

"Everyone went their own way today." He left it at that.

"Sure you don't want to just come down yourself?"

"Alone?" Wyatt got a strange, uneasy feeling that made alarm bells go off in his head. Maybe there was something more than he'd originally thought behind Alex's behavior.

"Yes, just the two of us."

He tried to be as polite and professional as he could. "Listen, do you need me to do anything before we start back tomorrow morning?"

Alex was quiet for a moment on the other end of the line. Her voice mirrored his crisp, professional tone. "Not a thing," she replied, "Charles has everything arranged. I'll see you and the whole cast—sorry, staff—tomorrow, bright and early."

"Good night, Alex."

Wyatt hung up, setting his phone aside again. He heard the doorbell ring through the open sliding glass door, and he stood, his heart leaping again in his chest. He hurried in through the screen, shut it behind him, and practically sprinted to open the front door.

Instead of Delaney, he found his aunt standing there. "Ursula? What are you doing here? Everything okay?"

"Oh, yes!" she said, returning his hug when he bent to give her one. "I just left my glasses here yesterday. Have you seen them anywhere?"

Wyatt shook his head. "I haven't. Where did you last have them? The porch, maybe?"

They went to the back porch but had no luck. They next tried the backyard, then finally walked down to the firepit, where they found them sitting in the drink holder of a folding chair.

"Aha! Here they are." Ursula held the pair up triumphantly. She slipped them into her skirt pocket, and Wyatt offered her his arm as they climbed back up the hill to the house.

"You want to stay for a bit? I can make some tea. I have that jasmine kind you like."

She nodded and went ahead of him into the house when he opened the door. "That sounds nice, Wyatt. A last quiet night before we've all got to go back and see what Miss Fancy-pants has done to our place."

Wyatt saw his aunt settled in one of his plush, oversized chairs before he went into the kitchen to start the tea kettle. The kitchen was open to the living room, so he was able to chat while he went through the cabinets, searching for something to serve with the tea.

"The renovations are just updates, Aunt Ursula. The property hasn't had anything major done to it since Mom and Dad... Well, since we lost them."

Ursula put a hand to her heart. "I miss my big brother every day. And your mother, what an angel. Taken too soon. I just don't want to see what they've built changed into something they wouldn't have wanted."

Wyatt found a package of chocolate-covered shortbread. He carefully placed the cookies on a delicate flowered plate—one of his mother's—and brought it over to the coffee table in front of Ursula.

"I know." He kneeled down in front of Ursula. "Please trust that I would never do that. I...I actually worry about what they'd have thought—about Alex, about all of the renovation, about the Pines being on TV."

Ursula reached out and laid a hand on Wyatt's cheek. It was comforting, but at the same time, it made him miss his parents all the more. She had the same kind blue eyes as his father, the same eyes Wyatt had inherited, or so Ursula had always told him.

"I know you'll do what's right by them. I'm just an old lady who's too sentimental. Sometimes, things have to change in order to move forward. I mean, the universe itself is in a state of constant change. How can we hope to avoid what even the stars can't get away from?"

Wyatt nodded, and she patted his cheek again.

On the stove, the tea kettle whistled. Wyatt stood

and went to make them two mugs of tea, dropping a fragrant tea bag into each mug. He carried their tea into the living room, trying not to think of the stars as they'd looked last night when he and Delaney had walked by the lake.

Wyatt had the urge to confide in Ursula about Delaney, but what would he say? How could he describe what the real problem was when he didn't even know himself?

"Thank you, dear," Ursula said, taking the mug he held out. Wyatt sat across from her and picked up one of the cookies, biting into it. The chocolate melted on his tongue, and he washed it down with a sip of tea.

"Those are good," Ursula said, sipping her own tea. "But they're not as good as those butterscotch cookies Delaney makes."

Wyatt nodded his agreement. "Pretty much everything's better when she does it."

Ursula took another sip, arching a brow and peering over the rim of her cup at her nephew. "Speaking of Delaney, how is she holding up with all of this? She does so much with the Pines, with Rachel, and now the show? I'm sure she'll be glad when things go back to normal."

Wyatt had to resist another urge—to say, Yeah, *if* things go back to normal.

"She seems okay. She's a strong woman, but I also know that she doesn't let it show when she's feeling overwhelmed."

"Sounds like somebody else I know," Ursula quipped.

"Hey! I admit when I'm stressed out."

"Like with the Pines? You didn't tell me until after

you'd agreed to let the TV show come that Bob at the bank had asked for the property to secure that loan."

"True," Wyatt admitted. "But I didn't want to stress you—or anyone else—out," he explained.

"So everyone carries around their baggage and never lets on. I wonder what else you keep to yourselves?"

"Aunt Ursula."

"I'm just saying." Ursula put her mug down and turned her palms up in the air. "We're only on this earth for so long, and we're meant to be here for each other. We should take advantage of that time. That's my point."

Her words hit home. Losing his parents was the perfect illustration of how no one knew exactly how long they had, of how lives, even well-lived, could end at any moment.

So what did that mean for Wyatt? And for him and Delaney?

The next morning, Delaney arrived at the Pines with what she thought was time to spare. Since Rachel had an outing planned at the water park today and had left with Bridget and her mom at an obscenely early hour, Delaney had been awake anyway. She'd wanted to get to work with enough time to find her phone.

She'd realized it was missing yesterday morning. The last place she remembered having it had been at the Bean Pot before they'd all taken off to Wyatt's. She'd managed to use a tracking app through Rachel's phone to locate hers, but the blinking dot sat right over the Pines. Delaney hadn't wanted to walk into a construction zone. Or risk running into Wyatt.

Play it cool, she thought as she parked in the newly paved front lot. Everyone's cars were lined up neatly in spots next to the one she was parked in. No one was in their car, but no one was in sight, either. What would she say when she saw Wyatt? What could she say about that walk at the lake, about that near-kiss?

A knock on her window startled her out of her intense thoughts. Wyatt stood at the side of her car, grinning. She gawked at him dumbly, her mind refusing to work. To prevent anything embarrassing from slipping out, she clamped her lips together.

"Get out of the car, Friday. C'mon!" His eyes were filled with a gleeful anticipation that made her rethink her nerves. He seemed happy to see her. Maybe things weren't going to be awkward. After all, this was Wyatt, her best friend. If two best friends couldn't brush off the fact that they'd almost ki—

"Del, seriously, where is your head? You've got to come see this!"

"All right, all right, I'm coming." When she stepped out of the car, she saw that the whole crew stood near the office. "Where did everyone come from? You guys were nowhere to be seen two minutes ago."

Wyatt put a hurrying hand on her back. "We were waiting for you inside. I tried to call you this morning. Actually, I tried to call you yesterday a few times, but—"

"I left my phone here before the barbecue at your place."

He stopped, and she stopped beside him. "Oh. That explains it."

She looked at him askance. "Explains what?"

"Why you didn't answer. Anyway, it doesn't matter. You have got to see the office."

From the outside, not much was different. The log building was freshly stained, the flower beds out front replanted, and the parking lot looked very nice, but it was still the same old Pines. The reassurance of the familiar old office—just a little refreshed—put Delaney a little more at ease as she and Wyatt reached the group.

"Del, you will not believe it!" Maisie squealed, already turning to lead the way.

Ursula and Slater stepped aside and shooed Delaney to the front of the line as they all followed Maisie. That left Wyatt in the back, and Delaney turned to see over the heads of Ursula and Slater as she mounted the office steps. Wyatt met her gaze and gave her a smile that was way too eager for this early.

Delaney turned back around and dutifully trotted after Maisie into the interior of the office. The building looked essentially the same on the outside, but inside, it was a whole new world. Delaney actually stopped short just inside the door, and Ursula bumped into her.

Laughing, Ursula gave her a gentle push. "Get in there, Del. You're killing my momentum."

Delaney stumbled into what had once been the waiting area. The dated armchairs and dusty racks that had held local tourist attraction pamphlets were gone. Instead, there was a comfy, L-shaped sectional with thick, dark-blue cushions. There was a bookcase full of paperbacks and a hand-lettered sign that read, *Take a book and take a seat.*

There were end tables made from tree trunks, with

the bark still intact but varnished until it was shiny. Delaney went over and ran her fingers over the glossy surface of the top of one of the tables, marveling at it.

The old hardwood floors had been refinished and resealed. The walls, which had been that dark, dated paneling Alex had criticized, were now smooth drywall, painted a mellow beige the color of a toasted marshmallow. There was a refreshments table set up with a single-cup coffeemaker, tea fixings, and a tray of cookies. The fireplace that had simply been decorative before because of a bad flue had been cleaned up and now burned cheerfully with a low, crackling fire.

"Why isn't it blazing hot in here?" Delaney said, feeling silly that it was the first thing she was able to say out loud.

"The air conditioning is fixed!" Slater said.

"And the heat," Ursula added.

Delaney moved to the front desk, which wasn't a countertop anymore, but an actual, substantial desk that jutted out slightly into the new sitting area. It was set up with a sleek computer that had no wires in sight. Delaney's eyes flicked up to the space that had been the storage closet, but her gaze was stopped by a new wall that sat where the storage closet used to be. Actually, it seemed that the new wall was set about halfway between where the old back wall had been and where the new front desk was.

"What's that?" she asked.

"It's your new office." Wyatt's voice was close. Delaney turned and found him standing next to her.

"What?" she gasped. "You're not serious."

He smiled softly and nodded. "I am. Go see."

Delaney looked at the rest of the staff, who were all

looking at her, anticipating her reaction. Feeling like she was in a slow-motion dream, she moved around the new front desk and toward the door set in the new wall. She reached for the door handle and twisted, pushing open the door and taking a hesitant step inside.

The room was small—no, cozy. The window that had been at the back corner of the old front room was now at the back of her office. The walls were the same color as the new reception area. An ornate white desk faced the door. A laptop rested on top, and a cushy, light-colored leather office chair was tucked behind the desk. To the right of the desk was an armoire, the same antiqued white as the desk. At the very far end of the room, a tiny sitting area was set up with an oversized chair and ottoman. The morning sunlight would stream perfectly right through the window into the little nook.

"That armoire opens up, and there's a bit of file storage inside and an extra desk that folds down for Rachel," Wyatt explained. "You know, for when school starts back."

Delaney fought hard not to cry. "This isn't something I asked for on my list for the show, I swear," she said, turning to Wyatt. The rest of the staff, all fanned out behind him, wore tearfully happy expressions that reflected exactly what she felt.

"I know," he said. "I asked Alex if it could be added."

When Delaney didn't respond, a look of doubt crossed his face. "You don't like it?"

"Like it?" She laughed, aware that she must look foolish laughing as tears spilled down her cheeks. "I love it. Thank you!" She reached for Wyatt. He opened his arms to her.

The walk at the lake, and any worry that it might have caused awkwardness between them, was gone from Delaney's thoughts. She hugged her best friend, awed by the sweetness of his gesture. When she pulled away from him, he reached up to wipe the tears from her cheeks.

"You couldn't work out of the golf cart your whole life," he said. And there, as he looked down at her, his arms still around her, was the same warm, intense expression that had preceded their near-kiss at the lake. Suddenly flustered, she stepped back just as a slow clap drew everyone's attention.

"Now that was some good TV." Alex stood in the new reception area, watching the exchange between Wyatt and Delaney. Her suit was cream-colored today, a choice that, in combination with her hair color, made her seem even more pristine than normal. "Too bad we weren't rolling tape. Do you think we might recreate that once we're all set up to film the reaction shots?"

Delaney laughed, too elated to care about having to playact for the show again. "Sure, why not."

"Wonderful!" Alex said. "Now, we do have to set up in here. And you all have lots more to see of the renovations. Just remember, you'll have to replicate every 'ooh' and 'ah' later!"

The group headed for the front door, the level of excitement and the volume of conversation rising as everyone began to talk at once, debating on what to go see first.

"Oh, Delaney?" Alex called. Wyatt stopped in the doorway, and Delaney stopped near the door, glancing back. Alex reached into her pocket and held out Delaney's phone. "One of the workers found this down at the restaurant."

Delaney took it, smiling gratefully. "Thank you! I thought that's where I'd left it."

As she turned away from Alex and back toward the door, Delaney caught a fleeting, strange look on Wyatt's face. When they were outside, she asked, "Everything okay?"

"Yeah," he said. "Everything's fine."

She had a strange feeling that there was something he wasn't telling her.

CHAPTER 17

His head was swimming. He was alternately happy and perturbed as they toured the renovated Pines, followed by at least one camera—sometimes several—for their entire walk around the property. There were new tables, booths, chairs, a new counter, and new appliances at the Bean Pot. The second walk-in cooler was up and running. The cabins were revamped on the insides with efficient, retro-looking kitchenettes, new drywall, and bathrooms that not only didn't leak, but also were repainted and clad in shiny new tile.

Wyatt's joy at these changes was only muddled by the fact that his mind kept going back to Alex, holding out Delaney's phone. How long had Alex had that phone? Had Alex known that Wyatt had been trying to call Delaney all day yesterday? Had Alex had the phone when she'd called to invite Wyatt out to the Pines?

He tried to keep his head in the game, but it was difficult. He wasn't sure of Alex's motives toward him, or his own feelings about Delaney. He had been relieved to see Del show up for work this morning, and his eagerness to show her the space he'd lobbied to have created for her had overridden any embarrassment he'd felt at how he'd acted by the lake.

Seated under the new cedar pavilion by the lake, Wyatt and the staff listened to Charles go over what would happen tonight at the open house. There would be a big bonfire in the fire circle—which was now surrounded by new concrete benches—guided nighttime tours of the new amenities, and a live band under this very pavilion. And Wyatt would be presiding over the whole thing with Alex on his arm. That little tidbit had been told to him by Charles just this morning.

"For the cameras, you understand," Charles had said, but Wyatt had seen in the other man's eyes that he'd known it wasn't the whole truth. Despite the joy Wyatt felt at seeing his parents' place in such good shape and the anticipation of having the campground filled with people again, he was equally apprehensive about spending a whole evening with Alex.

"Hey," Delaney whispered, tugging on his sleeve.

"Hmmm?" he said absently, still mired in his own thoughts.

"I've got to go."

His head snapped around. "What? Why?"

Delaney held up her phone. Onscreen, her text messages were displayed. "It's Rachel. She and Bridget are at the water park today, but Rachel's gotten sick, and I don't want to make Bridget's mom drive all the way back here."

Even though the water park was just over an hour away, Wyatt's first instinct was to hop in his truck with Delaney and hightail it to the place. "Let's go. Maybe we can make it a little quicker if I drive."

She put up a hand and shook her head. "Thank

you, but it's not an emergency. Please, stay here. Fill me in later on what I missed, okay?"

Feeling a surge of worry for Rachel, he nodded. "Get out of here. No one will know, and if anyone says anything, I've got your back. Go take care of our girl."

Delaney stood, gave him a quick kiss on the cheek, and snuck out of the row of folding chairs where they sat. Pleasantly surprised—she'd never done *that* before—he felt a big, goofy grin spread over his face. Charles finished his speech with a few last-minute requests for scenes only featuring Maisie, Slater, or Ursula. They were each taken off in a separate direction, leaving Wyatt and Charles—who was once again immersed in his clipboard—the lone occupants of the new pavilion. Wyatt didn't mind.

He stared out over the lake. He couldn't quite see his house from where he was sitting, but he could see the swimming deck that floated in the water just off-shore. Wyatt reached up to touch the place Delaney had kissed his cheek. What a great day they'd all had together.

Charles, who seemed to have gotten all his pages checked off, stood from where he'd been sitting in one of the folding chairs. "Wyatt, I think you've got a meeting with Alex in about twenty minutes."

Wyatt frowned slightly. "What about?"

Charles flipped up a page. Wyatt had never, before now, realized what an annoying sound that was. "She'll be discussing the offer with you—not on camera, mind you. That comes later. But she'll let you know what she's willing to put into the business, beyond the renovations, and what percentage of the business she'll want to receive for her investment."

Wyatt's trepidation grew. But he stood and nodded to Charles. "In twenty? Where?"

"Your office. They should already be set up in there. I'd just head there now."

As he trekked toward the office, Wyatt realized that Delaney wouldn't be in this meeting with him. That felt wrong, somehow. But it was one more step toward seeing the Pines successful again, and that would mean they were all—his aunt Ursula, Maisie, Slater, Delaney, and Rachel—taken care of.

To Wyatt's surprise, there was no camera in his office when he arrived. Alexandra was seated behind his desk with her feet up, talking on the phone. It didn't bother him. After all, the massive mahogany furniture piece was part of the renovation, and he had no attachment to it. But the level of familiarity her pose assumed did bother him. And the fact that she kept him waiting for another twenty minutes.

He spent those twenty minutes in the new reception area, lounging on the sectional, staring at the door to Delaney's new office. Man, he wished she were here. When Wyatt heard Alex hang up her call, he walked back down the hall.

"Charles said you needed to see me?" Wyatt said, standing in the doorway. The office still didn't feel like his, so he hesitated at the entrance.

"Please, don't be silly. Come in. Come in. Sit." Alex got up from behind the desk and came around it, gesturing for Alex to take his seat in the chair she'd just vacated. Once he was seated, she sauntered over to the office door and closed it.

"You don't need to close the door," he said. "I actually rarely close my office door."

Alex sat down in one of the guest chairs in front of his new desk. "I'd rather keep it closed, if it's all the same to you. I don't like to risk anyone eavesdropping when I'm discussing money."

Wyatt considered arguing but didn't. "No cameras?" he asked instead, probing at her purported reason for asking him here.

"Oh, not right now. We're just talking, businesswoman to businessman, hashing out what this place will need to continue successfully after the show has left. We'll film the 'making-the-deal' scene later. As you've seen, reality needs a lot of help to be entertaining sometimes."

"I see a lot that's faked around here, yes," he replied coolly.

She returned his cool stare with an arch look of her own. "We both know this place has a lot of potential. I mean, the location is great, despite the unfortunate bypass situation. It doesn't just need more clientele, though. What it needs is the right kind of clientele."

Wyatt leaned back, crossing his arms over his chest. "What does that mean?"

Alex flicked an imaginary bit of lint from the skirt of her suit. She'd changed from this morning, and her outfit was red now—the color of power, or intimidation. Wyatt didn't miss the symbolism.

"It means that you could leverage what you have here to an entirely new level. I have some interested parties who would love to tour this place and consider more renovating. Higher-end renovating."

Wyatt shook his head. "Our guests like what we

do. And, no disrespect, I'm extremely grateful for what you've done for us, but high-end renovating sounds like you mean guests would end up paying high-end prices."

"What guests?" she returned smoothly. "I had to put in money just to cover the payroll here when I first arrived."

Wyatt sat forward in his chair, spreading his hands over the desktop, ready to snap back. But he paused when Alex held up a hand.

"Just hear me out," she said. "High-end prices are exactly my goal here. This property is beautiful, and myself and the other potential investors see the value in it as a luxury destination. Corporate retreats, expensive weddings, you name it."

"The Pines isn't luxury, Alex," Wyatt said, exasperated. "It's down-to-earth. It's simple fun. It's getting back to what matters."

"And what matters is cable and internet? Those things were high on Delaney's list of needed upgrades. And where is your property manager, anyway? I'd assumed she'd be here with you."

Wyatt's stomach lurched, and a strong urge to protect Delaney rose. "Her daughter's sick. Otherwise, she'd have been here to back me up and defend herself. But since she isn't, let me tell you. Delaney gets what the Pines is about. She understands this place because she considers it home, just like I do. Just like Slater and Maisie and my aunt do. Customers requested those amenities you mentioned."

Alex nodded thoughtfully. "And I have customers who will vie for the amenities I'd put in place in a classier resort. And my customers would pay much better for them. Which would mean that your profit as half owner would be higher."

Half? Wyatt reined in his mounting displeasure and kept his voice firm but even. "We'll have to agree to disagree. My parents never intended for this place to exclude anyone."

Alex's mouth formed a soft moue. "It's a shame you're not more open about this. I'd hoped not to have to tell you in a way that was disagreeable..."

"Tell me what?" Wyatt couldn't imagine what she would have to tell him that would possibly make this meeting worse.

"I've invited the potential investors to the open house tonight. They've already flown in, and there will be cameras absolutely everywhere."

Wyatt's mouth dropped open. He stared at Alex. "I hope—for your sake, and for the sake of your business—that you play along and hear them out."

"And if I don't?" Wyatt clipped.

"Well, then, we have no deal. I'm not interested in investing in a common little woodsy playground. You'll keep your current renovations, of course, as part of the filming agreement, but there will be no extra capital. You'll be at the mercy of the studio's editing. What if there isn't any boost in business after your episode? You'll have to figure out how you keep your little camp family together when they're all out of jobs."

Suddenly, as if on cue, Wyatt's phone sent out a text alert. He dug it out of his pocket and swiped the screen. Delaney.

Rachel's really sick. I'm going to take her to the clinic here, but I have no idea of the wait time.

Wyatt fired off a quick reply, aware of Alex's eyes on him.

No problem. Do what you need to. And text me if you need me.

Her reply was equally fast.

Thank you.

Wyatt put his phone down, and his stomach sank as well. What if there was no increase in business after the show left, despite the publicity? What if the Pines actually had to close? He thought of Delaney, of Rachel. How would their lives change if Delaney worked somewhere else?

He couldn't picture Maisie anywhere but behind the counter at the Bean Pot, joking with her regulars and flirting with the guests. He wouldn't trust anyone but Slater to repair a darned thing on the property. And his aunt Ursula, who refused to accept a salary from him unless she actually worked in the front office, how would that go if there was no front office?

The pressure made his head throb. Alex was still watching him.

"Everything okay with Delaney? Her daughter?"

Despite their contentious meeting, Wyatt heard the sincerity in Alex's voice.

"I don't know yet. Delaney's taking her to the doctor."

Alex nodded and stood, smoothing the front of her skirt.

"Listen, Wyatt, I'm really not trying to be a bad guy here. I just see so much more potential in this place than it's fulfilling right now. And more guests with more money would mean you could pay your staff much more. Including Delaney."

Wyatt looked at her, at a loss. He was worried for Delaney and Rachel, conflicted now about Alex's offer. The open house was tonight. Maybe he should just hear Alex's investor friends out.

"I'll listen to what they have to say," he said. "But I'm not agreeing to anything without talking to Delaney."

Alex visibly relaxed. "That's fair," she admitted. Then she rapped her knuckles on his desktop and turned to walk briskly to the door. "You won't regret it, Wyatt. I'll see you tonight."

She started through the door, only to seem to remember something.

"Oh, and Wyatt?"

"Yes," he said, feeling tired, ready to be done with the meeting.

"Don't forget to wear something nice. We are filming!"

CHAPTER 18

"Delaney Elizabeth Phillips, you get yourself into this dress and leave this house." Ursula's tone was kind but firm as she stood in the doorway of Delaney's kitchen, her wild, red hair framing the expression of determination on her face, a hanger bearing said dress dangling from her finger.

Delaney sighed, leaning against the counter as she waited for Rachel's tea to steep. "I don't know, Ursula. It was so sweet of you to drive all the way over here and offer to stay with Rachel. But do I really need to be there? I saw all of the renovations already."

"Mom, gah, *go.* I'll be fine." Rachel hollered from the living room. Delaney grabbed a spoon from a kitchen drawer, added a bit of sugar from the sugar bowl to Rachel's mug, and stirred it before carrying it out to the living room. Ursula trailed Delaney, still carrying the dress.

The scene that greeted Delaney was at once familiar and amusing. Their small living room was filled with an overstuffed couch and loveseat, a small, round, oak coffee table, and an entertainment hutch that held their TV. Swamped in a nest of pillows and blankets with Duke in her lap, Rachel held court from the couch.

Delaney had been relieved to find out that Rachel's sudden illness had only been a case of an overload of junk food from the water park snack bar combined with a bit too much sun. A little rest, a little hydration, and everything would be fine. But Delaney still didn't want to leave when Rachel wasn't feeling well.

Setting the mug of ginger tea down on the coffee table near Rachel, Delaney put the back of her hand on Rachel's forehead. The slight fever that had come with Rachel's upset stomach was subsiding. "I don't know, honey. I'm not that keen on going anyway." Then, to Ursula, Delaney asked, "Don't you want to go?"

"Seriously?" Rachel picked up her tea and sipped it. "You don't want to see how people are going to react to all the new stuff? Everyone is going to freak out. Bridget and her mom are going. It would be weird if you weren't there."

"I want none of the hubbub," Ursula said. "This whole affair has thrown off my energy. Besides, Wyatt needs you there." Ursula hung the dress on the coat rack near Delaney's front door. The hem fluttered in the air conditioning. Ursula plopped onto the loveseat.

Rachel picked up the remote from the coffee table. "I'm planning a huge *Lovestruck High* marathon to-night. I mean, you could stay for that..."

Delaney thought hard about staying versus going. The idea of seeing the Pines filled with people again and the memory of the pleasant hum and bustle of a summer night on the campground, were tempting her to go. Plus, what Ursula said was sort of true. Wyatt had called Delaney about an hour ago to check on

Rachel, and he'd sounded seriously out of sorts. When she'd questioned him, however, he'd been evasive, telling her Ursula was on her way over and that Delaney should just stay home for the evening and take care of her daughter.

It was what he *didn't* say that made her think something was going on at the Pines. As she walked back to the kitchen, she recalled how he'd ended the call.

I'll see you tomorrow, Delaney. He'd said Delaney—not Friday.

"Let me see what Wyatt's doing over there. He probably has it all under control," Delaney said to the pair now glued to the television. When she got no response, she rolled her eyes and walked back to the kitchen.

Her phone sat on the kitchen counter next to the stove. Delaney scooped it up and texted Wyatt with one hand while she stirred a pot of chicken soup, made by Maisie and delivered by Ursula, which sat simmering on the stovetop.

Ursula says she'll stay with Rachel tonight if I want to go to the open house.

He texted back. *Is Rachel feeling better? Don't feel like you have to come.*

Rachel's threatening me with really bad reality TV if I don't go. I'd say she's feeling better. Thoughts? Once she'd replied, she set about gathering dinner.

Delaney turned off the burner under the soup and moved the pot to the back of the stove. She took a tray and two bowls out of the cabinet and ladled bowls of soup out for Rachel and for Ursula. Adding two glasses of lemon-lime soda and a large bowl of oyster crackers to the tray, she balanced it all and carried it out to the living room.

Rachel had started *Lovestruck High.* Ursula was staring as raptly as Rachel was. Delaney set down the tray, warning the pair to be careful of the temperature of the soup.

"Thanks, Mom." Rachel picked up her bowl.

"You're welcome, honey," Delaney replied, stopping to glance at the television.

On screen was a typical American high school classroom. A handsome teenaged boy in a letterman jacket made anguished faces just outside the line of sight of a pretty, waifish girl of about the same age. After a few moments of intense staring, he was called out by the teacher. The severe-looking older woman snapped her fingers, drawing the attention of the entire class.

"Scott, is the math problem written somewhere on Faye's face?"

There was general sputtering, embarrassment, and classroom hilarity after this statement.

Ursula was staring at the TV, her eyes wide, her hand on her heart. "Wait," she said to Rachel, "Faye doesn't know that this Scott person is in love with her?"

"No," Rachel replied, her voice thick with emotion. "He just keeps it all inside."

Delaney booked it back to the kitchen, smiling. How long had it been since she'd been that starry-eyed in love? There was something to be said for the butterflies in her stomach when she picked up her phone. When she saw that Wyatt hadn't responded yet, she typed out another text.

The teenage love-and-angst marathon has already begun. Please help me.

She almost laughed out loud at the quickness of his reply.

Thank you, meddling aunt and Lovestruck High. *How quickly can you get here?*

Delaney smiled. Some secret part of her was delighted at Wyatt's response, and if she set aside the fact that they'd been just friends for all these years, that same secret part could thrill at how he seemed to be longing to have her there. And it was nice to feel wanted.

"Rachel, Ursula," Delaney called, "You two okay if I go get ready?"

Rachel whooped in victory. Delaney laughed as she headed to the living room to retrieve her dress.

Wyatt couldn't wait for Delaney to arrive. He would never want to take her away from Rachel—he considered Rachel a priority over anything that the Pines or he would ever need from Del—but now that Rachel was on the mend and was even trying to terrorize her mother with *Lovestruck High*, he was all too happy to have Delaney back at the campground.

With Maisie down at the Bean Pot making last-minute preparations for the open house crowd, and with her having also recruited Slater to the cause, Wyatt was left alone in his office. The last rays of afternoon light filtered in through the blinds, giving way to evening. The quiet dark of the place was actually a welcome change from the recent daily frenzy of the show.

There was no film crew in the office. All of the filming would be out on the property tonight, right in the action of the open house. In fact, the doors to the front office were locked, and Wyatt was the only one in the building. He got up off his office couch—the only furniture to have survived the remodel—and wandered into Delaney's new space.

Sitting on her desk was an old, brown box marked "Records." Wyatt recalled that Delaney had been sorting through a bunch of these boxes when she'd cleaned out the old storage closet. This one must have been left behind when the construction crew had come in to complete their work.

He lifted the lid of the box. There, sitting on top of the contents, was the picture that he had seen of him and Delaney as children. He picked it up, trying to be careful of the yellowed edges. They both looked so joyous in the photo.

He sat down on the edge of her desk, staring at the picture. It had been taken at a much simpler time in the history of the Pines—in their own personal histories, as well. The picture showed them long before the struggles of adulthood, the heartbreak of love gone wrong, the tragedy of losing family. Innocent times.

Wyatt set the photo aside, sifting through the rest of the box. There were more photos. Some of them made him smile, and some of them made his eyes sting, but by the time he'd sifted through all the pictures, he was again feeling the weight of his responsibilities. Not only to his parents and their memory, but also, conflictingly, to Delaney and the rest of the people still here with him. The weight of each of them felt the same to him. It didn't help him decide what to do about Alex's ultimatum. In fact, it only made the decision harder.

If he accepted Alex's strong-arm offer, the Pines

would change drastically from what they'd always known it as. It would still be a haven, but it wouldn't be the one they remembered, and the memories made here in the future wouldn't be the same, either. But at least the camp and all the staff's jobs, would remain, and he could even offer them all salary increases.

If he declined, he had the sinking feeling that all the play-acted footage Alex had talked them into would be artfully put together to form a picture of the Pines and its occupants that was none too flattering. They'd be left with the legacy of the Pines intact but public opinion about them likely damaged forever. And then what? They'd been so close to closing before the show. An increase in customers would be absolutely imperative—the only thing that could save them.

Alex's investor friends had already arrived. Wyatt had seen the sleek black sedan that Alex had arrived in reappear about an hour ago from the direction of town. It had eased into the parking lot and sailed right past the office, heading toward the cabins. Wyatt assumed they were going to meet Alex at the cabin she'd moved back into after the renovations.

He resented that Alex had put him in this position. His stomach soured at the thought that Delaney had invited the show here with the genuine hope it would be the saving grace of the Pines, only to have it turn out to be the very thing that might hasten the demise of the place they loved.

Any misstep tonight would make Alex take the decision about her offer—and the decision about the fate of his business—out of his hands. Delaney would blame herself if anything bad came from inviting the show to the Pines.

Which led him to a very hard choice: should he talk to Delaney about taking Alex's offer, or should he make the call on his own, hoping that Del would see that he was taking all of the responsibility for whatever came after? He had a lot to think about.

But that didn't mean he couldn't have fun with Delaney tonight. He knew that Alex would be shuttling the investors around the property, showing off the changes she'd made, laying out her plan for future opulence. But she didn't need Wyatt for that. In fact, he'd kind of refused to participate. He was no stranger to playing hooky, though the last time he'd done it was junior year of high school.

Wyatt placed the photos back into the records box, all except the one of him and Delaney, and put the lid back on. His mind was made up. He would make this night about recapturing the fun of the evenings they'd had here at the Pines as children. He'd deal with what came out of Alex's meeting at the end of the night, just like he'd promised. He would hear out her new proposal.

He dusted his hands carefully to avoid messing up his outfit. He had dressed up a bit tonight, but it wasn't to satisfy Alex's request. He'd picked out a shirt Delaney had complimented him on previously and felt a little extra anticipation wondering if she would notice it again tonight. He slipped the photo that he'd held out into his shirt pocket.

As if on cue, his phone dinged. Delaney's name on the screen made him nervous and reassured him all at the same time.

I'm out front, by the campground. Where are you?

He walked out of her office, closed the door, and texted back as he made his way toward the front door.

In the office. Stay put, though. I'm on my way, Friday.

CHAPTER 19

T he Pines looked amazing at night. The moon shone full and bright, and where the trees blocked it, moonlight fell in dappled patches on the ground. Colorful lanterns were strung through the property, and new lighted signage, artfully crafted from wood and hammered metal, pointed guests to various areas of the renovated campground. The scent of new mulch reached Delaney's nose.

It was a dream, a wonderland. The camp had always seemed that way to Delaney when she'd been young, but she only now realized she'd stopped viewing it through the same lens—to some degree—as an adult. Especially since the decline in business, she'd stopped seeing the magic and started seeing leaky pipes, torn window screens, and a bare parking lot. She'd started feeling the burden of what had felt like insurmountable odds.

Now, with the path from the office to the campground once again lined with tiki torches and the smell of the bonfire rising in the air, the camp filled her with a renewed awe. They hadn't had enough people on the property lately to really bring back the mood of the old Cabins in the Pines. But as Delaney stood at the entrance to the campground, the office behind her, the parking lot filled, she couldn't help but feel the old magic again. The place was teeming with people.

A family wandered the path in front of her, headed toward the faint sound of music deeper into the camp. A young couple strolled past, coming from the parking lot, holding hands, pointing up at the stars. Delaney could hear the sounds of many more people further in—not just music, but also laughter, and a shout of, "Tag! You're it!"

"Remind you of anything?"

Delaney turned to see Wyatt standing behind her, his hands in the pockets of his khaki slacks. For a moment, she couldn't reply. He was dressed simply, but he looked so handsome that she didn't trust herself not to give away the way she was feeling. She knew, suddenly, the exact emotion that poor Scott from *Lovestruck High* was suffering under.

He smiled and walked toward her. "How's Rachel?" he asked. "And just to let you know right off the bat, I didn't send Ursula to convince you to come tonight, I swear."

"I know you didn't. I suspect that my little girl was just plain tired of my fretting over her. I wouldn't doubt that Rachel arranged the whole chicken soup delivery."

When he stopped next to her, she lost her train of thought. His golden hair was tamed for now, and in the flicker of a nearby torch, his blue eyes were darker, deeper, more intense. His face was smooth, freshly-shaven, and her eyes were drawn to his lips. She thought again about their near-kiss at the lake.

"I, uh... I love that shirt," she said lamely.

"Thank you. I thought you would."

He'd worn it for her? She felt her cheeks heat, and it had nothing to do with that nearby torch.

"And you, wow. You look absolutely amazing," he said reverently. The sincerity and appreciation in his eyes made her blush even further. There was no way she could hide her joy in his appraisal.

She fussed absently at the sundress she wore, smoothing the skirt. It was soft, butter-yellow, and sleeveless, with a gently scooped neckline and a skirt that fell in gauzy layers down to her ankles. It tucked in just right at the waist, and she'd put on a wide, brown leather belt she'd thought looked very bohemian. Ursula had approved the combination, telling Delaney that it evoked just the right summer vibe. The belt matched her strappy sandals, and she'd foregone any jewelry and kept her makeup subdued and minimal.

"Thank you." She parroted Wyatt's sentiment at her earlier compliment, trying to will herself out of the unexplainable nervousness she suddenly felt standing here with him. "No cameras?" she blurted, hoping he wouldn't notice her nerves. And then, before she could help herself, she added, "No Alexandra?"

"No, no cameras up here. Out there is crawling with cameras, though. They even brought in some extra ones this afternoon. There was a whole other equipment van. You really missed all the action."

"Sorry," she said. "I'm sure it was scintillating."

"It was. I feel bad that you were off being supermom and had to miss it. I mean, there was so much"—he seemed to be searching for something profound—"wire."

She laughed, and her nerves disappeared. She had always loved that Wyatt's sense of humor had the power to break her out of any negative mood she might be in, had the effect of easing her nerves, had always been a balm to any sadness or anguish she might be feeling.

"And Alexandra is somewhere around here. Who knows? Cabins, probably. But you never answered my question," he reminded her. "Does all of this"—he gestured to the flickering tiki torches and toward the noise of the open house—"remind you of anything?"

"It does." The smile that had been on her lips when she'd first seen the Pines lit up like old times returned. "Should we go see if there are s'mores?"

"Oh, there are. I actually helped Slater unpack a case of s'mores sticks this afternoon. Hundreds." He held out a hand to her. "There's one with your name on it."

She took his hand. His warm, strong fingers curled around hers. Her heart picked up at the fact that he had offered his hand. He hadn't offered her his arm the way he had at the lake a few days ago. This gesture seemed more familiar, more intimate.

"My name?" she teased. "How did you manage to write that small?"

"I have many talents," he bragged as he led her down the camp road toward the party.

She made show of examining the space above their heads as they passed into the canopy of trees. "One of which is beehive identification, right?"

Her laughter blended with the sounds of the party just over the next rise. She swung their intertwined hands as they walked deeper into the woods, elated at their closeness, feeling hopeful and carefree, and—she had to admit—a little in love. It was a scary feeling, but with the night air, the scent of the pine trees, and the nostalgia that being in this place with this man was evoking, she was willing to give into it, even if it was just for one night.

"You're just never going to let that go, are you?" he groused.

"Come on, Wyatt," she said, picking up her pace and pulling him along faster. "Last one to the bonfire gets trash duty in the morning."

She dropped his hand and took off ahead of him.

Trash duty really isn't all that bad, Wyatt thought as he held a long wooden skewer out into the roaring bonfire blazing in the fire circle. When both of his marshmallows had caught fire, he expertly twirled the stick, letting the flame burn the sugary confection all the way around. Then, bringing the stick close, he put out the flames with three quick puffs of breath.

Delaney stood next to him with a paper plate loaded with graham crackers and chocolate. Wyatt spun, deposited a toasted marshmallow on each of the s'mores bottom halves, then capped each with another graham cracker, finishing the second one with a flourish.

"You do have skills," Delaney admitted as Wyatt turned and tossed his wooden skewer into the fire.

"Well, I'm no you," he said, "but I have my moments." When she blushed—for the second time tonight—he put a hand on her elbow. He wanted her to know he was sincere, that he saw what she did for those around her, how devoted she was.

"I mean it," he said. "All of this started with you caring that this place continues."

She studied the crowd around them, and he took the opportunity to let his eyes wander over her face. Her hair was loose and down around her shoulders, curled and framing her face alluringly. Her dark eyes shone in the firelight. The flush in her cheeks only made her more beautiful to him.

"You're blushing. Again," he teased.

"It's the fire," she said, but she was smiling slyly. "And all of this is not just because of me. It's because your folks gave me a chance when I needed it. It's because Slater and Maisie and Ursula love this place as much as I do. And it's because of you. For you."

She looked as though she wanted to say more, but her eyes flitted to the people milling around them, and some spell seemed to be broken. Wyatt reached over and grabbed a s'more, biting into it. Delaney did the same. They both hummed in pleasure at the gooey, melty treat.

Unwilling to let the mood of the evening be derailed and too caught up in how wonderful it felt to just be here with Del in the festive atmosphere, Wyatt hurriedly finished his s'more and licked his fingers, mumbling around the last digit. "Do you want to go see Maisie and Slater?"

Delaney, too, finished her dessert. "Sure. That gets us closer to the lake. Maybe we could go down there and see the band in the new pavilion after?"

"Sounds like a plan."

Delaney deposited their plate in the trash, and they made the short walk to the Bean Pot in companionable silence. Wyatt wanted to grab her hand again, but he hesitated, afraid to spook her like he had at the lake.

As they neared the restaurant, he could see that,

just as with the parking lot out front, the newly paved egress to the restaurant was filled with cars. Wyatt was surprised—there seemed to be double the patrons he'd seen just an hour before. "Wow! It's even more packed than earlier. We should see if Maisie and Slater are doing okay in there."

They were inside in no time, and the place was rocking. The inside now had a cool, '50s-diner vibe that completely suited both the restaurant and Maisie. The layout of the dining room was essentially the same as before, but everything had been redone to be more organized and efficient, and the old flooring, booths, and counter had been swapped out for brand-new replacements.

Because of the increased business they had anticipated, Maisie had hired a few more servers for the evening, and every one of them was busy. Maisie herself was right in the thick of things, beaming with pride as she hustled through the dining room. When she caught sight of Delaney and Wyatt, she waved and came over to where they stood near the door.

"Y'all hungry?" she asked. Delaney and Wyatt both smiled at Maisie's customary greeting.

"No, Mais, thank you. We came to see if you needed help. Where's Slater?" Delaney looked around. Wyatt didn't see the other man anywhere.

"He was here earlier, but now he's actually off leading the night tours of the campgrounds. I never knew he knew so much about the land, the animals. He's a regular Ranger Rick. I just hope he doesn't run into any actual raccoons out there." Maisie seemed to stop and contemplate that, grimacing.

"So how can we help?" Wyatt asked.

Maisie waved nonchalantly at Wyatt, seeming to brush off his concern. "We're just fine. Besides, you gonna make Del wait tables in that pretty dress? No way. I've got everything handled, and everybody's happy. The place turned out great. I'm like a pig in mud."

"Is that a good thing?" Wyatt asked, unsure.

"It's the best. This is the best." She pointed a finger at the two of them, waving it back and forth between them. "This is a date, right?"

"No!" Delaney said, and Wyatt was surprised at the swift disappointment her denial sparked in him. "I mean... Why would you think that?" she asked Maisie. Wyatt was actually very interested in the answer.

"Well, this darned show has us all playing parts, right? With as much drama as they've made up, and as nice as y'all look, I figured that there was some love angle to the end of this episode. No?"

Wyatt shook his head. "No, nothing like that. We would never fake that, anyway. That would just be wrong. Right, Del?"

"Right," she quickly agreed. He didn't miss the strange, fleeting expression that crossed Delaney's face, but he couldn't place what it meant. Delaney poked at Masie playfully. "Besides, I'm surprised you and Charles aren't the 'love angle' on this episode."

"Nah. That's just a little summer flirtation, honey. I wouldn't call it true love," Maisie said, shrugging. "Anyway, I don't need either of you. Love you, but don't need you tonight. Go on down to the lake, see that band. It sounds mighty good."

"We will." Delaney hugged Maisie. Maisie warmly returned the hug.

Wyatt inclined his head in the direction of the music

that could be heard from even inside the restaurant. "Next stop, Lake Fairwood?"

They escaped the bustle of the restaurant, falling in behind a small string of people wandering down the camp road toward the lake. As they neared the lakeshore, the music grew louder. It was energetic, big band, swing-style music, and Wyatt didn't miss that it had likely been chosen to harken back to the time when the Pines had overflowed with visitors. Despite their friction, and her ultimatum, Wyatt had to admit that Alex was good at setting a scene.

They rounded the last bend of the camp road before coming out of the woods. The scene that greeted them was, Wyatt thought, just like something out of a movie. Delaney gasped.

"Oh, Wyatt. Isn't it beautiful?"

The same tiki torches that had lit their path on the way here were dotted along the shoreline. Hanging lights, with hundreds of tiny Edison bulbs winking from them, were strung around the existing docks. The new pavilion, where the band was set up, was a rustic structure, made to fit unobtrusively with its natural surroundings. But for tonight, the rough-hewn cedar beams were strung with more twinkling strands, giving it a bit of a fairy-tale appearance. A canopy of ivy was stretched out from the pavilion, curling across lattice that created a ceiling over a large, tiled patio space just next to the pavilion. At the moment, that space was being used for dancing.

He looked over at Delaney. The real beauty of tonight wasn't something he was finding in the newly renovated Pines, even as lovely as their new surroundings were.

"Let's go down and dance," he suggested. She seemed to hesitate a moment, but then nodded. They walked down the gentle slope toward the pavilion, but as they arrived at the dance floor, the lively song the band had been playing ended. Instead, a soft, jazzy, slow song began.

"Oh no," Delaney said, sounding disappointed, pausing where the grass bordered the tile. Wyatt caught her by the hand and tugged her off the grass and onto the dance floor.

"What? No one said it had to be a fast song."

Before he could lose his courage, he led her out into the center of the floor and pulled her in, looping her hands over the back of his neck. She turned her head, he assumed to hide another blush, when he steeled his hands at the small of her back. They began to sway to the music, and Wyatt's heart began to beat a little faster.

"It's probably better if it's a slow song," she said. "I think there's less of a chance I'll step on your toes."

"Shhh," he said. "Joking when nervous is kind of my thing, Friday."

She chuckled, and caused his racing heart to skip a beat or two when she laid her head on his shoulder. They stayed like that, swaying in the summer air for long moments. It was perfect. Wyatt realized it was perfect because of who was in his arms. He closed his eyes.

Oh, boy. He tried to keep Maisie's earlier question out of his head. What if this had been a date? What if he and Delaney were more than friends?

"Wyatt!"

"Hmm?" He was lost in thought, lost in the moment. The voice calling him didn't register at first, but it dawned on him that it wasn't Delaney's, and she had gone still in his arms. He opened his eyes, and what greeted him immediately soured the atmosphere he and Delaney had just created.

Standing at the edge of the dance floor was Alex, and behind her were two men and a woman, all dressed in the same power-status attire that Alex favored. Behind them was a cameraman with a camera hoisted onto his shoulder, pointed right at them.

"It's time," Alex said. Delaney looked at Wyatt, her face confused.

"I've got to go for a little bit," he said. *Please don't ask me to explain,* he thought. *Not here, not now.*

Thankfully, she didn't, though he felt like he was committing a million kinds of wrong as he slipped away from her. Without looking back, Wyatt followed Alex back into the campground.

CHAPTER 20

*W*hat *in the world had they been doing?*

Delaney wandered off the dance floor, a little out of breath, sinking into one of the chairs that had been set up under the pavilion. Moments before, when he'd pulled her close and she had sunk into him, what had been going on in Wyatt's head? That closeness, his voice, the way he'd held her...none of that had felt like platonic friends dancing.

Wyatt's mysterious, abrupt exit added to her confusion. Delaney took a moment to catch her breath and began to think a little more clearly. *Where was Alex taking Wyatt? Who were those people with her?* For the past few days, Delaney had suspected there was something going on that Wyatt was holding back from telling her. Whatever was going on, if Wyatt hadn't told her, maybe now just wasn't the right time. Delaney trusted him. He would fill her in later.

She decided to walk back to her car, where she'd left her phone, and text Rachel and Ursula to make sure they were doing okay. The walk took mere moments, seeming shorter now that Wyatt wasn't with her, and she retrieved her phone only to find that the battery was dead.

"Drat," she huffed, rummaging around her console for the car charger. When it was nowhere to be found, she let out an exasperated sigh. Her magical evening was quickly turning irritating. She contemplated just getting in her car and driving home but decided not to let a little interruption ruin what had otherwise been a very nice night.

Delaney thought a moment, trying to figure out how to find a charger without having to walk down to the Bean Pot to borrow one from Maisie. She wanted to get back to the lake as quickly as possible and not have to run all around the campground. And she definitely wanted to check in on Ursula and Rachel.

What to do...

Delaney suddenly remembered Wyatt kept a spare charger in his desk. She had her keys, so she could just let herself in the front door, sneak into his office, borrow the charger, and be back down by the lake by the time Wyatt got back from whatever secret mission of Alex's he was being roped into. Delaney practically skipped up the stairs, thinking about resuming the evening. She hoped Wyatt had actually put the spare charger back in his desk after all the moving involved with the renovations.

Her key turned in the lock soundlessly, and she noticed for the first time that the construction crew had removed the bell over the front door when it didn't sound as she walked inside. She'd have to remember to put it back up. That thing was practically an institution at the office.

Delaney was just passing the reception desk when she heard voices. She froze, listening, gripping her dead phone as she hovered between panic and curios-

...ve Resort, ladies and gentlemen. Let's go over some renovation proposals, and then we'll get down to the monetary offer we're prepared to give."

Cabins in the Pines Executive Resort? Delaney didn't want to hear whatever was about to be said. She had a sick feeling in the pit of her stomach. Should she back up, try to leave without being heard? She didn't want to be caught eavesdropping; she felt guilty even standing there right now.

But the next thing that drifted down the hall glued her to her spot.

"I understand exactly what you're proposing. Let's cut right to the money part of this." The tone was serious, firm. It was Wyatt, again, and what he'd said made her blood run cold. It was so unlike him. Cut right to the money?

Delaney *really* didn't want to be here now, didn't want to know what was going on behind the scenes. She turned and stumbled toward the door in the darkened reception area.

Near the door, she accidentally knocked into one of the end tables, sending a small wicker bowl that held an assortment of pine cones tumbling to the floor. She froze again, holding her breath, waiting to see if anyone back in Wyatt's office had heard her. The voices stopped.

She didn't waste time. She yanked the front door open and flew out of it. She didn't bother to close the door behind her, just ran to her car as fast as she could in her strappy wedge sandals. Hitting the button to unlock her car, she tumbled inside and slammed that door closed. She was parked a few rows back from the office, but she could see the front door swinging open in the hot night breeze.

Delaney's heart hammered in her chest. She didn't want to risk driving off now. They would be sure to see her pulling away. It had been a good decision. Not a minute later, Alex appeared in the doorway. Delaney gripped her steering wheel, hoping the distance and the dark would be enough to hide her from Alex's gaze.

Alex stood in the doorway, her eyes sweeping the parking lot. When the direction of her gaze moved to Delaney's car, her survey stopped, and she seemed to be looking right at—no, right *into*—Delaney. But she made no move toward Delaney's car. Delaney stayed as still as she could.

And then, behind Alex in the doorway, stood Wyatt. Delaney watched as Alex turned to him, and he stared down at her. Alex said something to him, and—Delaney gritted her teeth—laid a hand on his arm. Wyatt stepped aside and let Alex go back inside first. He pulled the office door closed behind him.

Delaney sat in her car, disbelief numbing her. She was a jumble of questions, of emotions, of doubt.

Take a deep breath. You don't know what's really going on.

She'd never been one to jump to conclusions, and it was true that she didn't know exactly what was going on. Heck, she didn't even know what was real and what wasn't since *The ABC's of Business* had crashed into their lives—since she had invited them in. But no good would come of Delaney crashing whatever Wyatt was involved in.

Rationally, she knew the Pines belonged to him. It was his to do with as he pleased. But with everything they'd been through together, with how close they'd seemed to be getting since the show arrived—Delaney couldn't help but feel hurt that he'd excluded her. He hadn't seen fit to involve her. She trusted him, but that trust was feeling a little shaky right now.

Delaney realized she was still clutching her dead cell phone in one hand. Plunking it into the cup holder in her car's console, she put her car key in the ignition and started her car. She backed out of the parking space slowly, then stopped. She rolled down her window and took a last, deep breath of air scented with pine and wood smoke and filled with the faint sounds of merriment.

Delaney needed some space. She didn't want to say something she'd regret. So she wouldn't be waiting for Wyatt down at the lake when he finished with Alex and the suited strangers. She pulled out of the parking lot, her eyes pricking with tears at how the night had turned from enchanting to upsetting.

"So, do we have a deal?"

Wyatt stared across his desk at the four imposing figures crowded into his office. There was Alex, of course, appearing as put together at this time of night as she did bright and early every morning. Then there were the investors, all of them equally staid, hands folded in their laps. They represented a large degree of money beyond what the show could offer, Alex had explained, but that didn't make Wyatt any more inclined to like being here.

Alex and her investors waited, looking at Wyatt expectantly. Wyatt raised an eyebrow at Alex, who had posed the question. Actually, despite the promise of all that money from the other participants, it had been Alex who had been the one directing most of the meeting.

He drummed his fingers on the folder that sat on his desk. This time, instead of rows of numbers that showed him the Pines was in dire straits, the folder contained one number that meant it would never have to be in financial trouble again—at least, not in his lifetime. But the deal only saved the Pines, not its employees. Wyatt's heart had leapt into his throat when he'd read that, under the terms of Alex's deal, the entire staff would be terminated. Even with the generous severance—much, much more than he could ever offer if the Pines simply went under—it would still mean that the family they'd all formed would be split apart.

"I have to decide now?" Wyatt shook his head in refusal. "No. Alex, that wasn't the deal. I told you I would hear out the details, but not that I would give you an answer on the spot. I want the chance to give this a once-over in the light of day and discuss it with Delaney."

Despite his earlier wavering, Wyatt knew there was no way he could agree to anything without talking to her.

Alex didn't seem pleased with his answer. She looked sideways at the other people in the room, then back at Wyatt. At this point, nearly an hour past when Alex had come to interrupt him and Delaney down at the lake, he was past caring what Alexandra expected. He had, again, the suspicion she was manipulating him, cornering him, and he couldn't shake the feeling. It was getting late, and he'd already texted Delaney with no response.

Though Alex likely wanted to argue, she didn't. She cleared her throat and smiled that wide, bright smile Wyatt was coming to think of as a front. She gestured to the others.

"Well, I think that's fair. Besides, we'll probably want to incorporate your acceptance into the show. If that's the direction we want to go."

Wyatt didn't miss the implication—it was heavy enough. He nodded, stood to shake hands with the investors and thanked them for coming. The three left, followed by Alex. Wyatt could hear her chatting with the others as she escorted them to the door. After a few moments, he heard the front door softly close, and firm, purposeful steps coming back.

Alex was in the doorway of his office a moment later. Wyatt thought back to when she'd first arrived at the Pines, how he'd been so impressed with her—her poise, her prestige, her big-city polish. What was behind all of that? Wyatt didn't think he had seen anything of the real Alex—or, if he had, that person hadn't ever loved something the way he loved this place. It didn't seem as though Alex had ever had someone who meant as much to her as Delaney did to him, either.

"I think that went well. They love the location."

"That's nice. Goodnight, Alexandra."

She didn't take the hint. Instead, she crossed her arms over her chest and glared witheringly at him. "Wyatt, I think once you realize this way is the most advantageous for everyone involved, things will go much more smoothly. I'll give you time to think, but I do suggest that you don't tarry. The rest of us are more than ready to move forward."

Wyatt slipped the folder containing the offer details into his desk drawer. He sighed heavily, not in the mood to make faux-pleasant conversation with her right now.

"I said I need time, Alex. So I'll let you know. Right now, I need to go find Delaney."

"Delaney?" The withering look turned to one of sympathy. "Oh, I'm afraid she's already left for the evening."

Wyatt's heart leaped into his throat. "What? When? How do you know she left?"

Alex shrugged, inspecting her nails. "When the door blew open earlier, and I went to close it, I saw her getting into her car. Didn't you say her daughter was sick today? I'm surprised she even came out tonight."

Something was terribly wrong. Wyatt felt it in his gut. Rather than stand there and argue with Alex, which he knew would get him nowhere, Wyatt grabbed his truck keys off his desk and brushed by her.

Her voice was shrill and indignant as she spun to watch him walk down the hall. "Where are you going? The open house isn't over for another hour!"

Wyatt threw back a reply over his shoulder, not bothering to stop. "I said I needed to discuss this with my property manager. I think you can see yourself out."

When Delaney arrived home, she was relieved to see Rachel had already gone to bed. Ursula had immediately seen that Delaney was upset, and it was only after Delaney had somehow convinced the other woman it was only stress from the show that Ursula had left for her own house. But now, alone and sleepless, Delaney sat on her couch, watching an episode of *The ABC's of Business*, replaying the night's events in her head and searching for a plausible explanation that didn't include her best friend selling the Pines out from under all of them.

The sound of tires crunching to a stop outside made her pause the television. It was late, and she wasn't expecting anyone. Drawing aside the curtains, she was surprised to see Wyatt's truck parked out front. She glanced down self-consciously at her yoga pants and oversized T-shirt. Well, if he showed up this late, he'd get her in pajamas.

She made it to the door before he knocked, Duke on her heels. She threw open the door and the screen door, and he caught the screen, taken aback.

"What are you doing here?" She was very aware

of how edgy her voice sounded, despite the fact that she'd calmed down significantly from when she'd left the campground.

"I, uh... You left the Pines."

"You're right, I did." She didn't owe him an explanation. She stood there, waiting for his instead.

Wyatt had the audacity to look confused, and, Delaney thought, a little annoyed. Duke ran out of Delaney's house and circled Wyatt's ankles happily before sitting down beside his owner. He whistled a sharp command, and Duke barreled off into the darkness and jumped up into the bed of Wyatt's truck.

Wyatt turned back to face Delaney. "Do you mind telling me why? Did I do something wrong? Was it the dance?"

She stepped out onto her front porch, closing the door behind her. She didn't want to wake Rachel. "No, Wyatt, it wasn't the dance."

He held up his hands defensively. "Then what's going on? I came out here because Alex said you took off from the Pines. I thought something had happened, maybe to Rachel. I texted, but you didn't answer."

Delaney raised her chin, felt her eyes narrow. "I am so sorry about that. I didn't get your text, actually. My phone died, and I came back to the office from the lake to borrow your extra phone charger. But your office was occupied. After I discovered that, I left. Did Alex tell you *that*?"

His eyes widened. He didn't say anything in response. So it was true. Delaney's heart squeezed painfully in her chest. She fought against the feeling of betrayal and anger that rose up and stole her breath. She had petitioned to get the Pines on the show, thinking it would preserve what they had—make it better, sure, but not turn it into something completely different. And Wyatt wasn't the type to care about money, so why? What else was he getting with this deal—Alex?

She laughed, but it was a bitter sound. "So when does it happen, this luxury upgrade? When do the Cabins in the Pines become the Cabins in the Pines *Executive Resort*?"

"I don't know yet, Friday. I haven't even decided if—"

"But Alex pitched it to you. And you're thinking about it. And you didn't tell me." He'd been meeting with Alex without Delaney, and the slick, upper-crust TV host had shown him a better world, Delaney supposed.

He was shaking his head. "Look, Delaney, Alex said—"

She cut him off again. "Then maybe you should be on Alex's front porch in the middle of the night—not on mine."

His face fell at her words. His voice grew soft. "Delaney, let me explain."

"Explain what? I... It's not like I don't understand. I'm sure it's a lot of money. I'm sure there are also... other advantages. I just thought we were a team."

"We were. No, we *are*," he said, stepping toward her, a hand outstretched. When she took a step back, he dropped his hand to his side. "The night of the barbecue, tonight at the lake, doesn't that count for anything, mean anything?"

She swallowed back the tears that threatened. "I thought it did. But I guess not. I think you should go."

She turned and let herself back into the house, giving him one last scowl through the screen.

He stepped forward and entreated her. "Delaney, please, just hear me out. I didn't come here to argue with you. I came here to tell you what's happened, so we could decide together."

She shook her head, though she wasn't sure he could see the gesture. She hoped he couldn't. If so, he'd be able to also see the tears that were now escaping, spilling down her cheeks. "Maybe it was naïve of me, but I do think—did think—that something was happening between us. Something that wasn't business or friendship. But after tonight, I don't know how either of us are going to feel once those cameras leave, and that really hurts."

The confession hung in the cool night air between them, and before he could respond, she took a deep, unsteady breath, and managed to choke out, "Goodnight, Wyatt."

She closed her front door softly, not looking up, afraid to see the same hurt or anger on his face that she was sure was on hers. She clicked the lock into place. She stood there until she heard the sound of his truck starting up, and, within moments, the sound of his engine faded.

CHAPTER 21

T he camp was strangely quiet. With the open
house over and the production crew packing up
the majority of the filming equipment, the Cabins in the Pines had the air of a fairground after the
fair had left town. Or maybe that was just the mood
Wyatt was in.

Ursula, who was sitting at the new reception desk,
squinted at the computer screen and alternated between frowning at it and consulting a book that lay
open beside it. She looked up at Wyatt.

"Are you just going to sit around moping all day?"

Wyatt, who was sitting in the new seating area up
front, Duke at his feet, closed the book that he hadn't
been reading anyway. "I'm not moping."

Ursula wagged an accusing finger at him. "I've
known you since your first mope, young man, and,
yes, you are. Are you going to tell me what happened,
and what it has to do with the fact that Delaney didn't
come in to work today?"

"Nope," Wyatt said stubbornly, refusing to buckle.
It was tough. He'd always been close to his aunt, and
she'd always been an excellent listening ear. Wyatt was
just too embarrassed to admit the mess he'd made by

not talking with Delaney after Alex had first dropped the bomb about her real plans for the Pines.

"Listen, sweetheart. I know this whole television show has caused quite the uproar around this place, but it'll be gone soon, right? Then everything will be back to normal. Back in balance."

"I don't know about that. I actually..." He paused, then cracked. "I messed up, Ursula. And now I'm stuck making a decision where the outcome might not be the best, no matter which way I go. Whatever I decide, things will change."

Ursula frowned at him over her sparkly, purple glasses. "What does Delaney think you should do?"

"I sort of...didn't include her in the process."

"Ah," Ursula said, realization dawning on her face. She shrugged. "Well, then, you make the decision that keeps the most important things unchanged and embrace the things that will be different, even if that's frightening. I mean, heck, if I can learn to adapt at my age"—she indicated the software training manual she had been working on—"you can."

Wyatt was silent, thinking. Ursula continued, "And whatever changes around the Pines, you and Delaney will be fine. Your friendship's been through much more than this whole television fiasco."

Normally grateful for his aunt's sage advice, Wyatt found her well-intentioned words actually didn't help him today. Instead, they made his heart ache at the possibility that his friendship—or the chance that there was more—with Delaney wouldn't survive, that the damage was irreparable, no matter what he decided.

"I'm going to go take a look at that new software,

too," he told Ursula, standing up. "It might take my mind off things."

"There's a copy of the training manual on your desk. If you need any help, let me know." Ursula's eyes sparkled as she teased Wyatt.

Wyatt smiled and walked back to his office. He'd been avoiding his office all morning, thinking of the previous night and the ultimatum bearing down on him. Settling in his desk chair, Wyatt picked up the photo that was propped against his new monitor. It was the picture he'd had in his shirt pocket just last night, the one that reminded him of all he had to lose if he made the wrong choice today.

A soft knock sounded on the doorframe, and Wyatt glanced up from the photo he was holding to see Charles standing in the doorway.

"Hey, Charles, what can I do for you?" Wyatt stood to greet the man, but Charles waved him back.

"Hey. Ursula said I should come back. Please, don't get up. I can't stay. Lots to get packed up today."

Wyatt sat and indicated one of the chairs in front of his desk. Charles sat. There weren't as many pages on Charles's clipboard today, Wyatt noticed. Wyatt was reminded, again, of how the end of the show was drawing very close.

Charles cleared his throat and read from the second page of his schedule. "I'm just here to let you know the final shooting schedule. We can get reaction shots of the staff very last, but the final important scene—the acceptance or declination of Alex's offer—will need to be filmed this evening in order to make it look as though it's been done the same night as the open house."

Wyatt nodded but couldn't bring himself to thank

Charles for the news. It wasn't as though it was Charles's fault. Wyatt knew that; he actually liked Charles.

Noticing Wyatt's discomfort, Charles leaned forward in his chair. "I know what Alex did put you in a bad position, but she isn't a bad businesswoman. She isn't a bad person, either. Sure, she can be a little cutthroat, but the moves she makes, well—they work. I've seen them work time and time again. She sees avenues others don't consider."

Wyatt frowned slightly. "And then what? She makes her audience see her way as the only way out for the poor, hapless people that Saint Alex has come to help?"

Charles winced. "That is an unfortunate aspect of it all. But people like drama, and I'm not sure how you can change that."

"We're not hapless, Charles. In fact, this place, this staff, has been resourceful and resilient from the day we opened. And I don't want to seem ungrateful for what you all have done because it's really been a blessing, but I'm not convinced that Alex's way is the best way."

"Have you asked Delaney what she thinks?"

Hearing Delaney's name for the second time this morning wasn't any easier than when Ursula had said it. Wyatt knew Charles had to be well aware that Delaney wasn't here. Charles had kept track of nearly every aspect of the day-to-day operations since he'd arrived. There was no way Delaney's absence had escaped his notice.

"No, I haven't," Wyatt said, leaving it at that. But Charles's eyes flicked to the photo of Wyatt and Delaney as children, the photo now lying on Wyatt's desk in plain sight.

Charles frowned slightly. "I see. Can I tell you something else I've learned over my last few years with the show?"

Wyatt leaned back in his chair. "Sure."

He was getting anxious, wondering where Charles was going with this, what the other man could possibly add that would convince Wyatt to see Alex's move as anything other than a smash-and-grab, a scheme meant to uproot and change everything Wyatt held dear. It seemed all Charles was doing was defending his boss.

"In all the places I've been, all the struggling small towns and businesses that are slipping, it's rarely ever been the people who have been the problem. It's been the times, the circumstances. The world moves faster every day, and you either keep up or you don't."

"Just like that? Sign of the times. So I should give up what my family's built here?" Wyatt was incredulous, and Charles shook his head.

"My point is not just that Alex's deal would renew the business. It's that it would take a lot of the stress out of whether or not the Pines does continue. Yes, it would be a change, but not everything would be lost. Change isn't always bad, and nd maybe if you weren't so focused on the Pines, you could focus on other things."

Charles stared pointedly at the photo on Wyatt's desk. Wyatt looked down at the photo that had caught Charles's eye. There was a lot that was valid about what Charles was saying. And his last point was one that Wyatt had caught himself thinking over since the scene on Delaney's porch.

Wyatt sighed.

"I know you mean well, Charles, but I still need some time to think. If I don't accept Alex's offer, she'll make us all seem like buffoons on national TV, and the Pines will probably still fail. But I won't be selling out. If I accept, everything changes, but I may lose the respect, the friendship, the..." He trailed off, his chest tightening.

"Love," Charles supplied.

Wyatt looked up, shocked. "I was going to say the family legacy."

"Okay. That works, too." Charles stood, tapping Wyatt's desk lightly with two fingers close to the photo. "It's your decision, and I know it isn't an easy one. I'll leave you to it."

Charles left Wyatt's office. Wyatt distantly heard him saying goodbye to Ursula and heard the pair of them making small talk about Charles heading down to the Bean Pot. There was laughter and a bit of teasing from Ursula about summer love. Love? If only things were as simple as a breezy romance like Maisie and Charles's. Wyatt thought of Delaney, of the wide-eyed, hurt expression on her face when she'd confessed what she'd been feeling. It was killing him that he'd hurt her.

Wyatt took the folder with the offer out of his desk drawer and laid it next to the photo of him and Delaney. The day would run out soon enough, and he'd be forced to decide. The folder or the photo—which way was right?

"Mom, stop pacing."

Delaney stopped her hundredth circuit of the living room, putting her hands on her hips, frowning absently. "Sorry, honey. I just have a lot on my mind."

Rachel, engrossed in the last episode of *Lovestruck High*, gave her mother a questioning look, but Delaney was saved from having to explain her angst to her daughter by the cheerful tone of the doorbell. Her heart leapt into her throat. She crossed the room quickly to the front door.

She was unsure of what she would say if it was Wyatt standing on her front porch again. But it wasn't Wyatt standing there in the late-afternoon sun. Delaney leaned against her open front door, reaching out to push open the screen.

"Maisie!" Delaney felt partially relieved and partially disappointed. "What are you doing here? Did you drive all the way here from the Pines? Why didn't you call?"

Maisie, pursing her lips, pushed past Delaney and barged into the house. "Hey, sister. When you don't show up to work, and Wyatt mopes around like a kicked puppy, that calls for more than just a little ole ring on the telephone. So I drove out here. And I brought y'all this."

Maisie hoisted a heavy, brown bakery box into Delaney's hands. The rich, ripe scent of peaches, followed by the warm smell of cinnamon and vanilla, made Delaney's mouth start to water instantly.

"How is peach pie going to fix my problem?" Delaney asked her friend.

"Well, it doesn't fix your problem. The pie is just a

treat for after we figure everything out. First, you're going to tell me what your problem is, and then, we're going to fix it."

Maisie turned Delaney and ushered her toward the kitchen, stopping only to give Rachel a quick kiss on the cheek. "Hey, sugar, feeling better?"

"Hey, Maisie. Yep, all better. Is that pie?" Rachel made grabby hands toward the box.

"After dinner," Delaney said, lifting the box out of Rachel's reach. "And then, you'd better get outside and away from that TV. We'll build a fire in the backyard."

Rachel nodded her agreement, turning back to the TV, and Maisie dragged Delaney the rest of the way into the kitchen. Maisie plunked her purse on the kitchen counter, and Delaney set the pie down beside it.

"Now, Del," Maisie urged, "spill. What in the world is going on?"

Delaney hadn't told anyone about the argument that she and Wyatt had been in the previous night—not even Rachel. But faced with the look of warm concern on Maisie's face, Delaney felt her resolve crumble. She told Maisie everything—from the near-kiss at the lake to the touchy-feely way that Alex had been with Wyatt since her arrival, to the dance Delaney and Wyatt had shared at the lake. Then, finally, Delaney told Maisie about what she had overheard last night in the front office—and about the fight on the porch.

When she was done, she was swiping at the tears rolling down her cheeks, and Maisie was hugging her and handing her tissues.

"There, now. Doesn't it feel better just getting it all out?"

Strangely, it did. Delaney nodded, sniffling. "It still doesn't fix things."

"You're right," Maisie said. "But now, you gotta let

me tell you what I know." Turning to her purse, Maisie rummaged around inside and came out with a clear DVD case, an unmarked disc shining inside.

"What's that?" Delaney reached for it, but Maisie snatched it back the same way Delaney had played keep-away with Rachel and the pie.

"A little reality, girl. Let's go." Maisie dashed toward the living room. Delaney followed. As they burst into the living room, Rachel looked up, startled.

Maisie hollered, "Rachel, make room!"

Obediently, or perhaps just as a reaction to Maisie's effusiveness, Rachel promptly scooted to one side of the couch. Maisie pointed to the empty spot that had opened up on the sofa.

"You, Del, sit."

Delaney sat down next to her daughter. Maisie hit eject on the DVD player, which made Rachel squeak in protest. "But, it was just at the part where—"

"*Lovestruck High* later, kiddo. This is an actual matter of life and love," Maisie explained.

Rachel's eyes grew wide, and she sat forward expectantly. "Whaaaat?"

Maisie took up a position on the loveseat, picking up the remote from the coffee table and pressing play. All three of them lapsed into silence as the screen filled with images. Delaney drew in a quick, sharp breath.

"This is the show, the episode—our episode! How did you get this?"

Maisie shook her head. "No, darlin', this is one version of our episode. And as for where I got it, let's just say I have an inside man on the production crew."

"Why would Charles give this to you?" Delaney was aghast as she watched the roughly-edited video unfold. It was as if the worst parts of the Pines, plus the faux flubs Alex had incorporated, had all been cut together to make the campground—and all of them—appear absolutely terrible.

"This is what's gonna get out if Wyatt doesn't agree to let Miss Posh and her fancy investors turn the Pines into some highfalutin joint. Wyatt's got to decide whether to tell Alexandra no and let this air, or tell her yes and get a much happier ending—as far as the show, and Alex, is concerned."

Rachel made a sour face as she watched the events playing out onscreen. "Mom, this is totally not how the Pines really is. It's awesome. Why would they want to make it look like this?"

Everything made sense now. Well, not everything. Wyatt had still shut her out of what was going on. They could have talked things out and presented a united front, whatever the final decision had been.

Except you kicked him off your porch when he eventually tried to.

"And Charles wanted you to bring this here to show me?" Delaney was still confused about how Charles fit into all of this.

"He thinks you'll help convince Wyatt to take Alex's deal. See, Wyatt's been holed up in the front office all day, tearing his shirt about what to do. And the decision has to be made, oh"—Maisie checked her watch—"in the next hour. They want to film the final offer tonight."

"So what do I do?" Delaney jumped up from her couch, her mind racing. She couldn't let Wyatt turn down Alex's deal, couldn't let anyone see the place she loved portrayed like this. The thought of having the Pines turned into a totally different place hurt her heart, but not as much as losing it completely would. And if this episode aired, they were done for.

"Wait," Rachel piped up. "This Alex lady wants to

turn the Pines into something fancy, but we just want to keep it the same as it always has been—well, you know, except for having everything work."

"That's exactly the problem," Delaney sighed.

"So why can't we do both?"

Maisie and Delaney both looked at each other.

"What do you mean?" Maisie asked, pausing the DVD. The living room plunged into silence as Rachel seemed to consider her answer.

"It's a big place. If Alexandra has a lot of money, she could just take half the campground and make it fancy but leave the other half for regular folks. That way, everyone can enjoy it. People want the fancy stuff, Mom. But sometimes they need to be without it. Sort of like how I get all crazy over my phone or my laptop—"

"Or reality TV," Delaney finished dryly.

"Yes, but then I have to put all of that away and go outside sometimes. What's that word?"

"Moderation," Delaney supplied.

Rachel nodded. "So why is everyone insisting it's only their way? Can't we make the best of both ways?"

"Out of the mouths of babes," Maisie said. The two women exchanged an astonished glance.

"You're right, honey. Maybe there is a way." Delaney took a deep, steadying breath.

"But not if he signs one of the offers," Maisie said, threading a hand nervously through her short hair. "And that might be happening, like, now."

Delaney was already reaching for her purse and her keys.

"Let's go. We can call Wyatt on the way."

CHAPTER 22

O*f all the times for Wyatt not to answer his phone!* Delaney's eyes flicked over to Rachel, who had just finished dialing for the third time. Rachel shook her head and handed Delaney back her phone. "No luck, Mom."

Trying not to speed, looking over to make sure Rachel had her seatbelt buckled, Delaney gripped her steering wheel hard as she drove. *Please don't have signed yet. Please don't have signed yet...*

"I'll keep trying on my phone," Maisie offered from the back seat. Delaney could hear the staccato tapping as Maisie brought up her phone screen and searched Wyatt's number in her contacts.

Delaney knew she should have stayed the night she'd accidentally stumbled into his meeting with Alexandra and the investors. She should have listened to Wyatt when he'd showed up on her porch. But her feelings had been hurt by the thought that he was in some sort of cahoots with Alex, that they were maybe even interested in each other, and she hadn't been fair.

"We'll make it. Don't worry," Rachel said, and Delaney smiled at the encouragement. Rachel bounced in her seat. "Finally. This is going to be *so* good. You'll stop Wyatt from signing the papers, you'll convince Alexandra to combine the two ideas for the Pines, and then you and Wyatt will kiss—"

"We'll *what*?" Delaney almost slammed on the brakes. She had actually lifted her foot from the accelerator before she realized what she was doing. She placed it back down, keeping her eyes on the road.

"Mom, come on. He obviously loves you. You obviously love him. Everybody knows it."

"Who is everybody?" It wasn't that Delaney was arguing, necessarily, it was just that she was in shock that, all of a sudden, her eleven-year-old daughter was a fount of life advice. "And where are you getting all of these notions of romance?"

Rachel shrugged. "TV?"

"*Everyone* is every one of your friends, duh," Maisie said, phone to her ear. "Even Ursula. And we've been trying to get both of you to realize that you're crazy for each other for ages." She pulled the phone away from her head and sighed as she pushed the end-call button. "And still no luck on getting him to pick up the phone."

"I doubt anyone thinks... I mean, I'm not even really sure that I... Wait, who's been trying to get us together?"

Maisie leaned forward as far as her seatbelt would let her and began ticking things off on her fingers. Rachel nodded along as Maisie spoke.

"Ursula is constantly late for work because she thinks that spending extra cozy, quiet time alone together in the mornings will encourage you and Wyatt to get closer. Slater makes you go in and put your head together with Wyatt's on all the camp repairs, when that man can danged well go in and figure it out with Wyatt himself. Slater just knows Wyatt gets starry-eyed when you do your problem-solving-juju thing."

Masie took a breath and continued.

"I put those blueberry-cottage cheese pancakes on the menu so you two would keep coming down to the Bean Pot to eat breakfast together before work, even though the things gotta be watched super close or they burn like that." Maisie snapped her fingers. "I mean, do you know what a pain that is during a breakfast rush? I took Rachel to get stuff in town so you and Wyatt could be alone during our day at his place. Heck, I even sent you two out to the lake the other night, under the stars, with a real live band playing, and somehow, y'all managed to miss that chance, too."

Delaney was pretty sure her jaw was somewhere down on the floorboard of her car. She sputtered as she searched for a reply.

Rachel joined in the fray. "You've never even gone out on a date with Wyatt, even after all the times I've stayed the night at Bridget's house."

"Rachel, please tell me you did not invite yourself over to Bridget's just to get me to go out on a date." Delaney knew her expression had to be one of horror.

Rachel made a *pffft* noise. "No, please. I would never do that. That would be so rude. I'm just talking about what Maisie is talking about. You know, all of those missed opportunities."

Delaney drove carefully through town, down the darkened main street, worrying her lower lip between her teeth. She knew she felt something for Wyatt, knew she could so easily call it love, but what about him—how did he feel?

"Let's deal with one problem at a time," Delaney said, signaling to make the turn at the other edge of town that would lead them, after another series of turns, in the right direction to get to the Pines.

"Have we tried calling directly to the front office?" Delaney asked, switching to problem-solving mode.

"Tried," Maisie confirmed. "My guess is they've either unplugged all the phones for filming, or they aren't filming at the office. Dang, I should have asked Charles where they were filming tonight."

Delaney seized on Maisie's words. "Oh! What about Charles? Should we tell him we're on our way back? Could he go stop the scene if they've started?"

Maisie shook her head at Delaney's question. "Can't do that, either. He's at the airport already. I saw him off in the cab at the Pines just before I booked it over to your place. He had to catch a flight. Otherwise, he would have come with me to bring you the DVD."

Delaney's brain was working overtime, trying to find a quicker solution that might get the scene stopped before they arrived. "Slater? Ursula?"

"I'll try Slater. Rachel, you try Ursula on your mom's phone." Maisie punched at her phone screen again, and Delaney handed her phone back over to Rachel.

Delaney signaled her next turn, but they still weren't close enough to the Pines to make her confident they'd arrive on time. Rachel and Maisie held their phones to their ears, and Delaney held her breath.

"Voice mail," Maisie said, disappointment and frustration evident in her voice. "Hey, Slater, get your behind to the Pines as soon as possible. We're on a mission, and we need you!"

"Ursula!" Rachel whooped excitedly—and promptly

dropped the phone. Delaney could hear Ursula talking on the other end as Rachel scrambled under the seat, feeling for the device.

"Hello...hello?" Ursula's voice was small and muffled.

"Get it! Get the phone!" Maisie yelled.

Delaney felt dizzy, then realized she was still holding her breath. She let it out in a whoosh at the exact moment that Rachel sat up, triumphantly shouting, "Got it!"

Maisie held out both of her hands. "Pass it here. Pass it here!"

Rachel handed back the phone, and Maisie whipped it up to her ear. "Ursula? Honey, you still there?"

At Ursula's reply, Maisie started talking a mile a minute. While her accent was still in place, Delaney was surprised her slow-talking friend could get words out so fast.

"Urs, listen. Wyatt's somewhere at the campground, and he's getting ready to do something real noble but real foolish with the Pines." She listened for a minute as Ursula spoke, then she answered. "We're not sure exactly what yet, but there are two choices he can make, and each one's got its noble points *and* its foolish ones. We're on our way from Del's, but we might not make it. Please, please tell me you're still on the property."

Everything fell silent for the second time since they'd started driving. Rachel reached over and patted Delaney's leg, and Delaney realized Rachel was searching for her hand. Delaney let go of the right side of the steering wheel and linked fingers with her daughter.

"Uh-huh," Maisie said. "Mmm-hmm. I'll wait."

Then, silence for a few moments more. Delaney focused on taking deep breaths and driving steadily on.

Maisie's disappointment was almost palpable when she next spoke. "Won't start? Yep. Okay. Ten four. Be careful, darlin'." She hung up, and both Delaney and Rachel gaped at her.

"Well?" Delaney said.

"Ursula's still at the campground. She's up at the office, but they're not filming there. She said she saw Wyatt, Alex, and a couple of others take the golf cart. They were planning to film down at the new pavilion. She jumped in her car, but the Bug won't start. So now she's hoofing it down to the lake. She *might* make it before we do."

"Let's hope someone makes it on time," Delaney prayed. Rachel squeezed her hand. Delaney squeezed back. Two more turns, and they'd be at the entrance to the Pines.

"Rolling."

Wyatt stared down at the open folder on the table in front of him. Norman had told him not to look at the camera at all. In fact, the director had told Wyatt to pretend only Wyatt and Alexandra were here. It wasn't a far stretch. The only people at the lakeshore right now were Wyatt, Alex, Norman, and the camera operator.

Under the pavilion, the folding chairs from the open house had been replaced with long, heavy, banquet-length picnic tables. The tops were smooth and glossy, and Wyatt absently ran the fingers of his free hand over the varnished wood as he stared down at the offer in front of him. In his other hand, he gripped a pen so tightly that his fingers were blanching. This was it: his decision recorded for all time, the move that would start the dominoes tumbling. His mind swam.

He should have tried to talk to Delaney again. This affected her, and she should have a say. And whatever would happen after this would affect them both—deeply, he knew.

But Alexandra and the crew were leaving. This was the moment of truth. He put the pen down. He looked up at Alexandra.

"I can't accept this," he said firmly. Alex, who had just minutes ago so eloquently laid out her plans to make the Pines into a luxe destination, was silent, a shocked expression on her face.

"What?" she said, sounding incredulous. "What do you mean you can't accept it? I came all the way out here, you—your property manager asked this show out here, and you're turning me down?"

Wyatt took a deep breath of the cooling night air, the scent of the trees and the lake filling him with resolve. "That's right, Alexandra. I'm turning you down. My grandparents and my parents after them put their blood, sweat, and tears into this place, and they always intended it to be for everyone. What you're proposing here would not only change the heart of the Pines, but if any of them were here, it would break theirs."

Alex stood from where she'd been sitting at one of the picnic tables opposite Wyatt and smoothed out the front of her jewel-green power suit jacket. "Mr. Andrews, I can't say anyone has turned me down in the entire course of this television program."

Wyatt closed the folder containing the offer. "I'm sorry we couldn't come to an agreement."

Alex shook her head in seeming disbelief. "But I don't understand. The money you'd be making from the new direction of the business could pay for a half-dozen other campgrounds just like this one."

Wyatt knew exactly what had tipped his decision. "I don't want other campgrounds. I want this one. The one where I ran as a child, the one where I grew into a teenager, the one where I finally realized that I was in lo—"

"Stop the cameras!" The deafening yell was courtesy of Rachel, who came running out of the woods from the direction of camp. Everyone froze. Rachel didn't pause. Instead, she barreled like a small tornado down the slope that led to the lake.

"Stop the show!" she repeated. She was so loud, so emphatic, that the cameraman actually reached for the controls on his camera.

"No," Wyatt heard Norman say. "Keep rolling. Pan over."

The camera swung to the edge of the woods. Wyatt could hear voices, riotous, coming up the camp road.

He heard his aunt say, "Keep moving!"

Maisie and Slater were bickering.

"You ran right into the bumper, Slater!"

"I'll fix it, Maisie. Let Del get in front of you, for crying out loud!"

Was that—his breath caught—was Delaney with them? He jumped up from the table, sending the bench he was sitting on crashing back. Seconds later, the whole group appeared at the edge of the woods.

Delaney pushed to the front, and they all moved toward the pavilion.

"What is the meaning of this?" Alex demanded, standing as they got closer. "We are trying to film the offer declination here, and this is not the atmosphere we were going for."

Wyatt came around the table, uncaring about any of the other directions he'd been given before they started filming the scene where he'd be turning Alex down. *We want your face to really show the conflict. You have to sell that you're giving it thought.* He gave his next move no thought, heading straight for the beautiful woman with the wild, dark hair who was marching toward him. His best friend.

"Wyatt," Delaney said, holding her hands out to him, talking fast as he came across the wide, grassy area between them. "You have to take the offer. You have to save the Pines. We—Rachel, really, had an idea that we could—oh!"

He reached her, and, his heart near to bursting, wrapped his arms around her, pulling her close to him and spinning her in a circle. He was filled with pure joy as he set her back on her feet. She was the most beautiful thing he'd ever seen.

Smiling down at her, he shook his head, still not quite understanding. "You came here to stop me from... Wait, what are you here to stop me from? I'm declining the offer. Isn't that what you wanted?"

"Well, if you would let me explain," she huffed—but her annoyance was put on. She was still in his arms, smiling widely, and her eyes shone as she looked back at him.

"I have a plan. But some things have to change around here. I don't actually have time to fully explain, so you'll just have to trust me, okay? And I'm sorry I didn't trust *you*, talk to you last night. I should have. You didn't doubt me when I asked you to let the show come to the Pines."

He didn't hesitate, just immediately nodded. "It's hard for me to accept that the Pines needs to change because I don't want to forget where it comes from. But I know it's true. And I *do* trust you. In fact, Delaney, I more than trust you. I—"

She pulled him close suddenly. Her arms came around him, and she cut him off, kissing him like they were in an old movie. The world around them disappeared. While he'd been aware of the cooling night air, the scent of the trees, and the lake just moments ago, now all he knew was Delaney's kiss. He faintly heard Rachel cheer, and Slater and Maisie stopped bickering. Wyatt didn't care that he and Delaney had seven other sets of eyes on them—eight, if you counted the camera. He pulled her in and kissed her back.

After a moment, he pulled away from the kiss, grinning at her.

"Sorry, Friday, you were saying something?"

"I... Wow... That is... Uh, yeah." She appeared breathless, disoriented, and a little confused. Quickly, she gathered herself and turned to look at Alex.

"We came with a counteroffer," she said, her voice strong. "Care to hear us out?"

CHAPTER 23

The camera was still running. Delaney could see the cameraman move to focus on Alex, who, for once, seemed to be scrambling for a response. Delaney didn't mind the moment of pause. Her heart was racing like the summer wind across the waters of Lake Fairwood. She clenched her hand in the fabric of Wyatt's shirt, and he smiled down at her. They didn't speak, but what she saw in his endless summer-blue eyes gave her courage.

"I don't know all of the details or all of the money involved, but there's a way we can both have what we want, Alex."

"I see you may have already gotten what you want, Delaney," Alex said icily.

There would be time for figuring all of that out momentarily, though Delaney was having a hard time focusing on the issue at hand when Wyatt had kissed her with such passion—and, dare she hope—such love?

Delaney stepped away from Wyatt and turned toward Alex. "Were you even interested in Wyatt, or was what you wanted the Pines? I mean, it doesn't hurt that Wyatt is kind, funny, handsome..."

"Thanks," Wyatt said sheepishly.

Delaney shot him an amused look. "You're welcome."

She turned her gaze back to Alex. "What I mean is that you're not angry that Wyatt is rejecting you because it's personal. No, what hurts you more is the business side of it all. You told me at the lake that it's hard out there for women, and you were right. I think you've had it tough, and I think you like to prove that you can be as successful as anyone else out there."

Alex was watching Delaney with ever-widening eyes, and Delaney pressed on before the older woman could interrupt her.

"But you don't have to do that by forcing us to do anything. If you had come to us with your ideas about making the Pines luxury, we might have been open to them. But you came in here and strong-armed us. Well, that won't work. That's not how it works in this family."

Delaney gestured around her, at Rachel, at Maisie, at Slater, and at Ursula. "We might not have it all here. We might have struggled and had to ask for help, but we treat each other right. We're here for each other." She looked back at Wyatt. "We love each other."

"That's all very well and good," Alex said. Then, her voice slightly thicker, she added, "And, you know, sort of right." Alex fidgeted, waving a hand at Norman. "Turn that contraption off. Get it out of here."

When Norman and the cameraman had made a hasty exit from under the pavilion, Alex continued.

"But it doesn't explain what this counteroffer is that you speak of."

Delaney held her hand out to Rachel, who came to her side. "My daughter, actually, had the idea. Alex, you want the Pines to be something you can show off to your friends in the city, somewhere they can come to experience the same lavishness they expect in their everyday lives. And the Pines is beautiful, a destination, and a plan like that could really bring in the profits we need to get back up and running on our own."

Alex nodded and gestured to the picnic tables. Delaney let go of Rachel's hand. Wyatt drew Rachel back and put his arm around her shoulders, stepping back slightly. Delaney came around to sit down at Alex's invitation. Alex took the opposite bench in order to face Delaney across the table.

"But the Pines has never been about that for us, and it shouldn't have to be about that for everyone else. Your idea would shut out so many people who could rediscover this place and enjoy it the way we have for all these years."

Alex took a slow breath. "So what do you propose, Miss Phillips? That I bankroll the Pines as it is now? I would seem like a fool to my investors."

"No," Delaney said. "I propose a compromise. We admit we need help. That's why we asked you here. And everything you've done so far has been so perfect, so in keeping with what the Pines needs. There's a way we can both get what we want."

"How?" Alex rubbed her forehead, sounding exasperated.

"You build your corporate luxury retreat here on the property, but you leave the old Pines as it is. We don't have to have the Cabins in the Pines versus the Executive Resort. We can have both."

Alex's hand dropped from her forehead. She looked

up at Delaney, something new sparking in her expression. "That's...not a bad idea. Go on."

Delaney glanced over Alex's shoulder at the group of people watching, and a fierce feeling of protectiveness came over her. "We don't want anyone portrayed badly on the show. If we can all agree to go forward, I'd say we should refilm the episode. We show everyone not how we disagreed and fell out, but how we worked together, how we figured it all out."

"I'm in," Wyatt said. Delaney saw Rachel smiling up at him.

"You know I'm in, sugar," said Maisie, who nudged Slater.

"As long as this new resort place doesn't make my trails too crowded," Slater groused. But then, he broke into a grin. "I'm here. Always."

Ursula stepped up to Alex, placing her hands on Alex's shoulders. "I think what Delaney is asking is... can we coexist?"

Alex's smile started small, but Delaney watched as it grew until it was wide, happy, and eventually, a little tearful. "I think that sounds lovely, actually. Quite lovely. And, you know..." She had to pause to dab at her eyes with the back of her hand, being delicate to avoid smearing her makeup. "I'm so sorry. I know I've behaved quite horribly to all of you."

"You're great at what you do," Wyatt said. "We just want you to trust that we're good at what we do, too."

Alex nodded and turned to address all of them. "I was wrong to not do that."

She turned back to the table and picked up the offer Wyatt had been about to decline as they'd all arrived. Opening the folder, Alex drew out the small stack, fanning it out to show that only the first page had printing on it. The rest of the pages were just blank paper.

"See? Even this offer isn't real. This is a prop. All of the real papers are signed off-camera with a whole lot of lawyers involved." She started to laugh, and the small chuckle grew into a full-bodied peal.

"But this"—she gestured around the pavilion, where the twinkling fairy lights shone down on the assembled group—"this is real. I see that now."

Alex looked around at all of them, and Delaney saw the expectation on everyone's face. It was the same expectation that Delaney was feeling, waiting anxiously to see what Alex would decide. If Alex refused, Delaney didn't know where they could possibly go from here.

Alex took a deep breath and set down the blank pages in her hand. "I'll call back the entire crew first thing in the morning, and we can start reshoots."

The group erupted into cheers. Delaney was glad she was sitting; if she'd been upright, her knees would have buckled with relief.

Slater and Maisie hugged each other, and Slater tried to stay upright as Maisie jumped up and down, holding onto his arm. Ursula and Rachel hugged. Over Alex's shoulder, standing out nearer to the lake, Delaney could even see Norman and the cameraman high-fiving each other. Rachel untangled herself from Ursula and threw herself against Alex, and Alex accepted the hug with an expression of surprise. From somewhere out in the woods, Duke came barreling onto the shore, spinning and barking.

Delaney got up from the table and walked to Wyatt, who held out his hands just as she had done earlier.

But instead of kissing him, Delaney leaned close to be heard over the celebratory clamor around them.

"How was that for fixing things?" she said, linking her arms around his neck. She leaned away to find those gorgeous eyes staring into hers, full of pride, amazement, and something Delaney wanted to shout from the treetops—just as soon as she heard it from his lips.

"Pretty darned good, Friday," he admitted. "But, just in case I didn't hear you quite right, did you say that we love each other?"

Delaney heard a triumphant voice behind them.

"I *knew* coming in late all those times was going to work," Ursula crowed.

If it was possible for the warm glow of the summer sun to be felt inside at night, Delaney felt the full force of it hit her heart. It was true. She did love him, completely. But that didn't mean she couldn't tease her best friend a little.

"Well, I said we all, you know, we *all* love each other like a family."

"Uh-huh," he said, sliding his arms around her waist.

"You, me, Rachel," she continued, taking a step toward him that closed any space that might have been between them.

"That sounds like a great family," he agreed, lifting a hand to cup her cheek. She turned slightly into his warm palm.

"Ursula, Slater, Maisie…and now Alex, and I guess we'll have to invite Norman and Charles, and I didn't catch the cameraman's name, but—"

"Hey, Friday," he said, running his thumb over her cheek.

She stared at him, swearing she could hear the orchestra music rising behind them. "Yeah?"

"I love you," Wyatt said. "It took me all of this craziness to realize it, but I do, and I have for a very long time."

Delaney had been overwhelmed by the events that had upended their lives for the past few weeks. But here, now, when those words left his lips, everything fell away, and the only thing she could feel was a deep, sure, answering emotion. Wyatt was her best friend, but he had slowly become so much more than that. They'd both just needed something to make them really appreciate it—a reality check.

"I love you, too," she replied, feeling as though her heart might burst out of her chest. Then, fighting sudden, happy tears, she teased gently, "Even if you can't tell a beehive from a hornet's nest."

He swiped at her tears with his thumbs, his warm laugh brimming with joy. It was joy that she wanted to inspire in him—and knew that he would inspire in her—every day for the rest of their lives. She rose up and kissed him.

EPILOGUE

"Just follow the drive past the parking lot to the camp road that splits two ways. Left takes you to the traditional campgrounds, and right will take you to the executive resort."

Delaney pointed at a glossy new map she had unfolded in front of the guest who was checking in. "Now, your group is booked into the resort side, but you can take advantage of anything on the property. I'd suggest at least one of the camp cookouts, maybe one of our nature walks or bike trail tours, and our sunrise yoga, which happens every dawn at the lake."

"I teach that class personally. I would love to see you there, dear," Ursula said to the woman.

Delaney folded up the map and handed it across the desk to their guest, who was dressed in a skirt suit she could have borrowed straight from Alexandra. With a big smile, the woman took the map, along with the key card Delaney handed over next.

"Thank you," the woman said, grasping the handle of her rolling suitcase. "What an absolutely beautiful place you have here."

The woman gave the handle of the suitcase a tug and rolled her luggage toward the front door, nearly skipping on the way there. As she breezed through to the outside, she set off the cheerful chime of the bell that had been replaced above the doorframe. Smiling, Delaney watched her go.

A few clicks and a flurry of typing noise drew Delaney's attention. To her left, Ursula was sitting in front of the reception computer, efficiently moving through screens on the booking software.

"That was our last guest for the medical supply conference. And we're about three-quarters full on the campground side. That's all of our check-ins for today."

Delaney leaned over to read the well-organized schedule displayed on the screen. As she scanned the schedule, a notification popped up in the lower right corner of the monitor.

"Oh, a reservation from online," Ursula said excitedly. "It's a family reunion for next month. And they want the week after the fall festival. That'll mean we're packed for two straight weeks. I'll let Maisie know so she can adjust her order for the Bean Pot."

"That's fantastic," Delaney said, grabbing the mouse and clicking to expand the view to a three-month spread. There were events on their calendar clear into the Christmas season.

Ursula checked her watch and stood, grabbing her purse from under the desk. "Come on, Del, time to close up shop and get down to the lake. Did you forget you've got a wedding to get to?"

Delaney looked down at her dress, which wasn't the formal affair one would expect at a wedding. In keeping with the theme of the event, a back-to-nature palette, everyone was dressed in muted, forest-inspired colors. Delaney's simple dress was a mix of soft greens, browns, and rusts that perfectly evoked the colors of the fall leaves piling up all over the property.

The bell over the front door chimed, and Alexandra and Charles came in. Charles had his head down and, predictably, was reading from his clipboard.

"So, these are the numbers from our first solid year of operation, and as you can see, surprisingly, we're doing about an equal profit between the traditional side of the Pines and the new executive resort." Charles ran his pen down the page as he spoke.

Alex dropped back to scrutinize the page Charles read from, nodding. "That's fantastic, but I'm not surprised at all. And we're past the point where we're getting bookings from the show alone, so I think these numbers show some real growth. We'll get another boost from this follow-up episode, but I anticipate we'll only grow from there, too. We're almost through year two, and I can tell you, the most recent numbers are higher than what you're showing me."

"It does seem promising," Charles agreed.

Alex tapped his clipboard. "Let's go through these a bit more in-depth. I'd like to see if our operations budget will allow us to add to the new fitness center in spring."

Delaney couldn't get over how different Alex looked. Instead of her usual power suit, she wore khaki shorts, a camp shirt, and a pair of broken-in hiking boots. Her hair was pulled back and tucked under a baseball cap emblazoned with the new logo for the Pines. In addition to supervising the construction and initial launch of the new phase of the business, Alex had also been spending a lot of leisure time here. She smiled more, she laughed more, and Delaney really felt that she was starting to become more than just a monetary part of the Pines.

"You two," Delaney chided, taking in Alex's outfit as well as Charles's equally casual attire. "Go get dressed. The wedding is in just over an hour! Alex, shouldn't you be down at the lake already? Aren't there angles and set ups and other TV stuff to be done?"

Alex pursed her lips. "Well, I'm fairly confident Norman and the crew have it all under control down there, but you're right about these clothes. I can't exactly show up on camera as a wedding guest in hiking boots. Now, my dress..."

"Is hanging in my office," Delaney reminded her. "And, Charles, Wyatt is down at cabin six with the other guys, so you can head down there."

Alex hustled into Delaney's office. Charles obediently turned and made a beeline for the front door. Delaney called to him, and he froze midstep.

"Just for today, leave the clipboard," Delaney suggested. With a sheepish smile, Charles came back over and handed his clipboard to her. She took it and slid it into a file pocket that hung on the wall nearby.

"See you at the lake!" Charles called merrily through the front door as he closed it behind him.

Alone in the office for the first time all morning, Delaney sunk into Ursula's chair and took a deep, calming breath. What a whirlwind it had been since the *The ABC's of Business* had first blown into the Cabins in the Pines.

The phone rang on the desk next to Delaney. She picked it up.

"Cabins in the Pines Family Resort and Executive Retreat, this is Delaney, how can I help you?"

The frantic voice on the other end got Delaney up and out of her seat. "Maisie, just calm down. I know you can't start without me, but we still have plenty of time. Don't worry. I'm on my way."

The pavilion by the lake was transformed, magical. Aside from the ever-present fairy lights, the structure had been dressed with wildflowers of all shapes and sizes, creating a canopy bursting with color that managed to still be in perfect harmony with the backdrop of the woods and the sparkling beauty of Lake Fairwood.

Delaney stood at the back of the aisle that stretched out away from the pavilion, beside Maisie, already struggling to hold back her tears. Staring out at the sea of faces—and trying not to focus on the cameras that surrounded the ceremony—she reached out a hand and found Maisie's waiting. The two women squeezed hands.

"Thank you for being my maid of honor," Maisie said. "I'm so stinkin' nervous, I would have fainted if you weren't here."

"I wouldn't be anywhere else," Delaney assured her. Her friend was stunning in a soft, cream-colored gown, the same muted color as the boutonniere Charles wore in the lapel of his tuxedo. Maisie let go of Delaney's hand and clutched her wedding bouquet as the first strings of the wedding march began to play. Rachel, who held a basket of fall leaves, stepped out onto the aisle runner, scattering the foliage as she walked up toward the pavilion.

"Showtime," Delaney whispered, and Maisie stifled a giggle. Stepping forward, the bubbly blonde took Slater's arm and walked slowly up the aisle with him, toward Charles, who was waiting at the altar. Delaney walked in measured steps behind them, keeping her eyes forward to avoid any sideways glances being caught on film.

Standing next to Charles up front was Wyatt, dressed to the nines and so handsome that Delaney kept having to remind herself that he was real. Wyatt's eyes had gone to Delaney the moment she'd stepped to the end of the aisle. The emotion on his face was one she still wasn't used to but doubted she would ever get tired of. It was one of adoration, devotion, and love. How silly that they'd gone all this time without acknowledging it.

Slater escorted Maisie to her spot and then took his place next to Charles, and Maisie and Charles joined hands. They stared at each other with reverence, joy radiating from them both. Ursula, who was officiating, addressed the gathered guests.

"Dearly beloved, welcome and thank you for being here on this very special day. We are gathered together to celebrate the marriage of Maisie and Charles. Just as it is in nature, so shall it be with them, that their two souls live in harmony like the wind and the trees, and that they cherish one another and live the rest of their lives as one heart."

Delaney wanted to look over at Wyatt, but she was afraid that if she did, the happy tears she felt threatening would simply spill over. Instead, she looked out over the wedding guests and then beyond. They hadn't closed off the shore for the wedding, preferring to let their guests have free access to the area.

Beyond the beautiful wedding setup, Delaney saw a family with young children playing at the edge of the lake. Down a few yards, a pair of teenaged boys threw a frisbee, running back and forth in the golden autumn light as they chased it. A man in a business suit was on one of the jetties, and Delaney watched as he walked to the end and sat down carefully. He took off his shoes and socks, rolled up the legs of his suit pants, and dangled his feet off the pier and into the water.

It was the perfect backdrop for the rest of the ceremony, and when the "I dos" were said, there wasn't a dry eye in the house. Alex, seated in the very back row, was weeping dramatically. Again, just like the night of the compromise, Norman and the cameraman were caught up in the swell. Delaney had to press her lips together to hold back a laugh at the two men shedding a few happy tears of their own.

"You may kiss the bride!" Ursula announced, and a roar went up as Charles did just that.

Following Charles and Maisie back down the aisle, ducking under the rainbow of leaves that the guests threw overhead, Delaney didn't even notice Wyatt had come up behind her until he snagged her by the waist, pulling her to the side once they reached the back of the assembly.

Delaney laughed as Wyatt swung her to the side and spun her around playfully.

"You know," Alex said, interrupting their embrace, leaning over the back of her chair, "we could do another follow-up episode. I can call and see what we have scheduled in spring, but I'll ask Norman to bring the crew back out and—"

"No!" Delaney and Wyatt both exclaimed at the same time.

Alex put up her hands, acquiescing. "Okay, okay. I get it. No need to shout." But she was smiling, and she turned back to survey the pavilion, seeming to get lost in the atmosphere.

Delaney looked at Wyatt, who inclined his head toward the dance floor. "We never got to finish that dance, Friday."

"You're right," she said, letting him lead her onto

wider at the ring that sparkled there. "I'm very happy for them, too. It *is* nice, it is going *so* well, and I am the luckiest guy in the world."

She raised up slightly on her toes and both of their smiles merged into a kiss.

THE END

COUNTRY COTTAGE CHEESE & BLUEBERRY PANCAKES

A Hallmark Original Recipe

In *Love on Location,* Delaney works for her best friend Wyatt at Cabins In the Pines, a rustic camping retreat. Even as the two try to save the struggling business, they aren't always sure where friendship ends and romance begins. One thing that is definite, however, is their shared love for the blueberry-cottage cheese pancakes at the resort's restaurant. Whether they are served with maple syrup or eaten plain, these tasty golden confections are perfect for bringing all your loved ones together at the breakfast table.

Yield: 16 pancakes
Prep Time: 5 minutes
Cook Time: 15 minutes
Total Time: 20 minutes

INGREDIENTS

- 1 ¼ cups all-purpose flour
- 1/3 cup sugar
- 1 teaspoon baking soda
- ½ teaspoon kosher salt
- 2 large eggs, lightly beaten
- 1 cup low-fat cottage cheese
- ½ cup plain yogurt
- ½ cup whole milk or half & half
- 1-pint (about 2 cups) fresh blueberries
- Butter or canola oil, as needed
- Maple syrup, as needed

DIRECTIONS

1. In a medium bowl, combine flour, sugar, baking soda and salt; whisk to blend.

2. In a second bowl, whisk together the eggs, cottage cheese, yogurt and milk. Add dry ingredients and stir just until blended. Fold in blueberries.

3. Heat butter or oil in a large heavy skillet or griddle over medium heat. Working in several smaller batches, spoon about 1/3 cup batter into skillet for each pancake. Cook until the

surface starts to bubble around outer edges, about 3 minutes. Carefully flip pancakes and cook an additional 2 minutes, or until pancakes are golden and puff up slightly. Keep warm in a low oven. Repeat with remaining batter.

4. Serve warm cottage cheese & blueberry pancakes with maple syrup.

Thanks so much for reading
Love on Location. We hope you enjoyed it!

You might like these other books
from Hallmark Publishing:

The Perfect Catch
The Secret Ingredient
A Simple Wedding
A Country Wedding
Moonlight in Vermont
Dater's Handbook
Like Cats and Dogs

For information about our new releases and exclusive offers, sign up for our free newsletter at
hallmarkchannel.com/
hallmark-publishing-newsletter

You can also connect with us here:

Facebook.com/HallmarkPublishing

Twitter.com/HallmarkPublish

ABOUT THE AUTHOR

With strong, relatable heroines and heroes too lovable not to fall for, Cassidy Carter crafts sweet, fun, family-centered romances that will win readers' hearts. When she's not writing, Cassidy can be found digging in the garden or lost in a good book. Originally from the South, she now resides in the desert Southwest with her husband, two daughters, and a cattle dog that has never seen a lick of ranch work.